Wild
and
Beautiful
is the
Night

Wild and Beautiful is the Night

a novel by

John Miller

Cormorant Books

The publisher gratefully acknowledges the support of the Canada Council for the Arts and the Ontario Arts Council for its publishing program. We acknowledge the financial support of the Government of Canada through the Canada Book Fund (CBF) for our publishing activities, and the Government of Ontario through the Ontario Media Development Corporation, an agency of the Ontario Ministry of Culture, and the Ontario Book Publishing Tax Credit Program.

LIBRARY AND ARCHIVES CANADA CATALOGUING IN PUBLICATION

Miller, John, 1968–, author
Wild and beautiful is the night / John Miller.

Issued in print and electronic formats.
ISBN 978-1-77086-510-5 (softcover)

1. Title.

PS8576.I53885W55 2018   C813'.6   C2017-904549-0
C2017-904550-4

Cover photo and design: angeljohnguerra.com
Interior text design: Tannice Goddard, bookstopress.com
Printer: Houghton Boston

Printed and bound in Canada.

MIX
Paper from
responsible sources
FSC
www.fsc.org   FSC® C103214

Body printed on 100% recycled paper.

CORMORANT BOOKS INC.
260 SPADINA AVENUE, SUITE 502, TORONTO, ON, M5T 2E4
www.cormorantbooks.com

For Robby, my rock;
for Debra and Vanessa, my solid footing, all these years;
and in memory of Kim.

*"In a real dark night of the soul,
it is always three o'clock in the morning, day after day."*
— F. SCOTT FITZGERALD, THE CRACK-UP, 1936

Rubble

DANNI WOKE WITH HER LEGS TRAPPED UNDER A HEAVY PILE OF bricks, and this time I wasn't there to pull her out of the rubble. It was too soon for her to contemplate how narrowly she'd escaped, but it could've been much worse. Anybody else surveying the ruins of her life might see only tough luck, crap decisions, or bad blood. I saw blessings. For one thing, she'd been chasing obliteration earlier that evening, and the collapsing wall could've done the trick as permanently as if she'd injected one pump too many.

It was still dark when she woke, and the late summer air was — how'd she describe it? — chalky as it coated her face, cool and thin. What could she have been thinking about, lying there waiting for someone to find her? Her head hurt, and she sucked at her fingertips after touching her throbbing temple. Was she trying to taste her last hit of crack, worried she'd bleed secrets onto paramedics and police? The news report wouldn't mention her name. Maybe she longed for her mom. How many times had Danni announced she wouldn't be reconnecting, which only meant she was forever considering it. This calamity might've been the pretence she'd needed, after so much silence. Tangled in a building's hulk, this would be another disappointing slip-up to her mom.

Bricks covered her legs. One had hit her head. It must've been a crushing pain. How horrible if her skull had caved in. In those moments, she didn't know yet if the baby'd survived. Maybe she asked herself if the universe was telling her something: if she was gonna miscarry, there'd be no decision to make.

The stars sparkled, flickered, and blinked off.

Turf

WHEN I LATER VISITED DANNI IN THE HOSPITAL, SHE LET OUT A LOW rumble of a laugh, broken by coughing. "Lying. Under. Rubble," she said. Danni thought that the best way to defend against life's bleakest moments was to turn them into stories, and that she'd done, because here I am retelling it. Her crazy life turned into entertainment.

Danni'll be pleased. I've jumped into her plot line at a moment of big drama, and she's a big fan of the drama. Addicts all are; it's what we have in common, for all our differences. Also, she'll be pleased because it's her way to liven up a tale by sprinkling in details you doubt she'd remember. And also by bouncing through her life on a pogo stick, forwards and back. First she's in university describing something her professor said in a class, then she's fifteen years old recalling a blue line leading down a hospital corridor, then she's telling how we met and ended up sharing that crappy apartment in Regent.

When I tell my story — and I'll get to it — I'll do it in a more straightforward way: I was born in Hamilton, parents from Jamaica, left home and moved to Toronto, and so on from there. Or maybe I'll reconstruct mine alongside hers; we were together in this for a long time. Until a fault line cracked open, my fault, pardon the pun, and it separated us. I'll still tell those parts, Danni's too, because, after all, she did eventually build a bridge.

As for the gaps in my own memories — post-withdrawal something-or-other syndrome, they tell me — it's all in there somewhere. Storytelling helps. Drugs and detox flattened my brain, suppressing engrams, but they're not gone. I read that Toronto's like that too: the ground under our feet, pressed down by glaciers, is pushing back, bit by bit over time, to recover from all that crushing weight.

I only met Danni five years ago, but it wouldn't be bragging to claim I know her better than almost anybody. We've been closer than any lover I've had, way closer, and had bigger falling-outs. And still, how much can we know a close friend? On the one hand, better than she knows herself, and at the same time, not at all. We might miss the pressure building under the surface, the invisible fissures weakening her walls. What I can tell you of Danni is that finding herself in that pile of bricks — or some equivalent wreckage — was foreseeable, even if she missed the signs. And though I love her, I'll admit to snickering. After all, she lived, and she wasn't seriously injured. Here's hoping it was the wallop that girl has badly needed. We'll see.

Danni's troubles began long before we met, but perhaps I'll honour her and do a bit of pogo-sticking myself, first bouncing back only five years, more or less, to Maitland Street, July 2003. Maybe I'll embellish too, to paint a scene, you know, when I draw blanks. I was getting out of a car. I'd been turning tricks three years by then, and a guy had picked me up over on Jarvis. I was smoking, physically and metaphorically, in a sequined silver halter top. I wore a wig when I was working, 'cause my real hair was a flat-top. People said when I wasn't in work drag, I looked like Grace Jones in the poster with a cigarette dangling from her lips.

The man was youngish, with an eagle nose but the eyes of a deer mouse. New to Toronto and didn't know where he was supposed to be. Calling what I wore *drag* is getting to the root of what'd happened. I'd gotten into his car, he'd driven to where I'd said we could go, and, after reaching up my skirt, he'd yanked his arm back.

"You know it don't have teeth, right?" I'd said.

"I'm sorry. I ... I made a mistake." Well, mistake or not, I had a no-refund policy and told him so. "That's okay about the money. I just thought you were ..."

Feeling bratty, I'd let him flop around. "You thought I was what?" Lots of the women wore wigs on the stroll, but they didn't have my big hands. I'd arched a brow and crossed my legs, no easy feat in the skirt I was wearing or in the front seat of a Honda. Pine tree air freshener mixed with stale smoke. Honking came down the alley from the busy street.

"A he-she." He blushed.

"Ha! No, just she — and since birth."

"Oh, God." He'd smacked his forehead with an open palm.

"Actually, you might even call me a she-she. Figured that out at sixteen."

"Oh, God. I'm such an idiot!" His shoulders'd slumped.

The poor guy. "Nothing to be embarrassed about. If you're looking for the trannies, or even the ones who just dress up like them, you've gotta go a block over and a few blocks up from where you picked me up." He'd offered me another twenty to take him there myself.

On Maitland near the Catholic Children's Aid building, meaning to point him to his kind of girls, I stepped onto the sidewalk. A blur flew by going east, a streak of animal spots and a windmill of heels, followed by a slower jiggling mass of gold lamé: Babs, followed by Serena, two regulars. They were chasing after a new girl. Serena gave up, not up to her friend's fitness level, and caught her breath.

The pursued girl's arms flailed, and her hair was a matted nest. She'd teased it with hairspray, but I guessed either Babs or Serena had grabbed a fistful of it, pulled hard and twisted. And dragged her, before she broke free and they went after her in hot pursuit. Babs was statuesque and wore a spotted orange dress — it was like watching a giraffe chasing a wildebeest on *Animal Planet*. She caught up and grabbed the girl's arm above the elbow.

The girl jerked away, but this time stood her ground. She tried to fix her hair — complete fail — and tugged at the hem of her skirt. She spat lame insults at Babs, but I don't remember what they were because I was fixated on her makeup, horrendous and clown-like. A glue stick of pink goo dragged across the mouth, a spatula of red slop smeared over the cheekbones, a broom-full of light brown mud swept over the eyelids. All over top of a cement mixer of foundation.

"Bitch, did you not hear her?" Serena huffed but tried to stand tall after lumbering forward. "You need to move on from our corner." An impossibly long nail stretched behind her.

Babs poked the girl's chest and asked if she understood English. She took a step back on her long legs, and I expected them to bend backwards at the knee. The girl hesitated. She wasn't used to street fights.

I turned back, remembering their prospective customer, but his Honda was fleeing down the street towards Yonge. I approached the three of them and stepped in between the girl and her predators, telling Babs to back off and calm down. Serena came to Babs's defence and sputtered something about territories invaded and how neither of us should be there. She dabbed at her own copious foundation with a tissue she'd pulled from a micro-purse.

I mustered every ounce of fierceness and, in even tones, said, "If you two weren't so busy going all psycho-bitch, you'd've noticed that I brought you some business. Now you've gone and scared him off." Punctuating my point, another car screeched by.

Babs stood down, and Serena crossed her arms and let her eyes wander away from mine. In the silence, someone's godawful perfume hit my nostrils, a noxious slap of sickly strawberry that mixed with the rank odour of a nearby dumpster. I turned to the girl, who stiffened but remained ridiculous. "I will take whoever this fool is away and show her where she's supposed to be."

"Fine," said Serena.

I asked if we were cool, if there could once again be peace in the Pride Lands, and they mumbled, shifted on their feet. Before the truce fell apart, I grabbed the girl's hand and pulled her away. She stumbled, falling off a heel. "Girl, get it together. Can't you see I'm trying to save your ass?"

"I didn't know that was their turf." She recovered her balance, and, when we were out of earshot, I asked her if it was her first night. She looked herself over. "Is it that obvious?"

I laughed. "My name's Paulette, and you need to follow me before someone else tries to scratch your eyes out."

"Danni," she said, and stumbled behind, away from the conflict zone. She was the worst excuse for a ho that I'd seen in a long time. Wobbling along, she tried to pump me for information, asking if she was dressed too slutty, or not slutty enough. I didn't answer. She was already getting on my nerves. That I was helping her might've been residue from a Christian upbringing, because I can't say I was much impressed. However, I was intrigued. I could tell from the way she chattered that she came from money. I was curious: what crevice had she fallen through to find herself here, under the floorboards, with the rest of us?

Foundations

WE ENTERED THE BURGER JOINT AT THE CORNER OF GERRARD AND Jarvis. Known to everyone, even the hos, as Hooker Harvey's, it was a sad and sketchy place that interior designers and time had forgotten; we kept expecting the Harvey's corporation to sell it to a condo developer. But for the working girls on that strip, it was a refuge on a cold night, a place to sit, somewhere we wouldn't be turned away. A place other people would serve us — and without attitude — until we were ready to go back outside.

I ordered fries for her, my treat. We sat so that Danni could have a view of the streetscape. I was getting jittery 'cause my last hit was now some time ago, but I still wasn't hungry. Danni, who hadn't yet slipped to where I was, still had an appetite. She devoured her fries.

"That, there, is where we work."

She surveyed the corner outside the window. She was pretty, underneath the garish Tammy Faye Bakker makeup. Don't get me wrong, she wasn't my type, too thin and too flat-chested, but I had to recognize the bone structure. She'd probably never worn makeup before: in her case, her health and natural girlishness would've made it unnecessary. She tugged at the spider legs she'd pasted over top of her lashes, complaining that they were bugging the shit out of her.

Her lids pulled out grotesquely before the spiders released them and the lids snapped into place. Her real lashes were respectable; no doubt she had bouncy, shiny white people hair when it wasn't napalmed with spray.

"These are the basics: listen up. Maitland, and near there on Church? Cross-dressers and trannies. Breadalbane, and around Women's College Hospital? Boystown. On Jarvis and Gerrard, there outside? That's us. Only you'll have to find a spot for yourself because people get territorial here, too. For instance, this corner belongs to Olive."

"Who's Olive?"

"Trust me, you'll meet her. Don't be too anxious to."

She asked how to find a spot without getting bitch-slapped again. There was a spark underneath the nervousness. "Those girls were hostile. Now I know why they say the streets are mean."

She didn't have a fuckin' clue; she'd readily admit that now. I told her I'd let her work near me, a half a block south. We wouldn't be in competition because our looks were distinct, even if she managed to tone herself down.

I asked what her story was. I was trying to make her feel comfortable, though God knows why. It came across nosy, and if the tables'd been turned, I wouldn't've told her shit. She didn't want to share much either, at least not at first. She couldn't go home and needed money, which wasn't telling me anything I hadn't figured out. She mumbled something about screwing things up for good with her mom.

"I've been cut off, and this is a quicker way to make good cash. I mean, I assume it is. I'm not sure what I should charge."

"Seriously." I narrowed my eyes at her. "You just thought it'd be a trip to come down and do some hooking."

"I'm not saying it's a trip. I'm saying I need fast money." She pulled a cheque out of her purse and waved it about so that I couldn't see how much it was for. "This is all the money I have in the world. Once

I spend it, that's it. Anyway, it's just sex. No big deal." She stuffed the cheque back in her purse. "Besides, I don't have any employment experience, so, you know, who's going to hire me for a real job?"

She was full of it, for damned sure. Didn't the girl have any friends she could call? I shared with her more of the foundations, the basic menu of services and going rates. I warned her she wouldn't make much, especially if she had any habits to feed. She didn't mention any. I asked if she'd turned a trick yet.

"No," she said. "And I'd better get on it, or I won't be able to find a place to sleep tomorrow night."

There was no way I was taking her in. For one thing, I sublet in a good roommate situation, and there was no extra space. More to the point, it was gonna take something other than this poor little rich girl act to sucker me in. There are people in life whose main skill is to bat their doe eyes, tell a sad story, and get people to rescue them. I'd already pegged Danni for one of those, the more devious kind who isn't obvious in her desperation. Nevertheless, I remembered my first night three years earlier, how frightened I'd been.

"I know someone. She just kicked her roommate to the curb. But you'll have to pay rent. And her place isn't the kind of place you're used to."

"How do you know what I'm used to?"

It was glaringly obvious — the exaggerated way she'd chosen to dress, the way she used slang so unnaturally, to be clever. Now that we were sitting down and eating together, there was an ease to the way she accepted the food I offered. No hesitating. When she dropped the slang, her words were showy, sophisticated. I could speak like that too; I'd been at the top of my classes, took the Grade 11 English prize before I'd dropped out, but street talk was my second language, whereas Danni was unilingual, speaking a few phrases from a tourist brochure. And there was the way her words started crispy but crumbled like buttered shortbread in her mouth. It was how the rich kids spoke in the leadership program at Hillfield Strathallan College. Mama and some Trinidadian educators she knew had pushed me to spend a week there. The kids were friendly, but they lived in Ancaster, were mostly white, and things set them apart. Beaver Canoe sweatshirts. Talk of cottages. Casually mentioning driving a parent's car. And there was the usual crap. Like, "You're Jamaican? It's so beautiful there. We went there last Christmas." I used to fuck with them, say things like, "Oh, did you see Tivoli Gardens? No? Make sure you go next time; it's gorgeous." Awesome, if you're into visiting West Kingston slums.

"Carole-Anne's a heroin addict. Are you used to that?"

"No."

I told her she was harmless, that she wouldn't steal from her, which, from Danni's reaction, she hadn't considered as a possibility. "Don't worry. She manages to have a real job in a warehouse." Carole-Anne slept with our dealer to cut her costs and was racking up a huge credit card debt. Plus, she was spending down an inheritance she got from her dad. So Danni'd be good for a while. But Carole-Anne was trying to keep her overhead down by taking in roommates, and unlike lots of addicts, she didn't put up with drama. She was maniacal about it. I told Danni that if she brought drama into her home, she'd be drop-kicked onto the street without a second thought. Which is what had happened to the last girl.

Danni paused before conceding that she didn't have a lot of options. I promised to introduce them in the morning, but there was Danni's first night to get through. If it hadn't been for Olive showing me the ropes, ignoring my tough girl act and telling me it got easier, I don't know what I would've done. She was Mohawk from the Six Nations Reserve, and was a good egg, when she forgot she had a reputation to maintain. What Danni didn't know yet is that it wasn't just about getting through that first trick, then sitting in a coffee shop and processing. She didn't have that luxury. If Carole-Anne was gonna take her in, Danni'd have to show her cash up front, and for that she'd have to do at least five guys in the next six hours. It was her first day at work, and she was already late.

Downpressed

DANNI DIDN'T TELL ME HER WHOLE STORY THE WAY THEY SEEM TO south of the border, flat out in one breath in the Piggly Wiggly checkout line. Why would she? I didn't tell her everything, either. Danni and I protected our stories with coats of varnish. What was interesting, what should've been a hint that we were to become good friends, was that we scraped the layers off faster than usual, which is to say more than a couple of flakes at a time.

We walked over to Regent Street. An early dawn light peaked above the horizon. A momentary flowery scent from the trees in Cabbagetown was wilted by the stench of a slaughterhouse from near the lake, dumped on us by a hot morning breeze.

"What would your stepdad think if he knew you'd just given a bunch of strangers blow jobs for cash?" I asked.

"Fuck if I care. He's not my father, just some craven loser my mom married. Hey, do you mind slowing down? I'm not used to sprinting in heels."

"You call those heels?" I was still fuelled by the sputtering fumes from my last hit of crack, which I'd done about a half-hour earlier when Danni was in a trick's car. I willed myself to throttle back my pace and to keep the conversation going because I was out of rock and wanted the evening to be done, but shit, it was hard to concentrate. I eyed a convenience store and considered getting a snack for mid-morning.

"I guess your dad's not in the picture either." I steered her into the store to buy chips and strings of licorice.

Danni crossed her arms around her waist. She told me when she was five, he was diagnosed with lung cancer from years of cigar smoking. I made a face. "You know how people smoked cigars in those days. It was all about ostentatious displays of wealth. Anyway, he died in '87."

She assumed we'd share cultural reference points, and maybe we did share one or two; the whole continent was drawn to those symbols of prosperity, even fake ones. Though I doubted the eighties hit us in the same way. In our neighbourhood of downtown Hamilton, my parents were powerless against the tug of the currents, heaving us up, but then, as my mama put it, *downpressing* us. They gazed up at the wiggling, promising surface. My mama came to Canada and became a personal support worker in a retirement home; in other words, she changed the diapers of bigoted old people. She watched news items glamorizing the spoils of the well-heeled and thought, they're just over there, how can they be so hard to swim to? We watched *The Cosby Show* and *A Different World*, where rich Black people I'd never seen in Canada had lives we couldn't relate to.

Danni's childhood was in one of those different worlds, though she was only an hour down the highway. Her father was a banker on Bay Street, she said. Mine worked in an auto body shop on Barton. My parents were full of rigid little rules too brittle to bend that filled me with frustration and made me want to rebel — though I rarely did. No playing with boys, ever. No cussing or you'd get a slap. No pants to church. Danni's dad was chill, and she'd inherited that quality — that was already clear. She was hardly shaken by her first night on the stroll.

I read about men like Danni's father; they were all over the news. He must've rode the storm surge of that decade and believed it'd rise forever and never crest. Meanwhile, down the highway, the water level dropped so low it left my parents flopping and suffocating in discarded waste. But in 1987, the wave curled and crashed down on Mr. Wexler, and for us, the undertow pulled us further down.

Danni and I'd lost our fathers the same year. One day, my dada up and left us, moved out and went to Toronto. I was mad as hell, but not half as mad as my mama. We kept in touch when he called, which wasn't often, but the conversation was awkward and stiff and had to be done when my mama wasn't around. Eventually, he started a new family, and we started speaking less and less until months and eventually a year or more would go by without contact. The same year my dada left, my mama's wages were frozen for the third year in a row, and they went to the picket lines for weeks in a fruitless strike that left us visiting food banks.

Danni's loss was more permanent than mine. The spot on her dad's lung had grown and spread, until there was nothing to be done. When he was gone, widowhood left Danni's mom — how did Danni put it? — destabilized. The daughter of an Ottawa dry goods salesman, Barbara Wexler had met her husband at a Jewish summer camp, where they were both counsellors. The way Danni talked about it, her mom came from modest beginnings, married up and almost lost it all. She mentioned her modest beginnings like it was a badge of honour, or would help us relate. I never said a word, but to me, it sounded like her mom's starting point was somewhere my parents dreamed they'd end up. Small business owners who could afford to send their daughter to summer camp? Shit. Besides, those supposedly modest beginnings were in the past by the time Danni was born, so how would they have affected her?

I suppose the point was about almost losing it all. That if you're movin' on up to the east side, you've gotta make sure you don't fall from your dee-luxe apartment in the sky. And to do that, you have to open your eyes. Danni's mom believed her marriage'd been an upwards climb to a fortress. She had a great view, but in her nine years of marriage, she ignored the jumbo jets heading for the tower: her husband's line of credit, his caution that her Mastercard purchases were getting out of control, the excuse that the repossessed sofa was due to a late bill payment, the bonus payment spent on a new BMW instead of on paying down debt.

And most seriously, she ignored his worsening smoker's cough.

Danni wouldn't talk about how she felt about her dad's death, still doesn't. Maybe she was too young and is embarrassed she can't remember much of him. Maybe it's too painful. Instead, she talked about her mom, how Mr. Wexler's death left her panicked. After he was gone, Danni became her mom's means to prove to their la-di-dah friends that they still belonged. Danni was outgoing, beautiful, and close at hand, and her mom — especially after three gin gimlets — would flaunt her the way women show their girlfriends a new dress. It was a habit her dad had discouraged when he was alive, suckered in by Danni's complaints about upset stomachs. "Let her be, Barbara," he'd say, "she's not feeling well."

She dimly remembered how her dad had contained the consequences of her mother's drinking. A hand on his wife's arm, an apparently loving gesture to others, was a signal that it was time to settle down, to lower her voice and regain some decorum. Danni's faked stomach aches meant she could hide from the embarrassing unfolding display. But when her dad died, all of that changed. If her mom had believed her dad's glossy stories of financial stability, she was less gullible with Danni. And because she suspected that the stomach cramps were a sham, Danni couldn't escape the guests. She didn't like being on display. (I could easily imagine how she'd been feeling about putting herself on the street corner all night) and disliked more the sight of her mom making a fool of herself after her fifth drink.

"It was brutal," she said. "She'd want me to brag about my track and field medal, or say some random phrase in French, and I'd do it — because it would take people's attention away from the drunken mess."

"So, like, are you totally clean?" We'd crossed Parliament Street and were headed to River.

"Hell no. But if I'm drunk, at least I've got the sense not to inflict it on anyone."

"Alcohol's never been my thing." I tried to say it casually, like I didn't care that she might be a drinker and I was a crackhead, because I shouldn't've. But Danni was happy talking about her mom, or maybe it was more that the subject triggered the uncoiling of a spring. If she was fazed by her first night — and she hardly seemed to be — talking got her head out of what she'd just done, and listening helped distract me from finding my dealer. I pressed her for more.

"Mom picked herself up eventually. When she was done grieving. And when she was ready, Holt Renfrew gave her a chance as a saleswoman."

"Shit. Just like that? No experience?"

"All they cared about was that she was pretty and well put together."

"And white! If my mama'd walked in there for a job, they'd've assumed she got lost on her way to the Sears cafeteria."

"Huh! I guess you're right." She became quiet. Was it occurring to her that, despite a blank resume, she might've taken a similar chance, used a pale face and nice clothes to her advantage? Instead of this? "Well, however she got her job, she was good at it, and for months she managed to keep her drinking under control, which was a relief. It was the one time in her life that she was optimistic. But then sales took a dive, and the pressure from her boss eroded her confidence. She kind of descended into melancholy."

That's the word she used. Another reminder of our differences, even when bringing up a point in common. My mama didn't have *melancholy*. She'd come home from work, mutter, "Rain a fall, but dutty tough," and disappear into her room. For months. We didn't know anything about depression. An auntie on our floor said, "She just sad," and checked in on us to make sure we had supper. My older brother was nowhere, off with his friends doing hell knows what. My mama never recovered for long.

Whatever she called her mom's sadness, I didn't have to imagine much to know that those must've been hard years for Danni too. But her mom's melancholy was situational, not biological. She pulled out of it and started entertaining again.

"She called them 'visitors', never 'company'. I only realized that later, isn't that funny? Maybe it was a good thing, because with only the two of us alone in that house, talking about company would've been tragic."

Danni had an interesting way of looking at things. A car whizzed by, too fast to be rushing anywhere good at that hour of the morning. "Wouldn't it've been more tragic if nobody'd come by at all?"

"Maybe." She paused for a minute. This girl was a serious chatterer, and the power I had to clam her up would come in useful. We crossed an intersection, ignoring the red light because the streets were empty again. "What I think," she continued, "is that she consciously avoided the word *company* 'cause she didn't actually want any — companionship, I mean — even from me. *Visitors* is all about social niceties. That word shifted the focus away from us and onto the person arriving at our house." Danni moved her hands from left to right in front of her body, as though pushing aside a piece of furniture. "At least that's my theory. It probably wasn't even conscious."

She lost herself in thought, dragged her soles on the pavement as we walked. She'd wanted to be alone with her mom, I get that. Maybe her mom was the only person who missed her dad as much as she did. I know when my dada left, almost everyone tried to cheer me up, except my mama. I wasn't happy she'd barely spoken to me, but I was grateful she hadn't tried to raise my spirits. If Danni's mom was anything like mine, she would've been lonely and afraid of the future. And neither of us measured up as company, not in our mothers' eyes.

The self-absorption of checking out like that, leaving your children to twist and turn and fend for themselves, it wasn't something I could relate to. Not yet. With both of us having drained our need to talk about family, we dropped the subject and walked in silence.

Shelter

I TOOK DANNI TO A BREAKFAST JOINT NEAR DUNDAS BEFORE CALLING Carole-Anne and warning her we'd be coming over. She slept lots, and she wouldn't've been ready for a knock at the door at six.

After downing eggs and toast, we went to 200 Oak Street, the building where I also lived, and took the elevator to the ninth floor. On our way up, I almost reconsidered and asked Danni if she wanted to sleep on our sofa. It might've helped with the rent, but Yen Mah, whose name was on the lease, wouldn't've gone for it, even as easygoing as she was. Instead, I stuck with the original plan and warned Danni about Carole-Anne. She'd lost three kids in a custody battle and her ex-husband had moved to Dartmouth, so God help Danni if she mentioned them, or any other children. The subject of childhood was to be avoided. "Oh, and she's nutso about the green armchair. Never, ever sit in it."

After scrutinizing us through the door viewer, Carole-Anne unlocked what sounded like ten deadbolts — heroin made her paranoid — and opened her door to exactly the width of her head, which she pushed through the gap, appearing to trap herself in a vise. Carole-Anne was a not-bad-looking woman, in her early forties then, with sandy brown shoulder-length hair. She was gaunt but solid.

Despite being no more than five foot seven, she managed to haul stock at the Gerrard Street Home Depot, which she called "Domestic Despot." Her arms were impressively buff.

Her eyelids drooped behind reading glasses, but it was hard to tell if she was sleepy or if she'd already slammed her first needle of the day. She examined Danni up and sideways, and if it was to establish her trustworthiness based on her appearance, that didn't bode well for Danni. But Carole-Anne saw the same pathetic naïveté that I had. She opened the door and waved us in. I nearly tripped on her enormous cat, Sir Purrsalot.

Her apartment was surprisingly well kept, no less tidy than anyone's might be if you dropped in with little notice. What I mean is it wasn't drug addict messy. Danni and I sat on a lumpy chesterfield covered in cat hair, and the first thing Carole-Anne asked was if Danni had any money to put down. Danni handed her most of her night's haul. Carole-Anne walked to the television console where she snatched a pad with a list on it and clutched it with both hands, a pen hooked in her pinky. She sat in her precious green wingback to begin a grilling.

The gruffness was put on; Carole-Anne was a softie with a Nova Scotian sense of hospitality, but she'd been burned too many times. The interview was something she'd coached herself into, to avoid future grief. She asked a series of questions, head lowered to read her list, lifting her eyes but not her head to meet Danni's responses. She didn't use the pen except to hover the tip of it over the question she was asking.

What were her work hours going to be? (Working nights, was Danni's answer.) In that case, was Danni a light sleeper, not that Carole-Anne was going to be loud, but she didn't intend to pussyfoot around her own apartment because Danni was sleeping in? (No, Danni wasn't a light sleeper.) Was she okay sharing grocery bills?

(Of course.) Did Danni do needles? (No, but she didn't have anything against it.) Carole-Anne's pen lifted and skipped over her next question. Did she intend to bring back tricks or boyfriends to the apartment? (Never.)

Carole-Anne squinted and cocked her head, perhaps assessing if Danni was shovelling a huge load of shit. She continued. Did Danni have any furniture that she'd be bringing with? (She had nothing.) Did she mind smoking? (She hesitated, but cleverly said no.) Who was Danni's *faahther*, Carole-Anne asked, her East Coast drawl emerging. Danni gave a name, and Carole-Anne snorted, said she didn't know him. Maybe this was to signal that this put Danni on thin ice. I caught Danni's puzzlement, but she didn't state the obvious: having grown up nearly two thousand kilometres apart, there was no reason their worlds would have intersected.

Carole-Anne asked her last question while stroking Sir Purrsalot. She hoisted him onto her lap with her Domestic Despot arms. He'd have been good off-hours training for tossing lumber and heavy boxes off the back of a van. Furrowing her brow, daring Danni to answer unwisely, Carole-Anne asked if Danni was allergic to cats. (She was not.)

Poker-faced, not fully trusting that Danni'd work out, Carole-Anne got up and put the list and pen away in a drawer. She shook Danni's hand and said, "Welcome. Mi shithole es su shithole. Unless you break any of the house rules, in which case you're gone."

When she rhymed off those rules, I caught Danni's flicker of surprise; she'd assumed, as I had, that the rules had been covered by Carole-Anne's list of questions. Those things were on the list, but there were more: She didn't have herpes, so Danni didn't have to pee from a crouching position like those crazy germophobes do in public toilets — but Danni was to wipe down the seat anyway. Don't put her toiletries on the right side of the bathroom cabinet.

She wasn't fussy about what to watch on television, except for *Coronation Street* and *The Sopranos*, which were like church — missing them was sacrilege, and she didn't have a DVR or a VCR or any such thing. Don't feed Sir Purrsalot treats no matter how much he begs you and sucks up because he has a weight problem that we're trying to control. I guessed that by "we" she meant her and Sir Purrsalot, as though she were his Jenny Craig consultant and they'd hatched the plan together. From the size of him, he wasn't enthusiastic about it. No long-distance calls unless Danni paid up front. They'd share chores equally. Rent was due a week before the end of the month if she planned to write a cheque. The day of, if it was gonna be cash. Garbage day was Wednesday. And, confirming my warning, she said, "There will be no drama in my house, do you understand?"

Danni understood, and Carole-Anne's shoulders relaxed.

Danni exhaled. "Thank you so, so much. You don't know what this means to me."

Carole-Anne harrumphed. "I have some idea." She picked up her cat, pressing her face into his coat, and I don't know if Danni was unsettled, but I sure was: Sir Purrsalot had not purred, not once.

Bagga Nonsense

DANNI AND CAROLE-ANNE DID WELL TOGETHER AT FIRST. THE LIST of house rules grew, but Danni, not wanting to screw things up, did her best to comply. If she was bothered by Carole-Anne's slamming heroin, she didn't let on. Carole-Anne described the heroin high as being really, really stoned while also having mind-blowing sex, while also eating a chocolate cupcake with vanilla icing. I assumed she was lying, that the feeling she described was from her first time, the high we all chase and can never get back. Remembering that new drug high nearly made me switch over from crack, but the prospect of learning how to manage a whole new habit exhausted me.

In 2003, when she met Danni, Carole-Anne called herself a functional addict. I'd never heard of the term until I met her. If you defined a functional addict as someone who worked while taking drugs, you might've lumped those of us who turned tricks into that category too, and you wouldn't have been wrong. Some of us happened to work nights and irregular hours is all. But I wasn't considered to function because I didn't hold down a respectable job. Lord only knows how people did that. The hiding it'd take. They felt superior, those so-called functional addicts, but, like us, they were taking their chances in a condemned building. Yes, they lived a few storeys up, but that only meant they had further to fall. It pissed me off, still does, the lack of respect given to eking out a living on the streets, dodging police, ducking danger, living by your wits. I'm not saying it's thriving, but if that wasn't functioning, what was?

Being self-employed, with no boss to tell you what to do and no secure paycheque for putting in a solid night's work, meant you had to try harder, but it was a simple choice. I was scared about a lot when I landed on the streets, but I would stay pimp-free if it killed me. And by that I mean if *they* killed me. Too many Hollywood movies depicting nasty metal-toothed, gun-wielding bullies scared the bejesus out of me. Staying a free agent wasn't as tough as I expected; I stood my ground when the guys came by to offer protection or better pay or the promise of fewer arrests. In the long run, I'd been better off. They left me alone. I figured they had enough girls willing to accept their protection that they didn't sweat the one or two pigheaded ones.

It was one of the first things I learned from Olive, and one of the first that I passed on to Danni, because she was like us in that way. Olive was a lone wolf like me, except the hardened, snarling kind with scars from too many fights. There was another one who came along before Danni, a Métis girl from Winnipeg named Tammi, but she attached herself to me like a bloodsucker. I slept with her once, big mistake, and after that the only way to un-suction her was to become a huge bitch, which came surprisingly easily. Tammi moved back to Manitoba.

With Danni, it was a relief to hang with someone I wasn't attracted to and to not worry that her feelings for me would become romantic. There wasn't one iota of girl-on-girl vibe. What's more, she wasn't the kind of straight girl who needed to set her markers down aggressively, or, sometimes when in the presence of a dyke, defensively. It was refreshing. There's nothing that bores the shit out of me more than a girl whose focus on men pulls every topic of conversation back to them.

Danni settled into her spot south of me, about a third of the way between Gerrard and Dundas. I had steady work, and Danni's arrival didn't cut into it. We worked the west side of the street, where we caught the southbound guys going down to the Gardiner Expressway headed to the suburbs. On Saturday and Sunday nights, we'd switch sides to catch the guys coming into town on their days off. Danni and I weren't in competition. Mostly I got the white guys wanting something "wild." I didn't give a shit if they held stupid notions about Black girls and sex, so long as they weren't *kumoochin* assholes and paid without a fuss. I played it up, wearing my Tina Turner lion's mane wig. If they saw through the war paint and teased hair and wanted that lezzie lie that pornos fed them, they never let on.

Danni, once I sat with her in front of the mirror, managed to come away halfway decent. Slutty but not cartoonish. I had her up to my place, and we bought blonde dye from Shoppers Drug Mart. Her hair wasn't nice and easy as I'd thought it might be. It had a mind of its own, not quite curly, not quite straight, just messy. We tamed it. Once she'd wriggled into a stretchy one-piece, she was Julia Roberts wearing that wig in *Pretty Woman*. I was proud of my work.

We set off together every evening at sundown. It was the natural thing to do since she was only two floors away. When it was clear we weren't attracting the same clientele, we inched closer to each other on the stroll until we stood side by side. I had someone to talk to, to pass the time with.

After a while, for all of us, what we did at night became second nature. I'm not saying we learn to love it, but lots of people put up with shit for the sake of a paycheque. You could get used to almost anything. It doesn't bother you in the same way, is what I mean. For me, it never bothered me much at all, but how was Danni coping?

I didn't want to pry. In the beginning, Danni'd offer up that she didn't expect this or was taken aback when a guy said that. Once, she popped out of a car and said, "Okay, he was disgusting ..." but there were no tears. No fear, not that I saw, anyway. Was it bluster?

I asked Carole-Anne how her roomie was doing, if she was handling things okay, but Carole-Anne didn't have much to offer in terms of intelligence, maybe too stuck in her own muck to notice. I kept a closer eye on Danni that first coupla weeks than I needed to, and while I consider myself good at reading people, she didn't show much cause for concern. Maybe she snivelled into her pillow at night, in Carole-Anne's apartment, but I doubted it. That girl was not soft.

At the end of week number two, as we took a break in Hooker Harvey's, I asked, "Hey, is everything okay out there?" The restaurant smelled of fry oil and bleach.

She said, "I can't say I love it. But it's only sex. Just because people say we're pitiful or degraded doesn't make it so. Not unless we believe it."

"Uh-huh. Where'd you read that, in a fortune cookie?"

She chuckled. "In a course at Trent, actually. I did Anthropology and Women's Studies."

"Of course you did." It was a sweltering August night. I had sweat running down my *ears-corners*. I pulled at the fabric of my tube top, holding it away from my midriff so that the air conditioning could get at my tits.

She reached across the table and poked at my arm. "But I happen to agree with it!"

My fingers lost their grip on my tube top and it snapped against my skin. Re-glued itself. I took a plastic fork and speared a stray piece of iceberg lettuce that had escaped Danni's hamburger and popped it in my mouth. "Sounds like feminist bullshit."

Her eyes widened. "Don't tell me you're not a feminist."

I crunched on the lettuce. "Not particularly." I stabbed another piece, this one from her burger itself, while I half-listened to a lecture about something she called "the Backlash," a concept I was supposed to've known about, as if it were global warming or the Y2K scare. About how we'd distanced ourselves from our mothers' generation, too afraid of being labelled unfeminine. Our mothers' generation? My mama, listening to this, would've laughed and said, "Yuh a chat bagga nonsense!" When Danni started to teach me how much feminism had given us, I reached my limit. I swept my arm across the fast food joint. "Yeah. So much bounty, I don't know what to do with all of it."

Truth is, I was intrigued by what Danni said, but the curiosity was trumped by her pissing me off. Since mentioning her anthropology degree, it'd clicked: she was on a fascinating research expedition, which by extension made me one of the natives being observed. Besides, sex wasn't the point. Getting into a car and wondering if this was the guy who was gonna strangle you and leave you for dead: that was the point. When I'd asked her if everything was okay, I meant did she feel safe. If she was gonna pretend that turning tricks was like falling into a big fluffy pillow, fine. She could've at least given me credit for stuffing the pillow. As for her malfunctioning sense of fear, I hoped it wouldn't land her in a dumpster. I made a mental note to ask Olive to give her more survival tips.

But if there was one thing I could count on with girls like Danni, it was their guilt. I knew how to end this foolishness. I picked lazily at my fries. "Come to Hamilton with me and tell my mama how feminism has helped her."

Danni lowered her eyes to her plate, and I got a moment's reprieve from the lecture. "I guess I wasn't prepared for how boring it can be."

"Boredom. Seriously. Well, if that's your concern, crack does help with the tedium."

"Maybe I'll join you someday," she said. "But now I've gotta get going or I won't have enough for rent next month."

An ambulance whined past, a mosquito flying by my ears. "Then eat up, 'cause this conversation is making me jones real bad. I need to go find my favourite stairwell."

She gobbled the rest of her burger.

Great Equalizer

I DID ADMIRE DANNI'S WORK ETHIC. AND HOW LONG SHE RESISTED crack. She bought coke to snort from time to time, and Xanax — at my recommendation — to sleep later, but I mostly partook on my own. When I was high and she wasn't, she'd keep her distance. Being around someone who's zooming when you're straight is not much fun; she'd made that clear. Maybe she didn't wanna be tempted.

One day in mid-September, I was off to meet my dealer. She sidled up. "Mind if I ask you to get me some? I need to economize; blow is too expensive, and I need a little somethin'-somethin'."

"You sure you want to go there? You know when I suggested you do it? I wasn't serious."

"I know. But I'm crawling out of my skin. And besides, I'm already doing coke."

"Okay, but to be clear, crack is different. If you try it, that's on you. Don't come back to me later with the blame and the finger pointing."

We went to Ülle, an Estonian guy who hung around that neighbourhood to do business and who didn't live far if you needed to call. He wasn't my only dealer; I also had a guy named Mario who lived near my apartment. Ülle didn't like that I was splitting my coin, but I told him he couldn't be everywhere at once. If I was at home and was tapped out, I couldn't be traipsing across town or waiting for him to make his way to me.

Ülle was more than happy to sell to a new buyer; he knew this wouldn't be the only time. Danni came to my stairwell, a parking entrance near an apartment off Church Street. When she smoked her first hit, her eyes went wide and she screamed, "Wow!" and stamped her foot. I had to hush her. It was that lightning bolt of the first high. I felt sorry for her. I warned her it wouldn't strike twice.

Later that night, riding the last wave of the last hit from the small amount of rock she'd purchased, Danni picked up a guy who lived in south Etobicoke and who worked in the business district, long days. She told me it'd been a straight-up blow job, but that the guy'd been chatty and wanted to tell her all about his day. He worked in an accounting firm. We got guys like that once in a while. They had a need to talk, and whether they wanted to beforehand, to make themselves comfortable, or afterwards, to offload their day's stress, if they kept it to under ten minutes, it didn't matter to me. This was the kind who got lively afterwards, and when he came up for air he asked Danni if she'd be there, same time, two days later. She said yes, unless she was with a customer.

In two days, he returned, good as his word. Same thing. Then two days after that, Danni was with a john. He said, "Fuck." Checked his watch. "Will she be long?"

"I'm not her secretary." I leaned onto his windowsill. "Anything I can help you with?"

"No thanks." He gripped his steering wheel, checked his watch again. A car honked and pulled around him, its engine revving. Another car honked. The man turned his blinkers off and drove away.

The next night he was back, and this time, Danni was free. Shawn, he told her his name was. Then he missed her the next night. When he returned again, he asked if he could meet her weeknights at seven.

Danni was savvy enough to say that it'd cost him double for prearranged appointments. He argued: she'd be getting regular business, so she should give him a discount. She held firm: she didn't need the business, she lied; if he wanted to make sure she was waiting for him, it meant giving up other johns. And she didn't mind talking, but if it went on more than fifteen minutes, it'd be another twenty bucks. Shawn said he didn't want to go hunting for someone new. It was worth it on one condition: if she had any diseases, even a cold sore, she needed to tell him. He'd pay her anyway, for her honesty — unless it happened over and over, and he suspected she was playing him. They shook on it.

Danni'd gotten her first regular not two months into the life, and had a sweeter deal than any girl I'd met. I'd been at it for three years, and the only so-called regulars I could claim were one or two guys who showed up once every coupla weeks, if I was lucky.

Despite pulling in more than she had since she'd begun to turn tricks, she didn't go back to her occasional coke snorting. She'd come with me to Ülle and pick up a quarter of an eight ball. He tried to get us to choose him over Mario by offering a tiny discount. It was laughable. He of all people should've known that when you need it, you need it. Unless he slashed rates, the discount wasn't gonna convince us to delay our high. Crack is a thousand times more powerful than that candy bar at the checkout counter, and who can resist those?

I watched Danni inhale. Her back broadened, her shoulders settled, she shook out her head and arms and straightened her neck. Crack puffs you up, makes you invincible. When Danni smoked, she was taller and she lost the awkwardness of her gait.

When you're facing the fear, the danger, and the boredom of the streets — and its go-nowhere days and nights — there aren't that many options to make you feel better. A TV program recently profiled a desperate community in the far north. A father and his four young kids were living in a one-room, badly heated tin shack. They had nothing, but on the wall hung a forty-two-inch TV, and on their roof, there was a satellite dish. People might judge that father for buying luxury goods while they lived in squalor, but I got it: that TV was survival by fantasy.

Wearing her own inhaled fantasy like a cape, Danni strutted down to her piece of pavement, workin' it, like Missy herself. And she boasted. We all said stupid shit when we were high, made promises we couldn't keep. My boasts were about getting my kid back, the one I'd given up at seventeen. Stupid things that I knew were impossible. Danni's goals were grander, in a different class, and stated with more certainty. She was gonna put her money away. Get an apartment of her own. Go back to graduate school to finish her master's. The swagger and swell of the crack highs made Danni feel more like her old self, is what I guessed. Back on top, in control.

Based on my advice, she was able to manage her money better than most of us, until I, too, believed her desert mirage. She handed over her rent to Carole-Anne in increments. She maintained a bank account but cut up her ATM card to eliminate the temptation of withdrawals in the middle of the night. She made more than I did, what with her income from Shawn and one other less frequent regular that she'd nabbed.

None of this helped her manage her habit. Addiction is the great equalizer, and she got hooked, little by little, as I had. An unending production line of men stretched up Jarvis Street into the late fall and early winter. Crack was an invisible down coat when the temperature was bitter and icy and we still had to work. It was that pot of fresh coffee in the break room, always there, always hot. Danni's mug was newer than mine, with a pretty flower design and no chips on the rim to cut her lips, but she filled it from the same pot.

In the mornings, coming down from her high, she'd throw a blanket over her thin drapes. The noise was harder to block out than the daylight. Carole-Anne'd be stomping and storming about getting ready for work, while Danni buried her head under a pillow. Working the graveyard shift is one of the hardest adjustments. It's one thing to pull a teenage all-nighter; it's another to live like that all the time. She was prickly.

"It could be the drugs or the sleep deprivation," I said, "but frankly, anyone'd be irritated by Carole-Anne."

"Now you tell me this?"

"What were your choices?"

For the most part, Danni avoided her roommate. They didn't have the same schedule. Carole-Anne'd leave, and Danni'd find sleep, vaguely aware of loud conversations in the corridor outside the apartment. When she woke in the late afternoon, she'd find Sir Purrsalot sleeping at her door — silently, of course, never purring. She'd watch television, maybe walk in Riverdale Park, go home for dinner.

At the table, Carole-Anne yammered about the daily soap opera of the Domestic Despot's loading dock. This person was taking too many breaks. That person was faking a bad back to get Worker's Comp. Another was dating a girl in Lighting, but he didn't know that she was cheating on him with a guy in Kitchens. When Carole-Anne came up for air, it was to suggest improvements to something Danni was doing. "You know, if you put your index finger on your knife, you'd get better control of it." Or, "You shouldn't leave the water running like that when you're doing the dishes; it's a waste." Or, "You know, I find you don't need to cut both the ends off beans, only the stems."

Danni held her tongue and released it when we met. A coupla times a week, we'd cook a dinner at my place before going out to the stroll. "Why does she give a shit about the ass end of a string bean!"

Yen Mah moved through the kitchen to open an old margarine container filled with leftovers. She was hovering somewhere around forty, no children, and worked at one of the Chinese grocers on Gerrard East. One night a week, she volunteered for an organization that worked with Chinese immigrants, doing I'm not sure what. Her English was accented and awkward, so I hadn't learned much about her story, why she didn't have family in Toronto and why no friends ever came by. But she was the perfect roommate: quiet, undemanding, understanding if my rent was three or four days late. I rarely had a friend over either, but when I did, she let us be and did her own thing. Definitely more easygoing than Carole-Anne.

"She's particular, is all." I didn't know why I was defending Carole-Anne, except that I felt some responsibility for Danni's predicament and hoped that they'd settle into a groove. And they did, not that Danni's complaining let up. By Christmastime, Danni was no longer bothered by Carole-Anne's early morning thumping. She'd become used to it, aided by a pre-sleep cocktail of over-the-counter non-caffeinated codeine tablets and melatonin. Sometimes she chased those down with Nyquil. It knocked her out well and good, which had a moderate effect on her grouchiness.

The four of us — Danni, Carole-Anne, Yen Mah, and I — celebrated Christmas together, and we kicked things off by buying a fake tree at the dollar store. Normally Yen Mah was emotionally flat, but she perked up that evening. She forced smiles and put a barrette in her hair. Carole-Anne set up the fake tree in her apartment, and we decorated it with coloured condoms and a bag of regular ornaments she'd tucked away. I bought stewing meat from a guy Yen Mah took me to in Chinatown — more expensive than I'd hoped it would be, but I splurged — and cooked us some Jamaican Christmas favourites: curry goat, oxtail, rice and peas. It was terrible; I'd only ever watched my mama making it and did it from memory, but it made me feel good to do it, and they didn't know the difference anyway. Carole-Anne made a chicken. After a fruit cake for dessert — Danni's contribution that she'd bought and submerged in rum — and three bottles of wine that Yen Mah brought, we went quiet, each of us transported to estranged families. I thought of my mama's holiday table, how they'd've finished with glazed fruitcake and were probably dipping into a nice glass of spiked sorrel while they got out the dominoes. How she'd be fielding calls all evening from relatives back home who'd received the barrels of food she'd shipped weeks earlier, dry goods and staples she'd saved all year to be able to afford.

I didn't expect the holidays to affect Danni the way they did, her being Jewish and all, but she missed her annual pilgrimage to the movies and for Chinese food. Carole-Anne had a so-called date with Mario the drug dealer, and Yen Mah wanted to go back to our place to listen to Chinese Christmas music, so Danni and I took the night off — a terrible one for business anyway — and rode the subway to a theatre where we were sure not to run into anyone we knew. We watched the late showing of *Elf* with Will Ferrell. It gave us a few laughs.

By February, the coldest month for turning tricks, the month during which people were at their testiest, I could tell that the grim reality of outdoor hooking was wearing on Danni, not to mention the added lack of daylight hours. It's a special skill to dress to keep warm and yet somehow show off your assets. Leggings. Skin-tight under-layers. A fuzzy over-the-shoulder wrap. Cute earmuffs hidden under a teased mane of hair. Danni claimed to be a true Canadian who loved winter, but she'd never had to love it this much. On those dark evenings when she soon had to go out, it was harder to let Carole-Anne's advice roll off her back.

One night, readying myself for work, there was a knock, a sharp rat-a-tat that lasted longer than usual.

Danni stomped in. "So I'm getting ready, and she criticizes what I'm wearing."

"Hello to you, too." I shut the door behind her.

"Sorry. Hi." She gave a token hug. "It's just that she drives me. Fucking. Insane!" Her hands mimicked explosions. "'You're going to catch your death of cold,' she says, like this is a revelation. Am I supposed to wear a freakin' parka? I'm not a ten-year-old fairy princess on Hallowe'en. Nobody's gonna give me any candy if I put anything else on, is all I'm sayin'. So I lose it. I say to her, 'I'm not your fucking daughter, Carole-Anne!'"

"Oh no you didn't."

"I wasn't thinking!"

"What did I tell you!"

"And she started crying."

"Oh, God. Danni."

"Seriously. Less than two seconds. Rivers of tears. She says, 'My daughter is almost your age,' and she's weeping, and I say, 'I'm so, so sorry,' but she runs into her room."

I shook my head. "She'll be okay. The woman has hair-trigger tear ducts. It's been a while since this has happened. You might wanna bring her a peace offering."

"Such as?"

"Baby slippers?"

We laughed, but neither of us was proud of it. Carole-Anne's sadness I could understand, but not the magnitude of it, except in the abstract. I'd given up Chantelle, but I wasn't ready to be a mother, and my pain was more a dull ache whereas hers was a gaping, sting-ing gash. Clearly. Her husband had taken her children when they were young, when her slamming was on the upswing and their marriage was in its death rattle. She'd been too ashamed to fight for custody, even joint custody, and he soon moved back east to Nova Scotia to be nearer to his parents and sister. Carole-Anne hadn't seen those kids in years. They never returned her calls. She suspected he'd poisoned their minds against her.

We got ready and headed to the stroll. The previous week had been savage, down to minus seventeen, but that night was mercifully warmer, only seven degrees below freezing. Still, I was jealous that Danni was gonna be seeing Shawn, her regular, so soon after we reached the curb. It meant she got to be in a warm car while I worked for my first trick. Soon enough, Shawn showed up and off they went. I took in an icy breath and approached the curb ready, trying to catch the eye of passing men. This time of night was tricky. There was no street parking on that section of Jarvis, and in the still heavy traffic after work it was difficult for cars to stop. You had to position yourself near the semicircular driveway of a Ryerson building. If someone was interested, you could motion him to pull in there for the negotiation. It wasn't safe to stay there long, either, or security would ask you to leave, though sometimes we could bribe them to let us be. Despite the potential hassle or expense, it was better than having a guy lose his nerve and drive off because cars were honking at him to get moving down the street.

I wasn't lucky that night. Not one customer in the first half-hour, and then as I was readying to go to Hooker Harvey's to warm up, Danni stepped out of Shawn's car up near Gerrard. She crossed the street and headed east. Something was wrong; we always met up after a trick. Her shoulders were hunched, and from more than cold. I hollered, but she didn't react, so I went after her, careful not to slip on the ice. I caught up at Sherbourne Street.

"Danni! What the hell!"

"I'm going home."

"We just got here. He couldn't have tipped you that much. What happened?" I got ahead of her; she had to stop.

Her eyes focused off in the distance, and her jaw was slack. "I'm an idiot. I was horrible to Carole-Anne. The way we made fun of her for reacting the way she did? I'm no better."

I asked if she'd been crying. She didn't answer. She tried to move around me, but I grabbed her arm and pulled it. "You're coming with me. We're getting a coffee, and you're telling me about it." I let go and shivered, waiting for her to protest, but she didn't. "C'mon. Before we freeze to death."

Trick Candle

SHE FOLLOWED ME BACK TO THE COFFEE SHOP. SHE NEVER TOLD ME what happened in the car, except that Shawn had freaked her out. We bought double-doubles and sat staring into them for a long while. I didn't wanna push. Fan heaters sputtered and ticked like old diesel engines. A girl at the next table took forever to finish a plate of fries. When she left, I said, "Nobody's listening now."

Danni sipped her coffee. "Remember I told you about my mom, and how she was after my dad died?" The light in Danni's eyes was a trick candle, burning hot one second, dying, then bright again. That night it was a wild flicker.

"Yeah, I remember."

"Well, she started dating again. Not right away — but in a couple of years, when I was nine, she decided it was time to get another husband."

Sitting still when I was due for a hit wasn't easy. I wished she'd blurt it out, but I smiled when Danni needed sympathy and shook my head or nodded when she needed shoring up. I took a package of mustard left on the table and ran my fingers back and forth over its surface, moving its contents into a bubble from side to side. Danni dealt with her stress by crumpling a napkin, smoothing it out, and crumpling it once more.

Like most children who've lost a parent, Danni'd viewed her mom's suitors with suspicion. Sometimes outright hostility. Maybe that's why she remembered so much detail. Saul Deutsch was her mom's first suitor, from the same family that makes the pickles. He ignored Danni. She'd be all, "Pass the potatoes," and her mom would chide her: "Say please, Danni. I didn't raise you in a barn. Saul, would you mind passing the potatoes to Danni?" He'd hand her the bowl with a flash of contempt. Danni knew why. He was annoyed that she hadn't been sent to a friend's house, or that she'd taken the spot at the head of the table, in her father's old chair.

Another guy, whose name she'd forgotten, shook her hand with a clammy palm and a nervous smile, then spoke to the babysitter more than to Danni. "I promise not to have her home too late," he'd said, laughing at his own joke.

Then she told me about Stan Abel, a tall man with groomed, wavy hair, who had greeted her in a curt, friendly, but too adult manner, as if she were a prospective business contact. He was good-looking enough, but had a smooth, oily way with her mom. Money and gifts spilled in a slick from his pockets. This one stuck around for a while.

The man imported and distributed chemicals used in refrigerators and fire extinguishers and was grumpy about the coming ban on some of those chemicals. When he spoke about his work at the dinner table, Danni wanted to jab a fork into her eyeballs.

"But what about the ozone?" her mother asked.

"The effects are overstated. Besides, do you want to go back to using iceboxes and sawdust? Or toss that extinguisher you keep by the stove? My company brought those chemicals into the country."

To compensate for his discomfort with kids, he heaped compliments on Danni like a dump truck. "Danni knows what we're talking about! She's a clever girl, and I can tell she has a head for business, too — might even grow up to be the head of a company one day."

The praise was about things he couldn't possibly know she shined at. Its phoniness piled up and stank.

In response, her mom dreamed up ways to help him relax around Danni. By their second month of dating, her mom had them setting the table together and chopping vegetables for salad. Because Stan had a business degree, she asked him to help Danni with her math homework. By the third month, at her mom's insistence, he'd begun hugging her. It wasn't until the fourth month that he relaxed, and even then barely so.

Once, her mom and Stan had come home from the theatre to find Danni still awake because she'd fussed with her babysitter. Stan hung around longer than usual after bringing her mom home, and in the awkward clinking of teacups, the air got heavy in the dining room.

"Why don't you go make us some more tea," he said to her mom, "while I tuck Danni in." Danni wondered if he was sleeping over.

"How sweet of you!" her mom enthused.

"But you always tuck me in," Danni protested.

"Danni, you have no right to argue. Janine was supposed to tuck you in, and you gave her a hard time, so go with Stan and get ready."

She grumbled. Stan followed her to her bedroom. To let her change, he turned. She put on her favourite T-shirt and underpants. The smell of his cologne gathered in the room. When he tucked her in, she lay on her back, arms at her sides. Sitting on the bed, he held her left arm and leaned in to kiss her cheek, giving her chest a rub through her shirt. He was icky. She didn't want him there. She felt a chill and wiggled to turn over, but he reached to pull the sheet tight on the other side. Her movement was halted, but only briefly. She writhed and squirmed onto her stomach, away from him. He rubbed her back once, up and down, and left.

After that, tucking her in became one of Stan's regular jobs, along with vegetable chopping and helping Danni with her homework.

Danni tried jumping into bed and landing on her stomach, her face away from him, her knees to her chest, but it didn't help. Each time, his hand lingered longer on her back, and the rub he gave went farther up, and farther down, until his hand rubbed all the way down to her bum, where she felt a small pat.

She didn't want that to happen again, so she switched back to lying on her back, and one day, while his hand was up to its usual business, Stan slipped a finger between her legs and retracted it. Because there were two layers of covers and her underwear between his finger and her body, and because it lasted a fraction of a second, Danni asked herself afterward if it had happened on purpose. By the time she'd flinched, clamping her legs tight together, shaking her head no, the finger was already gone. Why couldn't she say anything? She rolled sharply away and looked to the wall. She'd often touched herself there, but nobody else ever had — save her mother, when she was giving her a bath. But that was different.

The next time he was over, when she felt him coming towards the bed behind her, it was like when she'd been playing in a field once and had seen a line of rain rushing towards her. No way to avoid it. A hard wall of cold and a frightening, mounting roar from which she couldn't find shelter. It happened again, the finger, and not so quickly that she doubted its purpose. This time around, clamping her legs didn't help. But she could tough it out. Later, the rain would stop.

When for two weeks he did nothing, Danni hoped he'd sensed her discomfort. But one night he slipped his hand under the covers. Her breath rose in a whooshing updraft, and she was unable to pull it back. She wanted to push his hand away — to tell him to stop — but the words circled in her windpipe, his expression, intent, almost angry, making her stop. Her right arm felt like it had withered at her side, useless as the left one he held firm.

She counted: one one thousand, two one thousand, three one thousand, four one thousand, a tornado was moving up and down inside her, hurting, drowning everything out, drawing her up into its eye ... He pulled his hand back, and she released a faint whimper. A finger, the same one, to his lips in a shushing gesture. He left the room without a word.

That night, stabbing cramps woke her. She screamed. Her mom found her curled into a ball on her mattress. She'd never pretended to be in this much pain. "We're going to the emergency," said her mom. To Danni's dismay, Stan drove them. He was now regularly staying the night.

At the Hospital for Sick Children, a doctor examined her. He palpated her belly, checking for acute pain. There was none. He asked if there'd been any vomiting or diarrhea, and she answered no. "And we all had the same thing for supper," added her mom. "We're both fine."

"Is something bothering you?" asked the doctor. "Are you worried about anything at all, Danielle?"

Stan stood behind her mom. In the silence, while they waited for her answer, he shook his head ever so slightly.

"No," she said. How could she say what it was, even if Stan hadn't been standing there; it was disgusting, and what if he said she was doing something that made him think it was okay? She'd die from the shame of it.

The doctor turned to her mom. "Has she had any bleeding?"

"Of course not. She's only ten!"

"It'd be unusual, but not unheard of, for girls this age to get their periods. But I didn't mean that kind of bleeding." He prescribed pills in case the pain came back and referred them to a specialist. "Give these sparingly; they contain codeine. But they'll relax the cramping."

They exited the hospital. Her mom's body was stiff. "If I discover you faked this to get attention ..."

They filled the prescription on the way home. The pills took effect. Danni described a sensuous trickle of heat, remembering when she'd drunk steamed milk and her father had stroked her head as it lay on the pillow. This was the warmth she'd hoped for, but wasn't sure existed.

The next evening, when they were alone, her mother went to the basement to do the laundry, Campari and soda in hand. Danni followed her and tugged at her blouse.

"Ma," she began, hesitant. She scuffed the linoleum with her shoe.

"Yes, darling?"

"I've decided I'm too old to be tucked in."

"Too old? Don't be ridiculous."

"I'm big enough, now!"

"Don't be too anxious to grow up, honey. When you get to my age, believe me, you'll wish you'd spent more time enjoying being a kid."

Her mom folded clothes while Danni sat on a family-sized box of detergent. Her mom spent more time on each item than she usually did, her mouth a straight line. "I thought you liked having Stan tuck you in," she eventually said. She snapped out the same shirt she'd folded three times and began again — a motion not so different from what Danni was doing to her napkin as I listened to her story.

Danni told her mom she didn't like it, careful not to appear angry. Or else her mom might fight her instead of sympathizing.

"Aren't you two getting along?"

Fourteen years later, telling me this story, Danni couldn't remember exactly how much she'd told her mom. At first, she was sure she'd stated that she didn't like the way the man touched her. With the passing years, however, the firm, reliable conviction she'd held about that conversation softened and became porous. When she tried to grab hold of the memory, it compressed, and when she released it, it soaked up all kinds of uncertainty.

Hadn't she said that his hands were too rough, hadn't she said "on my skin" and that she hated his cologne, that he hurt her arm where he pinned it on the bed? She knew she didn't say where he touched her. Did she really need to? Danni was plagued by doubts, but she never doubted that the touching had happened. And there was one other thing she felt sure of: after she'd spoken, her mom became unusually quiet and continued to fold clothes until Danni left. In retrospect, Danni was certain her mom knew. What mother wouldn't work it out, or at least worry, right?

Her mom didn't ask her boyfriend to tuck her in anymore. But she also didn't break up with him, and Danni never forgave her for that, even if that man no longer came to her room.

The intense stomach cramps continued. If she asked for one of her comfort pills, her mom would ask if the pain was that bad, if she was absolutely sure she needed something, before handing one over. Her mom wasn't rationing the pills because of the doctor's advice; she still worried Danni was faking. Once or twice, she was.

Two months later, Stan left. Things weren't working out, is what her mom told her, giving her hope that her mom had eased her way out of the relationship. That she'd finally taken Danni's side. But the next day, she overheard her mom crying on the phone with a friend. "Maybe it was because I've gained all this weight." Later, Danni caught sight of her mom drunk in her bedroom, wiping tears and pinching belly fat in the mirror. Danni didn't feel she could console her, so she went to the living room and turned up the television extra loud.

"I'm a freakin' cliché," she said, and got up from her chair. What had happened to Danni wasn't my story — not all the girls on the street suffered that kind of abuse — but it was one I'd heard before. I put a hand on hers. "You were right. You should take the night off." There was no point in empty words.

Anthropologists

WE MADE IT THROUGH THE WINTER, AND BY APRIL, SHAWN WAS NO longer coming by. Since February, his appointments had petered out. I didn't wanna ask, but I suspected it had something to do with that night, with how Danni'd reacted. When she hooked no other regulars, she settled into the reality: Shawn had been her one lucky break. A few weeks later, she recognized his car picking up another girl north of where Olive worked. She sank into unstable ground that day, and I can't say I didn't enjoy it. It put us on a more equal footing, what with my ground having been pretty mushy and uneven for some time. It might've made us closer, which is admittedly fucked up.

We spent more time together after that. Danni and I'd go and do hits at least every other night. Cooking meals took a back seat to pizza slices and cracking open a can of this or that. We'd go to Mario's Drop-In, the name he gave to an apartment he rented in our building. Mario didn't live there; he provided the place for regular customers, with the threat that if they caused or brought any trouble, he'd ban them. He had a huge fan installed in the living room, venting smoke out through a window. The apartment wasn't rented under his name, but he was wary nonetheless. Three years prior, a place he'd owned over on Jones was raided and he did time.

The idea of his banning us was a joke since he was never there. How would he know who might've been making trouble unless he had an informant, and he was too cheap to pay one. He lurked in or outside of the lobby, making deals with a broader range of clientele. I suppose he might've cut us off from our drug supply, but in all of my years knowing him, the only buys he'd refused were from suspected cops.

This apartment was shabbier than most in the building because despite his supposedly careful screening, a lot of people were coming and going, and he didn't clean it nearly enough. In its large living room, there were two sofas, a big armchair, and mattresses near the walls.

The first time I brought Danni there, she said, "Cool." The anthropologist had made a brief reappearance: it was anything but cool. The place was repulsive: odd stains on the wallpaper, roaches (the insect kind), and, despite the noisy fan, it smelled rank, a mix of crack smoke, must, and a faint odour of cat pee. It didn't help that it was overheated and stuffy because most of the windows were stuck closed and the balcony door jammed shut. Even if that door hadn't been jammed, it led to a balcony that nobody'd've dared step onto because it appeared structurally unsound.

Mario's Drop-In was a relatively safe, neutral place in which we could get high, away from where we lived. I didn't like doing anything at home and encouraged Danni to draw that line too. I'm not saying I never slipped up, and Danni could've done the same at Carole-Anne's given that Carole-Anne regularly shot up in her own apartment, but it felt more contained to do it elsewhere. An activity that was only one part of your life.

I'd bring my works — I'd been doing needles for years already when I met Danni — and she'd bring her pipe, screen and push sticks. Not that I didn't still like to smoke, but injecting was easier on my lungs and the hit lasted longer. I was smart about it; I got hooked up early with a worker from Street Outreach Services who gave me clean needles and who told me about citric acid. The vinegar I'd used in the beginning caused abscesses at the injection sites on my arms and legs, which, aside from being revolting and painful, was not good for business. Danni hated needles and still enjoyed the quick fix she got from inhaling.

We had our laughs in Mario's Drop-In. Mostly, we'd sit and shoot the shit about nothing — a good *labrish*, my mama used to say — or joke at the expense of others Danni gave unflattering nicknames. There was Flo-Jo, named after track star Florence Griffith Joyner, a wiry sistah with long fake nails who paced back and forth and took deep breaths, shaking out her arms and legs as though she were psyching herself up for a sprint. There was Grumplepuss, a fat guy who complained about a lot of things, including the state of the building, how it was poorly kept up. To which Danni said, "You're in a fucking crack house!" and he replied, "So? We don't deserve nice things too?" Grumplepuss moaned about being the only crack user in the world who couldn't lose weight.

There was Jump-Start, a wispy heroin addict with hair the colour of a corroded pipe who sat on one of the mattresses, her back against the wall, legs splayed, shoulders slumped, her works scattered about her. She'd nod off, and slept lots, but when she awoke, she'd yell, "Holy crap!" and look around skittishly. Our hearts raced every time. There were two other regulars who preferred privacy and kept to the bedroom: Poodle Do (a picky-picky head who tried hard to pull her nappy hair into tufts on the sides) and Boo Radley (a gaunt white guy with hollow eyes).

On her second visit there, Danni went to the kitchen and grabbed a pizza slice from the box we'd brought with us. On the counter was a nearly empty bag of dry cat food and beside it, a small plastic bowl holding two lonely nuggets. She filled it with kibble, laid it on the floor, came back to the sofa, and we did a hit. When next we returned, the food in the bowl was gone, as was the bag. The next day, Danni bought a small bag of cat food and brought it with her. She filled the bowl. Whenever we arrived in that apartment, the bowl was empty and one of us filled it. This continued visit after visit until Danni's bag ran out three weeks later. For me, it normalized spending time there: we were taking care of a friend's pet while house-sitting. Responsibilities while satisfying our needs.

The next couple of times we came, we forgot to bring more food, and the bowl stayed empty. "Poor kitty cat. It's gonna starve if I don't go to the store," said Danni, and she went to the corner and bought another small bag. She filled the bowl and smoked a piece of rock. I cooked myself up some and stuck a needle in my arm. At the peak of her high, Danni drummed her fingers on her thighs. "Paulie, have you ever actually seen that cat?"

"Of course I have," I answered. "I think it hides in the bedroom. Poor thing's freaked out with everyone coming and going. Can you blame it?"

"Oh." She got quiet.

A while later, when Danni was in the bathroom, I searched for the cat but couldn't find it. Now that I thought about it, it'd been months since it'd mewled its way through the apartment.

That day, Flo-Jo was pacing in the living room and Grumplepuss was on the sofa jiggling the flesh on his legs by vibrating them while keeping his feet planted on the floor. Danni, finished in the bathroom, knocked on the bedroom door — she was on a search of her own. When nobody answered, she turned the handle, and I followed her in. Poodle Do was out cold and drooling on a nasty stained pillow, one of her side tufts sticking straight up at the ceiling. Danni checked the closet, where there was kitty litter, smelly but not too bad, boxes, and extra IKEA furniture parts. We checked under the bed — nothing. I hunted for that cat in every corner, Danni following me and helping.

"Fuck!" I shouted. "Where is that stupid thing?"

"Calm down. So we can't find the cat; who cares?"

"Must've gotten out when someone left the door open."

"Maybe," she said, her hand on her chin. We sat again, but she bounced back up and beckoned me into the hallway. We took the elevator to the lobby and approached Mario, now outside. He had a foot up on the edge of a planter to tie a shoelace, and the waist of his jeans gaped in the back, thank God revealing no more than black underwear. Off in the distance, a couple argued and the woman yelled, "Fuck you!" and pushed her boyfriend in the chest. Mario's T-shirt was unusually clean, and a cigarette dangled from his lips.

Danni said, "Hey, Mario, just letting you know someone may have let the cat out of the apartment."

He took the cigarette from his lips and held it between a nicotine-stained index finger and thumb. He ran the other hand through his jet-black hair. "Did someone bring another cat in there?"

"Oh. Maybe," I said. "We thought it was yours. We've been feeding it."

Mario shook his head. "There was a cat, but it died six months ago. If someone's brought another one in, they'd better be changing the litter. I don't want that thing peeing or shitting off in some corner."

Danni said, "The litter's clean, no worries," and hooked her arm in mine, pulling me away before we let our jaws drop. She took me for a long walk, across the bridge on Gerrard and up into Riverdale Park East, back across the footbridge over the Don Valley into Cabbagetown and back south to the building. She was testing a theory.

When we got up to the apartment, the same three people were there. In the kitchen, the bowl was empty. Flo-Jo squatted in a corner of the living room and muttered.

Danni asked Grumplepuss, "Has anyone opened that door since we left?" Nobody had. With anyone less paranoid, we might've doubted his certainty. "The balcony?"

"Nope. Everything's still stuck shut, and nobody seems to give a shit. The whole building's gonna fall down around us one day."

Danni pulled me into the hallway. "Holy fuck!" she whispered.

"I'll bet it was Flo-Jo. With all that pacing, that girl needs energy."

"Or maybe Poodle Do is in a cat food coma. Like when you eat too much turkey — what's that chemical called?"

"Nah, my money's on Grumplepuss. Maybe that's why he can't lose weight."

The alter ego of Kaptain Kibble — as Danni called him or her — remained a mystery despite our hyper-vigilance to everyone's behaviour.

That was a great memory, a funny puzzle we almost didn't want to solve, and it comforted like a silky mug of hot cocoa flowing down the gullet when the harshness of life became difficult to swallow. Like in September, when the TV showed terrorists taking hundreds of schoolchildren hostage in a small Russian town and massacring them. Later in the month, Hurricane Ivan hit the Caribbean, flattening Grenada, Jamaica, and Trinidad. It was all over the news. Flo-Jo shook her legs and paced more than normal; her family was from St. Vincent and the Grenadines. "Shit, shit, shit." She banged her fists against her head.

My mama was probably on the phone with relatives. I wondered if any of them might've lost their houses, or worse. This'd be a good reason to reconnect with my mama, a safe excuse that could be about other people and not about us.

My breathing quickened with each ring; it'd been ages since I'd called. My brother answered. I hadn't expected him to be there; he didn't live at home.

"Eddy? That you? It's Paulette."

"Bean-Pole?"

"What are you doing there?"

"Oh my God, are you serious? What am I doing here? Says the girl who hasn't been by in years." He nearly spat on the word *years*.

Already I regretted calling. "I heard about the hurricane. I'm ... Is Mama all right? You know, she has people down there."

Eddy paused before answering. "Bean-pole, Mama's sick. She doesn't know there's been a hurricane. She's got fucking Alzheimer's, which you'd know if you weren't too good for us now, with your life in the Big Smoke."

I kept it cool. I didn't want to get into it, but God, if he only knew. I asked how long this'd been going on, and he said it'd progressed slowly for two years, and then sped up. He checked in on her sometimes. I doubted it was often, but I was in no position to take the moral high ground. Mrs. Johnson down the hall looked in too, which I did believe. The woman was a saint. Eddy arranged for visiting nurses to go in.

I asked about Mama's mood, if she was angrier or more depressed than she'd been before, but apparently, she was more cheerful. All of her worries and troubles had been lost in the mist of her disease, and she didn't care to search for them.

Once my brother moved past his snarkiness, he asked about me. I lied my face off. Told him I was working at a restaurant, bad hours, long hours, hard to get to Hamilton. I made promises I wouldn't keep. If he knew I was lying, he didn't press. Besides, Eddy much preferred talking about himself, so I changed the subject. He named a packet of troubles, troubles of a whole different species. Back-talking preteen son (what goes around comes around), child support payments to his ex, and a live-in Ivorian girlfriend. Eddy mentioned something about keeping her happy and avoiding jealous fits. And good luck to him, I thought. I'd met this crazy-ass girl once at a rave years ago, watched her tear braids off a rival in a drag-down fight over a guy. He didn't say, but it wouldn't have surprised me if he still had connections to his old gang of dirtbags.

After the call, I was raring to punch something, bite someone, scream, or cry. Alone, not with Danni. I made an excuse and ditched her at the stroll, and when I got enough for a fix, I stepped down into my stairwell. I don't know if it was bad luck or if maybe I was careless, messier, and someone had reported me, but I was picked up by two cops. In the early hours of the morning, with the dark barely holding on, I was coming up from my hole in the ground when the flashlights blinded me. I stepped up, and there were those starched uniforms. Pulling into the station, the female officer said, "Don't you want to live a normal life? Be part of the world?" I raised an eyebrow from the backseat and smirked. She shook her head. "Don't you care about yourself?"

Terrorists in Chechnya killing children. Hurricanes flattening countries. Alzheimer's sweeping a lifetime clean off its shelf. My life was shitty, but the supposedly steady world outside was shaky and dangerous, too. That cop didn't wanna hear my answer, so I buttoned my lip. She led me to the holding cell.

Tremors

IT TOOK SIX MONTHS TO GO TO TRIAL, AND SINCE I DIDN'T KNOW anyone who could afford bail, I cooled my heels in the West Detention Centre and they applied that time to the eight-month sentence. Danni was able to help Yen Mah with the rent for a month until Yen Mah found someone to sublet. I promised to pay Danni back.

It wasn't my first time inside. I'd done time for possession the year before I met Danni. That first time was a shock. It wasn't fear; I made myself fierce, and most of the scary ones kept their distance. It was the boredom. Deadening. Two crooked guards smuggled in drugs and occasionally new needles, but not enough of either. I'd go into withdrawal over and over, never quite long enough to reach full detox. Boredom made the jonesing worse — muscles trying to burst free of my skin, worries like hornets whipped into a frenzy by a foot in a nest. Sure, the stroll, standing there like an idiot waiting for johns to come, that was monotonous. Prison monotony was of a different kind.

It's not that there weren't activities. There was an educational program, but I wasn't gonna be there long enough or I might've finished my high school diploma. I spent time in the library, and outside, when it wasn't too cold. It didn't fill enough hours. On the streets,

I got slight comfort from thinking of activities in the big city — a trip to Centre Island, a jazz concert, or shopping in the Eaton Centre — even though they were financially out of reach. In prison, there was an outer edge to my world that thickened the tedium to near concrete, like the walls surrounding us. I waited for the next batch of drugs to get smuggled in.

Danni visited me and did her best to cheer me up. She asked if I was getting any action in jail, and I scolded her for believing that stereotype. She stammered an apology, and I smiled, came clean, told her I was fucking with her, and that I was getting action from time to time. She smacked my arm, bringing the guard forward to reprimand her. I was getting more than I'd had on the outside. I asked if there was anyone special in her life, and she said, "Hell no." It didn't surprise me. She'd mentioned only two boyfriends, guys she'd dated in school. The pool from which she and I had to choose was shallow — pretty much bone dry for her, a bit better for me if I could pick someone up at Pope Joan on a night off, but that was a lot of effort without much guarantee of success. Besides, they'd closed the year before, and I didn't have much success at Slack Alice. In that respect, jail was better. Whether it was from curiosity or maybe Sapphic girls had more of an anti-social bent, whatever the reason, there was a core contingent of us. I was popular. I let a couple of bees land in my honey and get stuck there for a while until I tired of them and shook them free. It reminded me what an orgasm during sex felt like, after faking them for so many years.

Since Danni didn't have any boyfriend news to share, she complained about Carole-Anne and told me how Olive had been in a fight with a new girl who'd tried to take her corner. Olive had kicked the girl's ass all the way down to Dundas. Danni mentioned how she was still trying to figure out who'd eaten the cat food. She'd laid traps, but Kaptain Kibble was too embarrassed to snack with anyone around. By process of elimination, she had it down to Flo-Jo and Grumplepuss, but one day when neither of them was there, and Poodle Do, Jump-Start, and Boo Radley were alone in the apartment, the cat food was eaten.

"A second culprit!" I screamed. The same guard shushed me, told us if we didn't behave she'd bring the visit to an end.

I told Danni stories of the kooky cast of characters in the pen with me: A woman with a limp who whispered to her dead dog. A ripped girl with a craggy face who tried one arm push-ups in the yard but toppled sideways onto the pavement. An older Black woman with bleached blonde hair like Etta James but who, instead of having a smooth and silky voice, spoke in an irritating high-pitched nails-on-chalkboard way. Danni asked if I'd nicknamed them, but I hadn't. It wasn't right without her.

"I'm disappointed in you," she said and, on the spot, dubbed them Dog Whisperer, Jack Un-Balance, and Screechy-Bleachy. Okay, she was disappointed in me, but it had always been Danni coming up with the best names. It gave me an extra-sharp pang to know that she considered it a collaborative effort; at best, I'd helped her brainstorm.

The day I was released, in May 2005, I went to find Danni straight away in Carole-Anne's apartment. We hugged a long time. Yen Mah had been firm about giving notice to the renter who'd replaced me, but it'd be a week before the girl left. I asked Danni to ask Carole-Anne if I could crash there for a week.

We sat at opposite ends of the sofa. "Thank God you're out, Paulie. I was going squirrely."

"What you missed was someone to tell you that you can't go outside like that! Did you get dressed in the dark?" She wore a T-shirt, baggy sweatpants, and two different coloured socks. It wasn't only the outfit. She was paler. Her hair was still wild, but it was stringy, and her latest dye job was piss yellow from buying the cheapest product, like those Russian girls that sometimes showed up on the stroll. Her roots showed.

She said, "I wish I could blame it on that. The bulb is out in my bedroom, and Carole-Anne keeps saying she'll replace it, but, as you know, it's usually daytime when I get dressed."

Sooner than we should've, we visited Mario's Drop-In. It was hard to believe, but that ball had rolled further downhill since I'd gone to jail. Another smear on the wall, possibly blood. A new oily stain on the sofa. The chemical smell of crack smoke was more intense. Most of the same people were there, minus Poodle Do, who'd overdosed and nearly died. She was recovering at a sister's in Etobicoke. Grumplepuss had finally pried open the balcony door. He stomped on it, then came back in to warn us not to go out there, it didn't seem stable, we all might plunge to our deaths one day, stupid piece of shit building, etcetera, etcetera. There were two new French-Canadian girls from Hearst who, when they talked to each other, switched from French to English to French about five times in a sentence. None of the regulars noticed I'd been gone for half a year. Like when the cat's absence had gone undetected, these addicts were too busy fending off the itchy crawlies of their lives.

I watched Danni prepare for her hit. Her hand had a tremor. Her voice was heavier, deeper. I was alarmed by how seriously she placed a piece of rock in her pipe. Her forearm tensed and rippled. Her lower jaw jutted in concentration, her brow creased into cavewoman furrows. Had her nonchalance seeped out while I'd been inside?

We spent a lot of time together that first week after I got back, and much of it, when we weren't working, was in the Drop-In. On my second visit there, one of the new French-Canadian girls cut her finger on a carpet fibre while doing God only knows what down there on the floor, and within an hour her entire hand had become so grotesquely swollen that we had to take her to the hospital. "Gant de Baseball," Danni whispered in my ear while we waited for her in emerg, but the nicknaming was less joyful, even mean. Mario's Drop-In, injecting crack into my veins, finding cutesy monikers in a holier-than-thou way — it was losing its shine. My life on the streets had always been pretty crappy, but in jail that second time around, I'd had a chance to talk to people who'd been where I was and who'd gotten clean. I'd missed laughing with Danni, but this was our life together: laughing at other people no more pathetic than we were, except that laughing at them made us the more pathetic ones.

Danni was in deeper, and I was a bicycle wheel caught in streetcar tracks. If I didn't pull out of it, I'd land face-first and skid across the pavement.

Gateway Drug

WE EASED BACKWARDS INTO OUR OLD ROUTINE, AND SOMETIME during that summer of 2005, Danni told me she wanted to start slamming. I said no way, stick to the pipe, girl, don't fuck up your veins. I don't know why I was so adamant. On the surface, it was pretty much a burn-to-death or freeze-to-death choice, but I was worried that needles, for Danni, would be like Grumplepuss's two-legged stomp on the fragile balcony: a stupid strength test whose failure would kill the tester.

I also worried that Danni and I might not be so good for each other. She did help me keep loneliness at bay, and on the streets we had each other's backs, but getting high was that much easier, better, chummier with someone else. We egged each other on. Soon enough, despite the first budding urge to quit, my own drug use was more intense than it'd been before I went to jail. If I'd ever tried to hold off on the next fix for even a half-hour, I no longer bothered. I bought more, cooked more, nudged up the amount I'd slam bit by bit.

One slow night in late summer, on an extra-long break, we sat on a bench in the park near Allen Gardens. Danni pulled her mini-skirt down to cover more of the underside of her legs because the bench's paint was peeling and scratchy. A street cleaner drove by behind us.

"Paulie, how did you start?"

"Tricks?"

"Drugs." .

"Hmph." I was trying to buy time, avoid getting into the details. "Friends of my brother's. At parties. It was always around."

"Were you a badass?"

"I was a goody two-shoes. But my mom was always riding me: 'Study harder,' 'Don't be like your brother.' I guess I wondered how she'd react if I was like my brother. You know. I was fourteen and a fool."

"What did you do?"

"Mostly pot."

"Ah, your 'gateway drug'!" She made air quotes. "Mine was codeine."

I leaned back, crossing my arms. Getting Danni talking was the best way to deflect the questions. "Codeine was your first."

"I was a kid, and I lived in Forest Hill. Preteens aren't busy mainlining heroin up there as a rule."

"Okay, but how do you go from taking Tylenol Threes to doing crack on the streets? Did you have an injury or something?"

"No, it was the night they took me to emerg for my stomach cramps — that drug they gave me. I'll never forget the feeling. It was ... a ripple of heat moving through my body."

Like fish in a barrel. No, I shouldn't joke; it wasn't just to deflect. I loved the way Danni told a story. It reminded me of the way teachers would lean forward, holding their book, as we sat on the library floor. If I closed my eyes when Danni spoke, I had the feeling of watching a movie. She splashed bright images on my mind's screen, then cut away to something else just as vivid.

This is what she told me: When Danni's mother was ready to date again, her friends set her up with Dr. David Citron, the same pediatrician Danni'd seen that night in emerg. He'd never been married and was admired for the fundraising he did for the community. Her mom had tried to take Danni back to Dr. Citron after that first time, but he'd insisted she see a specialist, who also couldn't find anything physically wrong. This annoyed her mom. The specialist kept asking, was anything troubling Danni? Was anything wrong? Danni shook her head. It was too horrible for her to say, and anyway, the cramps were still coming even though Stan had stopped touching her. It would've been misleading to hand the doctor a connection.

Four months after that pervert left her mom, Dr. Citron started to come around. Danni's stomach gurgled more when he was there, so she kept her distance. She wasn't his patient, he'd treated her only the once, but it was still weird to have a doctor in the house making googly eyes at her mom. Eventually, though, Danni admitted that he was better than the pervert, or any of her mom's previous suitors. For one thing, he was comfortable around kids, but more importantly, when her mom had asked if he'd put her to bed, he'd said, "Oh, Danni doesn't want me doing that, do you, Danni?" Too shy to respond, she'd re-buried her head in her book until her mom had shooed her off to her room.

When Dr. Citron encouraged Danni to call him David, her mom protested, which she'd never done with the other guy. Was it because her mom hoped to make it easier, later, for her to transition to calling him 'Daddy'? This relationship was more serious, but never in a million years did she intend to call this or any other man Daddy.

"But 'Dr. Citron' is so formal," he'd argued. "If Danni and I are going to be friends, I can't have her calling me that."

She'd never heard of kids being friends with an adult, except in *Paper Moon*, which had been on TV earlier that year. She imagined herself a young Addie Loggins to Dr. Citron's Moses Pray, going door to door, swindling old ladies. But the truth was that Dr. Citron was far too respectable, her mom was still alive, and being Jewish, it'd've been hard for either of them to pull off bible sales. Still, to consider Dr. Citron — she gave in and called him David — a friend, well, Danni could stomach that more than a surrogate dad. If being a friend didn't involve tucking her in — and he'd laid that idea to rest — she didn't mind. He was funny and friendly, she said, and he was at least as handsome as Ryan O'Neal.

Her mom shrugged. "Suit yourselves. Nothing could make me happier than you two being friends."

"We're doing pretty well in the friends department, aren't we, Danni?"

"I guess," she'd said, before running to the living room to watch a cartoon.

Her mom's relationship moved quickly. Karen, one of her mom's friends who'd congratulated herself by calling David "a great catch" when they were over at her house for tea, said, "He's settling down, and how perfect that it's with you, Barbara. Danni needs a father."

"David's my friend, not my father," Danni'd said from the other side of the room, where she'd been doing homework.

"Isn't that sweet!" said Karen.

Within a year, her mom sold their home and they moved into David's, a two-storey red brick house with a small covered front porch on Russell Hill Road. They had a small wedding. Danni was a flower girl. Danni's bedroom window opened onto the backyard and the great big swing set he'd bought her. The room had a new princess canopy bed and a white desk with a vanity mirror. They let her paint the walls purple and paste decals on the ceiling. It was nicer than anything she could've imagined — the kind of bedroom I'd never stepped foot in, myself — but Danni still had trouble falling asleep. The house made noises, the metal chain on the swing creaked in the wind, and the silk curtains tied at the canopy posts cast frightening shadows. Before Stan Abel, she'd quieted herself to sleep by warming her fingers in the softness between her legs. But that didn't work anymore, so she tried to tire herself by counting the glowing stars on the ceiling and tensing and releasing her leg muscles until they howled.

In their new house, Danni grew to like David. Maybe more than her mom did. Her mom was impatient with her new husband and often short-tempered, particularly when he stayed late at work. Her mom was often left at home with Danni in the evenings, and Danni remembered this being a source of tension. "I can't help my work schedule," he said. "What do you think pays for this nice house? It's the life of a doctor, Barbara. I thought you understood that when you married me." Danni's mom didn't have a reply. In the next four years, she adjusted to the situation and complained less, but she wasn't pleased. She kept herself busy with charity work, but it didn't change the reality: her marriage hadn't turned out as she'd hoped. If from time to time she confided in Danni, her mom quickly dismissed her own complaints. Most of her friends had it the same or worse.

One Wednesday morning in April 1995, when Danni'd just turned fifteen, Danni convinced her high school vice-principal to send her home after first period. She complained of waves of crippling stomach cramps. Not her period, that had ended the week before. The school called her mom, and her mom reluctantly allowed Danni to come home. She didn't believe her daughter, but she kept that to herself; she didn't want Danni's reputation as a model student to slide.

When Danni arrived at the house, her mom had the television on. It blared horrific images: the bombing of a massive building in Oklahoma City. "Lunatics," her mom said, mostly to the TV. Danni waved a hand in front of her mom's face as if to indicate she was a human being needing to be acknowledged. On the set, the smoky building was in ruins.

The phone rang, and her mom took the receiver. "I know, I know. Awful. They're saying it might be a fanatic." A pause. "They don't know yet."

Danni's belly rumbled. Her mom ended her conversation, but before Danni could retreat to her bedroom to listen to music, her mom pointed to a small box near the door. "I need you to take that to the hospital. David called to say he forgot it, and I was going to go, but I have a million things to do."

"But, Mom, I'm really not feeling well."

"I'm sorry, dear. I have a Hadassah meeting tomorrow, and David's birthday is coming up and I have to get him a present. Plus, I'm sending you to a hospital. If those cramps get worse, well, what better place to be, right?" She smiled, pleased with herself. Danni tried one more time to avoid the errand, but her mom was unmoveable and sent her out the front door with an outstretched finger. She was making sure Danni left before she herself set off.

The box was small and contained some files that Danni leafed through on the subway. Disappointingly, they turned out to be about an administrative committee David sat on instead of someone's gory case notes. At the hospital, she followed the blue line on the beige floor all the way to a soft-serve ice cream kiosk that she knew well. Cool vanilla might relax the cramps.

She licked her cone, the box held against her side, then dropped it on the floor of the gift shop to browse through *People* magazine. The cover story was about the murder of pop star Selena. When she was done there, and with her ice cream, she found the bank of elevators to David's office, sucked the stickiness off her fingers, and pressed the button.

Her stomach continued its grumbling. The ice cream had possibly made it worse. If her stomach was punishing her for the years of pretending, the pain was real enough now, despite her mom's doubts. David's antacids, even though prescription strength, were a poor substitute for the pills he'd first prescribed — the comfort pills, she still called them — but he hadn't let her have those in a few years. It wasn't good for her to keep taking them, he said, when occasionally she'd made a plea for more. The tests showed nothing physically wrong with her. David said her pain was psychosomatic, which her mom interpreted as "not real" instead of caused by the mind. Proof that Danni was still faking for attention or, like today, to get her way.

The clock said eleven forty-five when she reached the wing where David kept his office. Jeannie, the regular hard-nosed receptionist, was not on duty. In her place was a lady with a Caribbean accent whom Danni'd met a few years before. She was less strict, if Danni recalled. Maybe her name was Marie; she seemed like a Marie.

"Hi there, Danni. I haven't seen you in a while. It's Sandy; you might not remember me."

"Hi, Sandy, yes, it's been a while for sure." She was disappointed it was Sandy and not Marie.

"My God, aren't you a beautiful young lady now. I can't believe how much you've changed. You're the spitting image of your mother."

Danni smiled thinly, displeased with the comparison, and thrust the box upwards and onto the counter. She told Sandy it needed to be delivered to David's office.

"Dr. Citron went for an early lunch, but if you want, I can give you the key to his office and you can put it on his desk yourself."

Danni promised to bring it right back. She turned left at the first corridor and headed down to the end, near the corner of the building that had a view of both University Avenue and Elm Street.

When she got to David's office, she slipped the key into the lock and pushed the door. What she saw when she walked into the room didn't make sense at first, like a puzzle with jumbled-up shapes in which you were supposed to distinguish a tree, or a dog, or a bird. David and another man in a white lab coat were pulling their hands from each other's underwear.

"Danni!" David exclaimed. The men drew apart. The other man's shirt was open. He was much younger than David. She glimpsed the tip of the younger man's penis, poking above the elastic of his underwear, but he turned and tucked everything back in, zipped himself up. David struggled with the zipper of his own pants. He was scared. Danni, startled, dropped the box on the floor near the door.

"Danni." David's hand told her not to come any closer. "This isn't ... Dr. Barnes and I were just —"

"Dr. Citron," interrupted Dr. Barnes, "excuse me, but I have a patient." He rushed past, his skin sunburn red.

David tried again, as he tucked in his shirt. "Danni, what you saw, it wasn't what it looked like."

Her insides churned. She bolted from David's office and down the hall, past Sandy at reception to the bathroom, which — thank God — was empty. Locking herself inside, she pulled the toilet seat down and sat.

"Danni?" David knocked on the door.

She didn't answer.

Sandy was outside the door. "Dr. Citron, I didn't know you were here. Is something wrong?"

David said, "No, it's fine. You can go back to the desk," and louder, into the door, "Danni, I'm going to wait outside until you're done."

She flushed the toilet to fake that she'd gone — the cramping had stopped as if slapped into submission — and while the water swirled in the bowl, she absorbed what she'd seen. A minute later, David knocked again, and there was no option but to come out. He put his hand on her shoulder, and she shook it off, moved her lower jaw left to right. "Come to my office for a minute. I want to talk to you." He was stern. A nurse stood nearby, concern wrinkling her brow. "It's okay," he said to the nurse, "she's not feeling well."

Danni followed him to his office, and he shut the door. She went to the window and stared down into traffic.

"Danni, sit down, please."

She didn't move.

"I don't know what you think you saw, but you're confused."

She turned. "I'm not confused, you and that guy were messing around!"

"Shhh. Danni, keep your voice down."

"Jesus, are you gay? Have you always been?" Her voice, lower, was almost defeated.

"No. And Danni, you mustn't tell your mother."

"Why shouldn't I?"

"She would ... This isn't who I am. We were just letting off steam. Men do that sometimes; it doesn't mean anything. But you know your mom, she'd make a big deal about this."

"It is a big deal!"

"Your voice, Danni!" She turned again to the window, but closed her eyes. In the silence, they each considered their next move. "If you tell your mother, she'd, well, I don't know what she'd do. It could get bad."

"What do you mean?"

"It could ... She might draw the wrong conclusion. She might not want you two to stay with me anymore. In our house. Do you want that?"

Danni sat on the chair. She lowered her head and tossed this possibility around. She wasn't an idiot. She was over the first shock of it and knew that what they'd been doing wasn't just two guys letting off steam. But the idea that she and her mom might have to move — it was unfair that something she accidentally saw might lead to that. To a new school, a new neighbourhood, a more modest home. Having to make new friends. Because of something that she might never have known about. The weight of it made her head heavy. Her presence in that spot, in that place, might make a huge difference in all of their lives. Change their future. Never before had she mattered in this way, to anyone.

She liked David's house, and she liked David, though at the moment she was angry at him — for hiding who he was and suggesting she lie about it, too. She was almost as mad as she'd been with her mom for leaving her with Stan and, later, for not breaking up with him. For waiting for him to break up with her. There was a pang of sadness for her mom, but maybe this was what her mom deserved for not standing up to that man.

"How can I convince you not to tell your mom?"

It hadn't occurred to her, until his question, that the situation was one that could be turned to her advantage. "What about those pills?" She'd just been thinking about them; they'd been on her mind all day, but she was shocked by her own nerve, by how quickly she'd come up with something.

His eyes were enormous. "Danni —"

"Those pills you keep saying I don't need. They're the only ones that work. My mom thinks I'm faking these cramps, but I'm not, and if she'd believed me —"

"— I believe you —"

"— I wouldn't've walked in on you. That stupid, fucking box." They both looked at it. It was on the floor where she'd dropped it, the files spilling out. Then she added, "You think I'm going to take them all the time, but I won't."

"I told you that drug isn't good for you."

"You don't care about me or my mom!" she shouted. "So don't pretend you're some good guy. You. Don't. Get. To. *Pretend!*" The force of her words: they were a sledgehammer, bashing away at him. Both her mom and David had distrusted her, and it'd led her to this situation and this dilemma, in which every choice meant either hurt or betrayal or both.

David put his hands to his face and rubbed it as if he were wiping off dirt with a washcloth. "Danni, Danni," he muttered.

He wouldn't talk himself around this, wouldn't weasel away. She stiffened her back and hardened her voice, but made sure her eyes conveyed a fury from which he couldn't shrink. It came from a well she'd never tapped. "You asked me how you could convince me not to tell. Write me that prescription, and make sure there are repeats."

He took his hands from his face and stared. His eyes were blood-shot and fearful and maybe a little sad. He flipped through his prescription pad without looking away. And she knew, from the way he watched her, like a person sizing up a dangerous and unpredictable adversary, that their friendship was done. Her childhood, too, such as it had been.

I leaned back and closed my eyes to inhale the scent of the trees in Allen Gardens, a sweetness I'd never come across before. It wasn't enough. Not for this. Like all highs, my last one had come crashing down; I needed another, and I needed to be far from Danni, to be in that place we all tried to go, with each swallow, each puff, each slow push of the thumb.

Danni, spent from her storytelling, sighed and bent forward on the park bench, her face between her knees.

Maybe the saddest part wasn't the threat those two had held to each other's throats. Or how young Danni'd been when she'd honed her wily ways. It was how securely she'd been hooked after tasting the lure of drugs. The lure of a fancy home.

Maybe she hoped I'd be more impressed, but all I could muster was, "And I thought I had a fucked-up childhood." I stood and stretched.

"That's it? That's all you have to say?"

She was hurt, but what was I to make of that story? That she'd been the victim? Sure she'd been a teenager, but it fit too well with what I knew of her at twenty-five. Clever. Used to getting her way. Making foolish decisions and throwing away a blessed future for the comforts of the here and now. Swallowing all of her advantages and shitting them out later.

"I need another hit, and we should get back to work." I walked ahead, pressing down an unsettling feeling about our friendship, something between disappointment and misgiving.

Recklessness

AUGUST WENT OUT SPEWING WAVES OF HOT, HEAVY RAIN, EACH NIGHT'S downpour washing the streets clear, but somehow not clean. Over the next few days, I did my best to pretend nothing was different. If Danni noticed my aloofness, she didn't mention it. When September came, I told her I'd try another spot for the evening. She made to come with me, but I halted her. "I'm gonna go off on my own tonight."

"Oh. Okay." She raised her palms, took two steps back.

I walked south to Dundas, where I took my heels off, tied them to the strap on my purse, and waited for the streetcar. It was warm, sticky, and the rain had become a stubborn drizzle, nearly a mist. I removed my wig, shook it, and stuffed it into my handbag. A tuft stuck out, making me feel like Paris Hilton parading an itty-bitty dog. At Jones, I got off and walked north to a crack house I'd been to once before.

In their kitchen, I got into a long conversation with a random junkie named Irene about all sorts of nonsense — city politics, the price of a Metropass, whether or not Fantasia Barrino had deserved to win last year's *American Idol* — she said yes, and I said no way, it shoulda been Jennifer Hudson — and a story on TV about rebuilding of the World Trade Center in New York, which led to an annoying conversation about 9/11.

"I was so scared that day, am I right?" said Irene. "I'm shootin' up in this high-rise, right, and when this guy mentions the second tower being hit, I freak, right? I'm thinking, like we probably all were, who knows where the next one's gonna hit, right? So I run down the staircase and into the street. Shit. That was some scary day, right?"

I stared at her. "You're a fucking idiot, right?"

"What?"

"Yeah. That shit-ass apartment building in Toronto was next on the Al Qaeda hit list."

"Well, we didn't know."

"Moron," I said. Irene told me to fuck off, and I did.

At four in the morning, my money depleted and feeling no better, I returned to Jarvis and sought out Danni.

"You're not wearing your wig," she said, as if it might've fallen off without my noticing.

"With this rain, I look better than you do."

"New spot not great?"

I leaned into the window of a car that'd already stopped for me. I could hardly believe it. This was the first time I'd tried working without my wig, and I'd waited all of thirty seconds. Why had I been duped into turning into every goddamned girl on the street? I'd lost my edge without knowing I was being dulled. Meanwhile, Danni'd been sharpening her blades since she was fifteen, and I'd mistaken her for an innocent.

My trick was a brothah in his fifties, hands big like my favourite teacher's, with a nice smile. We talked a short while, and he took me to a quiet street in the Port Lands. I lay down on his back seat, and when he went to put on a condom, I stopped him. "It's okay, I'm clean, I swear it."

He laughed. "Isn't that supposed to be my line?" and so I laughed too. We fucked, and at that moment, because I wouldn't have cared if the earth had split open into a gaping chasm, I let him come inside of me.

He was back twice the next week, and we did the same thing.

"So you have a regular now," said Danni, with a hint of jealousy.

In late October, coming straight from the Hassle Free Clinic, I knocked on her apartment door. Carole-Anne was gone, so it was safe.

She sat me down. "Shit, Paulie. Weren't you on the pill? Or at least using condoms?"

"Are you on the pill?"

"No," she said. "But I'm ninety-nine percent sure I'm infertile. I've fucked up lots of times and never had a single scare."

Why hadn't we ever had this conversation? "I wasn't on the pill because condoms protect against everything." When Danni made a face, I added, "Well, okay, if you use them, they do."

The nurse in the clinic had told me to wait three months for the HIV test, that it was more accurate that way. I should've been more nervous about that, but my pregnancy gave me a feeling of marvel and superiority, which would be bolstered when I later learned I'd dodged HIV.

Meanwhile, Danni was adding luck to the many other gifts she'd unwrapped and too quickly tossed in the trash. "Danni, you should really use them."

"You're kidding, right? You're lecturing me about condoms, baby mama? I use condoms a lot of the time. You're the one who screwed up. Nice try, trying to turn this on me."

She was right. I was in no position to judge, but I was bloated by a deluded sense of control. I was once again the ballsy girl from the wrong side of the tracks, finding my way to a more meaningful life. I'd taken a risk, but I'd snagged a sperm and I was sure I'd dodged a virus. In my recklessness, I'd been subconsciously planning my future. "Maybe I wanted to get pregnant."

"Bullshit," she answered.

Sir Purrsalot, still not purring, was staring up at me, so I hoisted him onto my lap. "I'm gonna make it work this time." I hadn't been trying to get pregnant, but I wasn't upset about it.

"Okay." She patted her thighs and shook out her arms like Flo-Jo did, a loosening up before the gruelling marathon we both knew this would be. "We can totally do this."

"Oh," I said. "Danni, I know you'd help. But I meant I'm gonna make this work. Me. I need to get clean for this kid, and I need to change things up if I'm gonna do that. You get it, right?"

She picked at her cuticles. "Yeah, of course."

"It's only that I've been thinking about this for a while. I wanna go into detox, then maybe join one of those groups, Narcotics Anonymous or something. Maybe I can ask Yen Mah if she can get me a job in her supermarket. Or maybe Carole-Anne'll find me something in her loading dock. I've got guns." I flexed my biceps, and we both snickered at their scrawniness. "Well, I used to, and I will again, if I get clean."

"Uh-huh," said Danni. "You'll be huge."

I stifled a laugh, because I needed her to hear me: "You understand, right? I just can't do this with you."

Danni's smile faded. She understood, and for the first time since I'd met her, she was afraid.

Encircled

I DIDN'T HAVE THE LUXURY OF MOVING INTO A NEW APARTMENT, which would've been the smart thing — making a cleaner break with my former surroundings — but I did check into detox, ready to make it work. It was in a large converted house in the west end, renovated in a way that ruined the house's charm without adding much comfort. The sickly-sweet orange of a super-strength cleanser clung to the walls, and cigarette smoke from the group of puffers on the front porch seeped into the front hall. I'd have joined them more often, if I could've afforded cigarettes. I couldn't make up my mind if the smoke made the citrus smell better or worse.

The first week was more gruelling than I'd imagined, equally from the strange physical symptoms, crazy sneezing, chills, and leg pain as from the despair, which blasted me and sent me tumbling. No matter how many people told me they were experiencing the same thing, self-doubt crowded me, keeping encouragement at bay. At night, I was sleepless, counting the minutes until the sun rose and a programmed activity — a meal or a discussion — would give slight relief. The staff prescribed magnesium, potassium, and l-tyrosine supplements to ease the symptoms and boost my energy, but it wasn't much help.

During a house meeting on the third day, a girl from Vancouver with a Downtown Eastside grit mentioned that things were becoming clearer, that nobody that she'd met through her habit was a real friend. She knew this now. The only thing they'd had in common was the drugs. The counsellors nodded, and so did everyone else. I did too, my throat tightening. Danni'd been my friend, truer than any I'd ever known, but my irritation with her was normal; she was a bad storm, and I needed to find shelter through an open door, follow those arms waving me inside. Leave her outside. From that refuge, I asked myself what she and I had in common. No two people had more different backgrounds. We'd met through hooking, but the drugs had kept us close. I didn't mention that I missed her. It wasn't good to enjoy running around in the wind and the rain. I had to cut my ties with Danni if I wanted to get clean and do right by my baby.

The memory of giving up Chantelle kept me motivated. This time'd be different. I tried not to be sidetracked, but during that first week at dinner, a hot girl named Washuka came on to me. She was a tall Kenyan with the prettiest eyes I'd ever seen. I'd promised myself no distractions, but she was too hot to ignore. She was lonely and scared, and I was the only one in reach: hardly flattering, but I gave in. I could resist drugs, but not this, too. We snuck away a couple of times, found somewhere private and did our best to keep quiet, though she was a screamer. I had to put my hand over her mouth while my other hand did its work.

By week three, neither of us was much into it anymore. The lust was gone, and there was only the longing for closeness. She approached me with a kind of resignation, a fake put-on sexiness I used on the stroll. Eventually, I took her hands in mine and said, "I'm not saying you're not fine, but I'm not here for that. I need to focus on my recovery." She moved seats, ate dinner in silence, and ignored me for the rest of our stay.

In the other girls, I hoped there'd be a good Danni substitute, a new bestie in sobriety, but there was nobody. It wasn't that they weren't nice — they were — but they lacked Danni's sarcastic snarl. Maybe that's where they were in their lives, the snarl temporarily or permanently muzzled for the sake of survival. Maybe it was dangerous, too dangerous in people like us, carrying with it a latent rabid bite that we couldn't treat, couldn't contain the way others did. The difference between addicts and regular people. It's how I felt about myself.

This was new to me, learning how different we addicts were from the general population. I took from this that we had faulty DNA, the kind that made us biologically unable to handle any drug in moderation. In the next breath, they described how drugs changed our brain chemistry, making it harder for us to experience pleasure without them. Aside from filling me with hopelessness, the messages seemed contradictory. Was it the drug's fault, or were we differently wired in the first place? When I asked the question, they told me it was both. What would it mean for my ability to raise my baby? Would those defects be passed on?

The plucky rehab counsellor, Jacqueline, a former crack user from France, tried her hardest to give us hope in spite of telling us our neurons were doomed. One day, we were sitting in the meeting room, its walls painted drab off-white and its tables a humdrum shade of orange to match the smell of the cleanser. Jacqueline said' that there were all sorts of people who find the strength to battle this double strike of bad genes and altered brains. "Dey fight dis battle for years, decades, living better lives. I am one of dese people."

Jacqueline was a slight thing; I could snap her in half without trying. If Danni'd been there, she'd have named her Meerkat. If you shaved, tattooed, and clothed one, that'd be Jacqueline: long snouted and hands resting flat against her thighs. She stood erect listening to us, sniffing the air for someone who might be making progress. Waiting for an unknowable signal. Maybe it was a phrase that showed we were committed to our recovery, something more than saying we were committed, naturally, because that would've been too obvious.

Jacqueline told us her story of ending up penniless, sleeping under a bridge in Paris, her family estranged, and turning her life around to immigrate to Canada, find a husband, and hold down that job for nearly five years already. She couldn't leave her face or her hair alone. She'd scratch her cheek or rub a finger under her nostrils to satisfy an itch, grab her hair and either pull it down in the back or take both hands from her thighs to run her fingers through it. She'd shake her head as if in a shampoo ad and return her palms to their resting position on her thighs. Some recovering addicts become champion soft drink guzzlers or obsessive gum chewers. Maybe Jacqueline's face and hair tics were her addiction trying to find a way back in, a prowler testing another entrance. When I managed my own addiction, where would my prowler find its entry point?

I tried to meet her expectations. She'd escaped hell and believed that we could too, so I hunted around in the debris of my past, sifting for insights that might satisfy her. I held the seat of my chair, to steady my wobbliness and the quaver in my voice, and offered up things like, "I'm too much like my mama," or, "I put on a tough show because it's the only thing I know that'll keep me safe. I don't know how to ask for help." None of it made me feel better, or steadier. Progress would be moving forward, but this was no more than reaching back.

By the third week, when I understood how deeply I was buried, I cried and couldn't stop. Jacqueline left me alone that week, checking on me from time to time. The tears stung my skin, leaving it puffy and raw. By week four, too exhausted to cry anymore, I caught my reflection in the mirror. Misery had walloped me in both eye sockets. I went back to the group, wishing for sunglasses.

I'm not sure I ever satisfied Jacqueline with what I had to say, what I could learn about myself. But by the fifth week, the shakiness had turned to numbness and our time was almost up. I hoped the worst of the withdrawal was over. At some point during my stay, I'd contacted Yen Mah to see if she could get me a job, and now I learned that she couldn't, and neither could Carole-Anne. It'd been a long shot. Yen Mah had, however, worked another miracle; she'd found an illegal worker to crash in my room for most of the time that I was away, and for the rest of it, Danni'd pitched in what she could. This'd make it harder to keep her at arm's length. Plus, she'd be in the same building.

I told Danni I'd pay her back, though how I didn't know. For money, I'd resigned myself to the dole, but before I was released, Danni called saying that a seafood store on Gerrard East had a Help Wanted sign. The day I finished rehab, I went straight to that store from dumping my small bag of clothes at the apartment and completed an application. I'd worked retail when I was fifteen and stocked shelves in a local corner store, and later, my friend Jaleesa and I got jobs in the Eaton Centre. Other than that, I'd spent time in the auto body shop where my dada worked before he left for Toronto, and I'd babysat kids in our apartment block. These were the only jobs I'd ever had; not a great resume, and *ho* wasn't something I could put down.

The seafood store owners, a Chinese couple, had kind eyes, and I hesitated midway through completing the form.

"I live in the neighbourhood," I said, "and I really need a job, but I ... I used to work in a clothing store, but otherwise I don't have much recent experience to put down. I do know fish, though." The man expected more, so I stiffened my back. "Hey, I'm Jamaican. That's what we eat."

His wife closed the register and gave a nod so slight I almost missed it. They must've been desperate, because they hired me. Maybe they imagined me growing up in a coastal village. Little did they know I'd been born and raised in Hamilton, and that my mama came from Kingston. I didn't mention that making salt fish involved unwrapping dried chunks you'd bought in a market and placing them in a dish of water to soak.

Luckily, my mama did love to cook fresh fish from time to time, and she'd shown me how to prepare it. That lesson must've lain dormant somewhere. When I came in the next day, my new boss, Bo Hai, showed me how to fillet a fish, and I picked it up quickly. It was a half-hour until the store opened. I tied my apron, and he gave me four nearly rotten fish to practice on in the back. The smell was fierce. He surveyed my work and gave a satisfied grunt. "Not bad. You'll get faster."

They started me on tilapia, a less expensive fish, and Bo Hai's wife, Mei Zhen, gave me gentle tips on how to improve my speed and efficiency, how to waste less in the filleting. Later in the week, I learned how to handle lobsters and crabs and how to make appealing patterns on the crushed ice in the display case. After two weeks, they let me ring orders in at the cash.

They must've harboured distrust, how could they not, but they didn't need to fear me. I'm not saying I wouldn't have been above scamming them had I still been drugging, but even if I'd wanted to, there was never the opportunity. This was a mom-and-pop operation, and they were always around. Also, they emptied the till at night, and I didn't have a key to come by after hours. These were kind people, and they must've sensed the struggle I faced. They never let me leave that store without dinner to cook, though for a change,

I sometimes froze it and picked up chicken or stew from Mr. Jerk on Wellesley. I got sick of fish after a month, but the savings were badly needed. I reminded myself how lucky I was to be sick of fish, until one evening back at the apartment Yen Mah said, "Too much fish not good" and pointed in the direction of my uterus. "Not good for baby because ..." and she couldn't find the word to explain so she brought me to her bedroom while she searched for something.

A Nana Mouskouri poster hung on her wall next to one of Cantonese pop stars. All around her bedroom were clues to the enigma that was Yen Mah: a bowl of thimbles on her dresser, each one painted in delicate, intricate patterns like Easter eggs, though I'd never seen her sew. A framed picture of an Indian man about her age in a kurta, whom I'd asked about once and she'd said only, "Old friend." A certificate on the wall, completely in Chinese and bearing a red wax seal. I'd also asked about that, and her answer was equally obscure: "Degree. No use here." She was probably a doctor or a nuclear physicist.

She pulled an oral thermometer from a pile in a drawer — the object she'd been hunting for. Tapped its red tip.

"Mercury. You're saying the fish has mercury."

"Yes!"

"Yeah? Well, starving is worse." My response was a touch dramatic; I knew I wouldn't starve if I didn't take Bo Hai and Mei Zhen's fish, but I didn't want to sink to food banks. Yen Mah and I had never shared food; we each took a side of the fridge. Her warning niggled, though; what would happen to my baby? I couldn't check if this was a real concern, because we didn't have a computer and I never had time for a library visit, to research this or the umpteen other questions I had about babies.

I pushed the mercury worry aside, hoping that Bo Hai and Mei Zhen's fish was of excellent quality, untainted. I focused on the work.

I enjoyed the new challenge, and the interaction with customers didn't involve more than a chaste smile, which I appreciated. I hadn't realized how much effort I'd put all those years into turning on and off sex banter or striking a flirty pose on the stroll, when sexy was the last thing I felt. I imagined it was like that for movie stars to step into and out of their roles between takes. In the seafood store, being friendly to customers was a cinch. Lots were pleasant, and if some weren't, did I give a shit? If there was any struggle, it was waiting out the day, its stiff stretch, which was stiffer when we weren't busy. I wasn't often bored in the shop, but with no fix to distract me, the minutes counted down with aching slowness.

I saw Danni from time to time, coming and going, in the lobby of our building, and she coughed and kept her distance, saying she was sick and didn't want me to catch it. One day, two months into my job, I ran into her. It was six o'clock, and she was heading to work as I was heading home. She had on a short skirt, teased hair that looked as if she'd put her hand on that electricity ball at the Ontario Science Centre, and everything was pushed up and out to her advantage. I was in jeans and a plain T-shirt, and it made me smile that she wrapped her arms around herself, that she might be self-conscious. My smile faded when she coughed again and held up her hand, to say wait, or maybe don't come closer.

"Sorry. Damn cough. Can't get rid of it." A raspy, wet hacking followed, too realistic to be faked. She looked like hell. And she was much skinnier. She unwrapped a lozenge and popped it in her mouth.

I asked how things were.

"Okay. Same old. Carole-Anne has a DVD player now and was given a new collection of old *Doctor Who* episodes, and so that's driving me insane."

"That'd do it."

"You look good," she said.

I liked that, and told her that she did too. I don't give false compliments as a rule, but Danni was sadder than I remembered. I told myself it was about us not being friends like we used to be, but maybe it had nothing to do with me.

"How's the fetus?" she asked.

"Everyting cook and curry, as my mama says." Used to say, when she was putting on a show of optimism. Did she bother anymore, or had Alzheimer's stripped her of those social niceties? "I'm in my second trimester. Not long before I get fat."

Danni puffed her cheeks.

"Hey, I can repay you. For the money you put towards my rent when I was in detox."

"Oh, you don't have to." She sounded disappointed.

"No, it's okay." She sat in the lobby until I returned with an envelope of cash.

She took it, felt its thickness. "Anyway, I've gotta go. Those tricks aren't gonna go screw themselves. Though I wish some of them would." She put the envelope in her purse.

In the elevator, its walls crushed inwards, the urge to slam a needle was stronger than it'd been in weeks. I put my fish in the fridge and took the elevator back downstairs. I couldn't stay in the apartment like that. I walked to Yonge Street and back, and back to Yonge Street, almost at a run. I had to keep moving, until it was time for my Narcotics Anonymous meeting.

Spiralling

THE URGES CAME AND WENT, BUT WERE MORE SEVERE LATE AT NIGHT. Sometimes, sleepless, I'd sit on the sofa, pull my knees to my chest, and rock back and forth in front of the TV turned down low. Other times, a more disorienting state would take hold. I'd wake as if I'd been on a bender, head throbbing, body hurting and achy, though I hadn't had a single puff of crack or touched any booze whatsoever. It'd last almost a week. God knows how much my bosses detected; it must've shown on my face. I'd forget things too. I took a shipment of waxed paper rolls and stored it in the back of the store one day, but had no memory of it the next.

"I'm sorry, I didn't sleep well last night," I said to Mei Zhen when she reminded me where I'd put them.

Most days after work, I rushed back to the apartment, dropped my things, and ran straight to a meeting. I admit the people there were a strange bunch, and it took a leap of faith to keep going back. The plain room smelling of coffee, chairs in a row like a classroom. I'm not at the best of times a sharer. In our community, growing up, we kept our dirty laundry in our homes. Opening up to a room full of people was not something I relished; it hadn't worked so well for me in detox. Thankfully, they don't make you do that straight away. There isn't the time crunch of the finite stay in detox. But dread welled up in me because at some point, I'd have to share.

In the meantime, I listened. A hefty guy with tattoos snaking up his arms always began his sharing the same way: "What a journey," he'd sigh, followed by, "When I first came here, I was a rebellious dog." People chuckled; they expected it, and he played it up. Another woman filled me with stress because she over-shared. One meeting, she detailed a childhood rape. I fidgeted in my seat. It was excruciating, much more so than when Danni'd told me what'd happened to her. I almost walked out. Someone did leave, and afterwards, the leader of the group reminded us that it was best to share in a general way, and not to sink into the details. I was relieved. The woman was mortified and didn't come back for a month.

At first, I couldn't sit still. I wasn't the only one. A young girl liked to hold a half-filled Styrofoam cup, dig a thumbnail into it, and turn the cup around and around. One day, when she was sitting two seats over, the older woman between us eased her hand over the girl's, and thus over the cup, to hold both still. The clear but calm gesture managed to avoid crushing the cup and spilling hot coffee. The pattern made by the girl's thumb, spiralling from the top of the cup, was halted midway to the base. I checked my behaviour and stayed my drumming heels so the woman didn't have to press down on my knee. It was a temporary measure; the drumming resumed without my noticing, and I'd repeatedly catch myself.

I was learning a new culture with new rules. I watched, trying hard not to judge, absorbing what I could and trying to be inconspicuous, something I appreciated after years on the stroll vying for business. It got so that I squirmed more avoiding the sharing than I knew I would if I opened up, so I talked. I gave people something that made them think they knew me, that I'd plumbed the depths of my soul. If I was supposed to talk the talk until I could walk the walk, that's what I'd do.

It was easiest to talk about the bouts of sadness that had hit me since my early teens, paralyzing me for weeks on end. The kind my mama had, except that I didn't want to see the similarities. Or a story from the streets that might shock them. Except it didn't shock. Lots of people had monstrous experiences. The worst of them got dumped on the floor and were left to wriggle about, while we all sat and nodded. None of us was allowed to poke those wriggling messes with a stick — twelve-step rules — no matter how much we wanted to test if they were good and dead or if they were gonna jump back at the person to take them by the throat.

Same as detox, sharing in NA meetings didn't make things easier. I did learn new things, though. When I talked about the bender-less hangover and the memory loss, I was told these were normal and part of a syndrome associated with having gone through withdrawal. But telling my story gave me no comfort. Maybe it was because I was chipping off the thinnest, loosest pieces. Trying to keep them skipping across the surface instead of letting them sink. I was congratulated and welcomed, and fellow group members tried to arrange coffee dates afterwards, which I rarely accepted. I was starting to show, so the women asked about my pregnancy. Did I have morning sickness, they asked. I told them I felt nausea, but had assumed it was my body getting used to being clean. Their interest was sweet, but getting close to them was pointless; how would I maintain friendships once I had a baby to take care of? How would I go to meetings?

I got my first sponsor: the older woman, Gwen, who'd calmed the girl who drove her thumbnail into the Styrofoam cup. Styrofoam Sally; the name came to me, and I remembered Danni with a pang. Gwen was a sphinx at our sponsor-sponsee meetings. Maybe her face was always like that, but I read disappointment with my progress. Could I be trying harder? Maybe, but it was hard enough just to get to meetings. Maybe if we had clicked more, it'd have been

easier, but Gwen didn't get me, not at all. When I mentioned Styrofoam Sally, when I used that nickname, Gwen stared, silent, until I
explained which girl I meant. "You mean Maureen?" The correction
reached over her cup of coffee and slapped my face. I swallowed,
ashamed of my pettiness but equally disappointed with the nickname. It was lame, not Danni-worthy. Given the designs this Maureen
made with her thumbnail, Danni might've chosen an artist whose
name started with an S, or — and it came to me too late — something funnier like Fidgety Fran.

It was possible Gwen had no sense of humour. She was dead
serious about NA's whole non-judgey thing. Or maybe I had to earn
the right to take the piss out of group members, an unspoken
privilege granted after a significant NA anniversary. Either way,
it wasn't only that attempts at humour were met with her brick
wall. There was always a lesson. Did I need constant teaching?
Was that how bad I'd become? Was that what it meant to be in a
twelve-step program? A never-ending series of life lessons without
any chance to come up for air? This new skin felt tight, like the
skin around my expanding midsection. Sometimes, I'd catch Gwen
glancing down there, damming up a pool of silent questions, maybe
judgments she wasn't supposed to have.

I went to get checked out at the Regent Park Community Health
Centre, made sure the baby and I were physically okay, and by mid-
February, Mei Zhen slapped her hand on my slight bump, which I'd
been trying to hide. "A little extra for the extra one." She handed
me my end-of-day care package. Her smile was huge.

"I'm sorry I didn't tell you."

"No, no, no. Why you tell me? Not good to tell too soon."

Feeling Mei Zhen's support made me miss Danni more. Each
meeting I went to, every workday felt like cement to a new foundation, but it wasn't a strong one yet, and Danni could destabilize it.

So yes, I was grateful to be around people who weren't drugging. But sobriety without the snarky and the snide was too cruel a punishment. I'd never lived in a world where people were so aggressively nice, so eager to help without any complaint. It was unnatural and creepy. To make matters worse, my one-more-time roommate Yen Mah had met a guy, and when one day an actual giggle penetrated her bedroom door, it was as if body snatchers had invaded. Cramped and stiff in my new life, all that cheerfulness was invasive, a sickly perfume clogging the air. Apartment, seafood store, NA meeting, shake your pompoms and repeat. How much smaller and duller would my life become once the baby arrived?

The issue of daycare was on my mind, how I'd afford it and how I'd make it to meetings when the ones after work were outside of normal daycare hours. What did addicts who were working mothers do? Maybe they had support systems. There was Carole-Anne, but she lived with Danni and was an addict herself; I didn't want to get pulled back down.

It got so bad that I almost called my brother, Eddy. We hadn't spoken since he'd told me about Mama losing her marbles. Not to ask if he'd help with child care, God no. More for a small window into another troubled life, one that might make me feel better about my own. At an even lower point, I almost called my mama, but her illness would've progressed. She might not know me. Did Eddy still bother to visit? I could see him giving up as soon as she no longer recognized him, there being nothing in it for him by that point. But who was I to judge? Obviously, the twelve steps hadn't worked their magic on me yet.

I focused again on my memory of giving up Chantelle. Although I'd given her up for her to be better off, I'd lost her. I wouldn't lose this child. I knew enough girls who'd had kids taken away that I didn't want to give Children's Aid any triggers to intervene. I had to avoid giving birth at St. Mike's, because I'd been in with abscesses in my leg, and they'd have me flagged.

The Toronto winter was easier than I'd expected it to be, a nice surprise. For one thing, the post-withdrawal symptoms eased. I wasn't working outside. The early dark and the work at the store sapped my energy, along with my expanding waist and its extra weight. I'd come back from meetings and crash. Sleep was fitful, and finding a comfortable position with my sticking-out belly was difficult, but it was sleep and I appreciated the rest. Mornings were still hard, the urge to use hitting before I'd unglued my top eyelids from my bottom, but taking a long walk in the cold before work distracted me, a self-punishment that made being back in the warmth of the store comfort enough to get me past the first jonesing of the day.

At the store, the three of us had a routine and squeezed past one another behind the counter in a practised dance. The biggest barriers were my baby bump and Bo Hai's own substantial belly. "Ha-ha! Mine is still bigger than yours!" he joked.

One day in early March, Mei Zhen brought me a small toy for the baby, three colourful interconnected plastic rings, worn by use. "I found a box in the basement."

"Who did this belong to?" I asked — it was the safest question.

"Our son," said Mei Zhen. "He died when he was a child. Car accident." Bo Hai turned away and walked to the back of the store.

"Oh. I'm so sorry."

"Long time ago. Our family is in Vancouver. You take this. It's no use to us."

I thanked her and told her I'd put it in the back. I went to my knapsack and placed it next to my lunch, a PB and J sandwich and a banana. Tears welled up. She brought other toys, a wooden train car and a doll with a Chinese silk dress. "We don't know boy or girl yet, so you take just in case."

When May came, and I was nearing my due date, I settled on Women's College, hoping there were no record-sharing agreements. A social worker at the health centre I'd been going to hooked me up with a church that gave me free baby clothes, more toys, and swaddling blankets. They hoped they'd gotten themselves a new parishioner, but I wasn't ready for those prying questions, and my relationship with God has always been between me and Him anyway. Don't need any preacher telling me what I know.

I got my room ready, choosing a nice cardboard box for a crib. The church people couldn't find one for me. Yen Mah's new guy, a fellow Chinese immigrant, stayed over sometimes. How would she be once the baby came? Would she feel pushed out of her own place by a wailing newborn? She said all the right things, but Yen Mah didn't strike me as the maternal type.

The daycare worry lifted, at least temporarily, when Bo Hai and Mei Zhen approached me one day and told me that if I was prepared to come back to work after three weeks off, I could bring the baby to the store, keep it in the back for when I needed to breastfeed or change its diaper. I knew the law said, technically, I could apply for mat leave through Employment Insurance, and have a whole year, but I didn't want that. I didn't know what I'd do with my days, and didn't trust myself to stay clean if I was sitting at home with a baby. "No need for daycare. Expensive," said Mei Zhen, and tears rushed to my eyes. Their kindness made me regret each grumpy thought that'd ever passed through my miserable, no-good head.

When the day came, I felt prepared, damn fool that I was. I was on my way to work, heavy but determined, and hopeful. In Toronto, spring is a spectacle in three acts: snowmelt, forsythia bloom, lilac burst. The lilac blossoms were in their full glory. I was walking to work, inhaling deeply, but I had to be close up, and the walk to the seafood store had barely a tree. I'd made it to the end of the block, the turn to the bridge, when the first pains hit. In that moment, after it passed, I went on instinct, turned back, took the elevator, and rapped on Danni's door. By the time she answered, another cramp had doubled me over.

"I didn't know who else —".

"Shut up and let's get a bag together for the hospital."

I didn't deserve any of it, but I needed someone, and Danni stayed, more or less, through twelve agonizing hours of labour. Wasn't the second one supposed to slide out? Apparently not. I refused an epidural despite wanting to pump ten bags of that shit up my arm or wherever the hell they put it. Danni left twice for a hit but came back in time to be in the room with me.

My baby was the most beautiful sight. A boy. More beautiful than Chantelle, I thought guiltily. May 28, only a week before I turned twenty-seven, but I suppose it was too much to ask that we share a birthday. Pudgy face, nub of hair, ten fingers and ten toes. Danni held him in one arm and put her hand on her chin, squinting.

I knew what she was up to. "So help me God, if you say another word before I've even given him his real name, I will kill you."

"I wasn't —"

"His name is Aaron. Okay, now you can go ahead."

"I can't. He's perfect."

She sat with me and held him a while longer, but she fidgeted more and more, and I was overcome with a stronger urge than I'd had in over six months. When her pacing got too much, I asked for Aaron back and said I needed sleep. I thanked her again, and, like she had before, she waved a hand in front of her face, batting away my bothersome, buzzing gratitude.

"I'll get going," she said, "but if you need me to babysit ..."

I smiled and hugged her. She understood I wouldn't be calling.

Magma

I'D FORGOTTEN THE FATIGUE THAT FOLLOWS CHILDBIRTH, A WEARI-ness in sinew and joints, a terrible pulsing surge that often pushed tears to the surface. And this was only the beginning.

I took Aaron home, where Yen Mah was waiting next to a plastic baby carrier. A present from her and Carole-Anne. I hugged Yen Mah; it was the first time we'd touched. Carole-Anne came by shortly afterwards and cooed over the baby.

"You be sure to call on Auntie Carole-Anne whenever you need to. When mine came home with me, I was desperate from lack of sleep. I was ..."

The tears started. I put my free hand on her shoulder and thanked her again, told her I truly needed sleep and I'd call her for sure. She left, apologizing for crying.

I barely remember those first weeks; they're a haze of bleary-eyed consciousness, tiny lips on my boobs, Yen Mah pulling him free of my arms and rocking him, my eyes drooping until I woke again with Aaron in bed beside me. Food appeared in the fridge or on a plate in front of me, with notes from Yen Mah or Carole-Anne. Once from Danni.

Three weeks later, I took Aaron to work, like Bo Hai and Mei Zhen had offered, but I was nervous about leaving him sitting alone in his carrier in the next room. It was steps away, and I could hear him if he fussed, but I was always keyed up. After lunch, he cried when I was with a customer, and my milk let down. Wetness seeped through my shirt. I grabbed an apron that I used when I gutted fish, while the customer pretended not to notice. When I went to check on Aaron, Mei Zhen put a hand on my shoulder, directing me back to the counter. Mei Zhen went to check on Aaron herself.

I was furious. Hadn't she seen my shirt? How dare she not let me go to help my child? But this was my boss. I clenched my fist and finished the transaction at the till.

At night, my group exhausted me, but I still managed to go. This is what I can say about NA. That program was founded by men. Men who had their women at home taking care of the kids. I asked my sponsor and other group members if there'd ever been any discussion of child care at meetings, and they stared back at me and scratched their heads. "Look, I have children too," said one guy, "but children are considered an outside issue, and we steer clear of outside issues." I wanted to punch him. Outside issue, my ass. I couldn't have been the first new mother to be in a group. A woman told me about a place where you could live and where they'd take care of kids for you while you did your recovery work, but when I called them, she'd been mistaken. You had to have schizophrenia.

Early evenings, when group took place, was the time of day when Aaron's colic kicked up. The crying gave me dark, worrisome thoughts. I'd never experienced such a thing, a love that could turn to seething resentment, then back to love, within an hour. None of it helped me focus on group. I was too busy going in and out of the meeting room, worried that Aaron would fuss.

Having him at work was not the simple proposition Mei Zhen had offered. Aaron didn't lie still, silent until break time. He was cranky and fussy and needed minding. All the time. I proposed wrapping him up in a sheet strapped to my back, the way aunties did when I was growing up. Mei Zhen and Bo Hai were nervous about how customers would react, but allowed it. Strapping Aaron to my back and moving around the shop calmed him. I didn't like not seeing his face, but I loved his warm little body against my back, his breathy coo into my ear. Sometimes, the tight sheet wrapped around me was the only thing holding my heart in its cage.

It turned out people loved a baby in the shop, women especially, who were most of our clientele anyway. It was a topic of conversation and made the shopping experience more pleasant. They praised my bosses for letting me keep Aaron at work. Sales increased. Mei Zhen and Bo Hai relaxed.

But it stopped working. A month later, instead of a cute baby carried about to boost the customers' mood, he was a wailing hellion making them irritable, and me with them. Too many times to count, Mei Zhen picked up the soother that wasn't working anymore, that Aaron had let drop on the fishy floor. She'd clean it and put it back because I was with someone. Or she'd push me aside so she could deal with the person herself, hoping to distract her from leaving the store to escape Aaron's screams. Several did anyway. After three days of that, she told me that if he cried, I'd have to put him in the back storeroom and leave him. "Shut the door and leave the light on. He'll be fine." I didn't have an alternative, so I gave in.

Shutting him in there didn't stifle the sounds. One customer, a lady with an expensive coat and a diamond ring, asked if someone would be going to the baby. "It's not good to leave them crying," she said. "My mother's generation did that, but now we know it releases a harmful chemical into their bodies and ..." I tuned her out because

I was close to clocking her. I wanted to ask if she wouldn't mind going back there herself, if she was so goddamned concerned, when Bo Hai said, "Paulette was just going."

In the evenings, after long days of this stress, I'd strap Aaron to my back and go to group, only to have him scream more. Members tensed their shoulders, crossed their legs, or stopped talking altogether. They stared, waiting for me to get my kid under control. I'd disturbed the calm and reflective space. Maybe hearing that sound — how we all felt inside — was unbearable. Annoyed that nobody offered to help, I whipped out my boob to breastfeed, but people looked away, and the meeting leader gently asked if I'd step outside to breastfeed, because not everyone was comfortable with it. So I agreed. Once, while Aaron fed, I fell asleep outside the meeting and was woken when someone left to use the washroom. The meeting was ending when we returned.

After two months back at work, I told Gwen I couldn't keep it up. I was talking about everything, but when a flicker of alarm passed across her face, I said, "The meetings, I mean." She offered to meet me by herself. It was sweet, and I took her up on it, but it wasn't enough. I could feel the ground underneath me loosening day by day, magma burbling beneath the surface. This scary, hot rage building up from below.

One day, when I was afraid it'd explode and I'd hurt my child, I went home from work and sought out Mario to buy a piece of rock.

"Girl, you sure you want to do this?" he said, tilting his chin at Aaron.

"Mind your own business." I hugged Aaron to my hip.

"This is my business. You're in my place of business." He pointed to the building entranceway.

"Just don't tell Danni." I held the worn twenty-dollar bill between my fingers, scanning in case she was leaving for work. He turned an imaginary key in front of his lips and took too long getting the baggie ready. "Hurry up!" I shouted. He gave it to me and backed away.

Back in my room, I cooked up the rock while my three-month-old slept beside me. I was a colossal failure. As a parent, a mother, a recovering addict. He started crying at the peak of my high. I jiggled him, walked back and forth in my room what must have been a thousand times, the only thing that calmed him. I never left his side, but when I came down from my high, I went to Danni. Again, she read my face at the door to her apartment.

Aaron was crying on my arm; I was rocking too vigorously. Danni reached out and took him. "What do you need?" She put her free arm around my shoulder and squeezed it out of me — the tears and apologies flowed.

We tossed about options. The best one was to get an apartment together. I was sure, fool that I was, that if I could get help with Aaron and be in a new building away from Mario's Drop-In, my relapse would be a one-time event. Danni was the central part of that plan. We searched the ads and found one we could afford in St. James Town, at 650 Parliament Street, overlooking the cemetery. While my legit job made us attractive on application forms, maybe one of those respectable gay couples that had babies together, we couldn't meet the first and last month's rent requirement. Even with Danni still working the streets.

So, before moving in together, we took turns taking care of Aaron while I went back to the strolls to earn more cash. Danni was still smoking, so she'd hand over money to me for safekeeping. Gwen, my sponsor, left messages, but I didn't call back. If I'd been tired before, working two jobs was stretching me to the limit, in spite of Danni's help. Two weeks into this insanity, Bo Hai asked if I was okay. "Oh, sure." My eyelids were lead weights. But he pointed to a half-dozen mistakes, sloppiness with my work. The magma roiled, bubbled up further. Aaron's crying, from back in the storage room. I clenched my fists. My jaw ached. Mei Zhen interceded, moved between us. My body sounded a primal alarm when she approached me: too close, too close! There was no way around her.

Mei Zhen said, "I understand. Difficult with a baby, but things have to improve." She was still standing there blocking me.

I shoved her away with both hands and shouted, "I'm doing the best I can!" Mei Zhen fell to the floor.

Bo Hai rushed to step between us, and he held up his palm while squatting down to help his wife. My arms were still extended. I dropped them, backed away, and stood against the wall. Mei Zhen's eyes were wide. Bo Hai helped her up.

"You go home now!" shouted Bo Hai. "Don't come back."

Mei Zhen put her hand on her husband's arm and said to me, "You go sleep and come back tomorrow. We'll talk then."

I took off my apron, smeared with scales and guts that may as well've been my own, and threw it in the corner. I grabbed Aaron and ran. Back at the apartment, I was relieved that Yen Mah was out. While Aaron screamed in his cardboard box, I left him there, red-faced, and found Mario. I bought half an eight ball, which I smoked on my bed, Aaron lying in the living room so he wouldn't inhale the smoke. I covered my ears when he wailed, the room spun, and I wished for the earth to open so that we could tumble into oblivion.

Charity

NO EARTHQUAKE CAME TO DELIVER ME THAT DAY. I PINNED MY hopes on moving in with Danni. It was unconventional; we didn't know anyone who'd tried anything like it, but Danni and I were smart women, smarter than most we met on the streets. We could make this work. When I made the decision and told Aaron, he smiled. I was getting concerned he'd never smile, there'd been so much crying. He didn't know what I was saying, but he'd mimicked me. I pressed his face into my neck, kissed the top of his head. It was a good omen.

I never went back to the fish store, even to collect the rest of my pay. Two weeks later, a cheque arrived in the mail. I was relieved there was no note in the envelope, angry, forgiving, or otherwise.

It took over two months to scrape together money for first and last, and by the time we did, the apartment on Parliament had been rented. We were turned down for another in the same building, but we snatched up an opening on Oak Street, in the building next to where we'd both been living. It was an illegal two-bedroom furnished sublet from a man named Christopher whom I'd met in the laundry room. He lived down on Gerrard Street now. The move was a kind of change, not a major one, but good enough. It was November, and we were anxious to find something before winter.

Yen Mah was poker-faced when I announced I was leaving. Maybe she was relieved. I'd been a millstone she was too kind to throw off her neck. On December first, Danni and I hauled our few boxes down the elevator, along the short-looped driveway passing in front of our old building and the new one next to it, and up the other elevator.

We set up house and settled into a routine that we'd make work for us — we were resolute. Alone, we were wobbly posts at risk of falling over, but we'd moved in together, and that'd shore us up. When I had Chantelle, back in 1996, I was seventeen and hadn't known what to do with a baby, but I didn't want my mama raising her, and, despite what she said, she didn't either, not really. She suggested an auntie, said that the baby should be raised by family, not strangers, but I was firm. I didn't want the reminder of how she'd come to be, and I didn't have any faith that I might change my mind. We put the baby up for adoption straight away.

Chantelle would've been ten years old by then, and wouldn't know I was ever her mama. I was determined things'd be different this time, despite the relapse. I couldn't bear losing my son. I was going to parent this child, care for him and protect him, shield him from the drugs.

Danni didn't say anything when I started shooting up again. She knew there was no point. We discussed the rules we'd live by, and I said, "I don't want us using in our own place." If ever Children's Aid came by, if someone tipped them off, they wouldn't find any evidence, needles or smoke lingering in the furniture or on the walls. The key to our plan was Carole-Anne. I didn't love it, but because Carole-Anne wasn't thrilled at having to find another roommate, we tempted her with an alternative: two hundred bucks a month, and spending time with Aaron. She was easily swayed.

She didn't need Danni's rent to keep her place; she liked the extra income.

This is how we worked it. We'd leave our drugs in our apartment; it would've been crack-brained — pardon the obvious description — to leave our stash with Carole-Anne, who was another addict, although crack wasn't her drug. I knew that however intrusive Children's Aid was, they weren't the police. They didn't search your underwear drawer. During the daytime, when Carole-Anne was at work, I'd slam at her place while Danni watched Aaron in our apartment and tried to sleep, and I'd spell her off while Danni got high at Mario's Drop-In — to minimize the smoke in Carole-Anne's apartment. At night, when at least one of us had to face the cold, the other'd take Aaron and go to Carole-Anne's if she had to get high. If it was Danni and she was smoking, she'd leave Aaron in the living room and light up next to an open window in her old bedroom. Carole-Anne got to cluck and fuss over the baby, if she was up. Danni and I'd take turns working, splitting the nights into what we called the early shift, five to midnight, and the late shift, midnight to seven in the morning. While one of us was on the strolls, the other was sleeping or getting high — but checking on Aaron, who was sleeping longer stretches at night, sometimes all the way through. In the morning, we'd feed Aaron and then crash with the help of Xanax.

This didn't work for long. One morning, I woke to Aaron's crying, to his trembling lower lip. How long had he been awake? He was sitting up in his cardboard box, a new trick he'd learned in the last month. The box was lined with blankets, and he grabbed an edge with both hands, bending it inwards with his weight. I picked him up and pulled him into bed, but he wouldn't settle. I'd weaned him when I started shooting up again, because I didn't know if the drug'd find its way into my milk, but I wished I could soothe him in that way. Even after I gave him a bottle and he stopped crying, he wasn't going to sleep. I'd had enough, but he hadn't. I got up and played with him, resenting Danni for snoring through it all.

But this wasn't her responsibility. Helping me with child care and her contribution to household expenses were vital to my parenting plan, for which I thanked Danni continually. This arrangement meant we couldn't work our old spot on Jarvis Street; we had to drum up business closer to home, along River, next to our apartment complex. Business wasn't great there, and it was less busy and poorly lit as if for Jack the Ripper. It was a scary but necessary compromise, and Danni made it without so much as a grumble.

Having a place to use that wasn't our apartment but was still nearby was crucial. An option that wasn't Mario's Drop-In. We made a joke of Carole-Anne getting too attached to Aaron, but it was a serious worry. Once, when Danni was in the other room doing her thing, she emerged to find Carole-Anne so overcome with grief for her lost kids that she had Aaron in a nearly suffocating embrace. Danni eased Aaron out of her arms.

Despite her neediness, Carole-Anne was our best bet. Keeping Aaron meant steering clear of other sources of potential help — community centres, doctors, and daycare — because these were the same people who might report us to child protection or the police. So far, none of them knew I had a new baby.

On Christmas morning 2006, we opened the small gifts we'd exchanged. First, alone, Danni and I each opened our presents from the other. We were gathering later for dinner in Carole-Anne's apartment, and both Yen Mah and Carole-Anne had wanted to give us our presents privately, so we'd agreed to pick Yen Mah up at her place on the way. This year, Carole-Anne said she didn't want to make it potluck; she was going to prepare the meal herself.

Danni's and my presents to each other, and to Carole-Anne and Yen Mah, were bottles of liquor — mine Bailey's and Danni's Kahlua.

Danni handed over a second small package, which turned out to be a new rattle for Aaron. He shook the rattle and giggled.

"You like Auntie Danni's rattle?" She picked him up and kissed him all over.

We let Aaron tear apart the wrapping for my present. It was a matching toque and pair of mittens that I'd knitted myself, in secret, in my room, embarrassed about how they might turn out. It was a skill my mama'd taught me, like preparing fish, lying dormant all these years. Did she herself still have those skills, or had Alzheimer's robbed her of body memory, too? Would she be in a home yet? How much joy she might've had knowing she had another grandchild. Now there was probably no point in bringing him to meet her.

"Beautiful," said Danni, when I pulled the toque over Aaron's head. "I didn't know you could knit." They weren't beautiful, but they were made with love. The stitching was wonky, and the colours were loud, but I'd had to work with what I could find: an old cotton sweater from a dumpster that I'd washed and unravelled.

Later in the day, we grabbed a bottle of wine and ran without coats the short distance between buildings. Yen Mah answered her door in a brightly patterned dress and waved us in. She smiled and did a shuffle-skip over to a side table where our gifts lay wrapped.

Above the table, there was a new poster on the wall, which was actually an old, faded poster newly framed. It was a simple but artsy design in black, red, and white, the silhouette of a fist in the air, with Chinese lettering in the top left corner and a thimble with a needle touching its tip in the bottom right. The needle was bending and about to snap, streaks fanning inwards to its breaking point.

Yen Mah grabbed two tiny gifts and handed them to me and Danni, and a larger one that she gave to Aaron. He tore it open and, triumphant, shook a teddy bear. Yen Mah bent over and kissed his cheek, pointing simultaneously to our presents. "Open, open!"

Inside the tiny packages were plain cardboard boxes, and inside those were a thimble each, from the bowl in her room, the two most exquisite of the bunch.

Danni and I had chuckled about Yen Mah many times, about how weird and mysterious she was. I'd tried once or twice to find out more about her, but not hard enough. Yen Mah's answers were always short and cryptic, and I hadn't wanted to pry. Danni tried to get me to pry more, but I'd convince her we shouldn't. "We gotta be respectful of her privacy; like my mama used to say, you don't wanna be too *fass!*"

In retrospect, we hadn't cared enough and were bad-mannered to boot. Yen Mah didn't speak great English. If Danni and I came from different cultures, Yen Mah's was the more foreign to us. It'd been funnier to make up stories, the way Danni always did. The coloured thimbles were tokens from a secret sewing group—slash—assassins' circle. The degree on her wall was in neurosurgery. The Nana Mouskouri poster was ... inexplicable. But hadn't she held my room for me when I was in jail, no questions asked, no judgment?

We were shitty to have taken her for granted. She might've been lonely. Lonelier than we were. She had lovers from time to time, but she'd never brought friends back to her apartment. I felt bad for caring, for the first time, if she had any friends.

"They're beautiful," I said. "Is there some meaning to them?"

Danni added, pointing to the thimble in the new poster, "Something to do with that?"

"Yes. Hard-shelled resistance against sharp stabbing needle of society."

"I don't understand," I said.

She smiled at the poster and swallowed the tang of a bittersweet memory. Its paper was yellowed, curling and torn at the edges. Maybe she was asking herself if she could trust us. She stroked the poster's frame. "My mother was opium addict in China. The Mao government said to opium addicts, 'Stop. Be good revolutionary. Avoid decadence of the West.' But my mother could not stop. Or maybe did not want to. Mao sent her to prison."

"Oh." Danni stood beside her to better view the design, its stylized lettering.

"Friends made this for protest. But no use."

"When was your mother in prison?" I asked.

"Cultural Revolution. I was a young girl when she died."

"I'm so sorry," said Danni.

"That was a long time ago. Now, I want you to have these. To help you have hard-shelled resistance."

She didn't say against what: society's needle, or the kind I used every day. Yen Mah had never used drugs. We'd had no idea what she thought of our habits. What's more, she'd never uttered a single political word before, but she was a serious activist, and we should've guessed as much from her volunteer work at the settlement agency. All it took for her to open up was for us to take the slightest interest. I shifted left and right on my feet, uncomfortable in my shame.

"Let's go," she said, clapping her hands. "Carole-Anne is waiting."

A few floors away, Carole-Anne unlatched her many deadbolts and greeted us in a hideous Christmas sweater. She brought out a pile of them and made us all put one on, loans she would take back for next year. She'd even bought a tiny one for Aaron but said pointedly, "That's not his gift; he won't fit into it next year anyway."

She sat us on the sofa, in front of two wrapped squares, obviously CDs. "Danni and Yen Mah, you open yours; Paulette's and Aaron's, I'm saving for after dinner."

They gingerly opened their presents. Danni's was a Barbra Streisand Christmas album, and Yen Mah's was one of classic carols sung in Cantonese. Yeh Mah seemed pleased with hers, but Danny said,

"Oh!" and then, "Thanks, Carole-Anne." I could tell from her tone of voice that there was an issue.

When Carole-Anne took Yen Mah into the kitchen to help her with one of the dishes, I asked what was wrong.

Danni waved the CD. "I don't fucking believe it."

I grabbed the case and turned it over. I shrugged, still puzzled.

"Anti-Semitic, much?"

"It's Streisand. She's a good singer. Besides, didn't she do the same thing with Yen Mah?"

"If Yen Mah were a Buddhist instead of a Christian — which at least we knew enough about her to know *that* — then yes, it would be the same thing. But Carole-Anne knows I'm Jewish."

I rolled my eyes. "You're insane. Shut up and put that CD in the boom box."

She mumbled something inaudible.

Carole-Anne called us to the table — she'd cooked green beans, potatoes, and a ham. "Anti-Semitic," whispered Danni, pointing at the ham, when Carole-Anne was out of earshot. I shook my head; I couldn't count the times Danni'd scarfed back a bacon burger at Hooker Harvey's.

A Vachon yule log was dessert. "I spent all day baking this," joked Carole-Anne.

We made dessert last, each of us having seconds. Aaron's cake ended up half on his face, half on the floor. We told stories of our best holiday memory. Mine was one before my dada left. Yen Mah's was of getting a rocking horse from her mother. Danni's was a vacation in Barbados with her mom and dad, before he died. Carole-Anne's involved spending time with her children, before she lost custody, but the tears came and she couldn't finish the story.

When she composed herself, she pointed to the bedroom. "And now your gift, Paulette — it's one present, for both you and Aaron."

I opened the door. Near the wall stood a beautiful wooden crib.

I could barely breathe.

Carole-Anne said, "I used the money you're paying me to let you use my place. He's going to grow out of that box soon. He'll tip it over and hurt himself."

The heat rose up my chest. She must've misunderstood my reaction, because she said, "Oh, it's collapsible so you can easily take it home."

I exploded. "Are you fucking kidding me?"

"What?"

"A crib? You bought Aaron a crib with my money? While meantime, I can't afford to buy my own son a Christmas present?"

"Paulette!" said Danni.

Carole-Anne was wide-eyed. "I only —"

"You only what? You thought it'd be nice to point out I can't provide for my own son?" I grabbed Aaron, who wailed from being jolted, marched past Yen Mah, put him in his carrier, and stomped down the hall. I was hammer-drilling the elevator button when Danni caught up.

"What has gotten into you?"

"Don't you see what she's doing?"

"What I see is a woman who's given you a generous gift that you badly need, unlike the gift she gave me."

"With my money!"

"Our money," said Danni. "And Carole-Anne has helped us at every turn. You've gotta go back and apologize."

"Not gonna happen." I got into the elevator. Danni disappeared behind the closing doors.

I went home and punched my fist into the wall of my room, imagining Carole-Anne's face, but my scraped and bleeding knuckles reminded me how mad I was at myself, too. How much money had

I spent on a habit I couldn't quit, instead of on my son?

The next day I put on my most sheepish smile and went back to Carole-Anne. I apologized for Aaron, because he did need a crib. Because I couldn't afford to get him one. I lowered my head and told Carole-Anne I was sorry for the outburst and for ruining Christmas. I was crazed, strung out from the drugs and from lack of sleep. She took my apology as sincere and hugged me. "You're a good mother," she lied.

But I didn't forget what she'd done, or Danni's lack of support. Carole-Anne'd taken that goddamned money, accepted it when clearly she didn't need it. Neither of them understood what'd happened, and it was because of how they were raised, both of them in middle-class homes, never wanting. I could forgive them for that, but my God, how little this new life had taught them. Had they still not learned how much it cost to accept charity?

Slam

LIFE SETTLED BACK TO NORMAL, AND ONCE IN A WHILE, MAYBE TO make amends, Carole-Anne'd say to me and Danni, "You two go off, I've got this," rocking Aaron in her arms. I took her up on it, no guilt anymore. In our arrangement, like traditional parents, Danni and I rarely had any time together, just the two of us. We ate as a so-called family unit, but there wasn't time for the kind of fun we'd had before. For a while, after the incident at Christmas, that didn't upset me, but drugs have a way of piling distraction on top of a grudge, burying it until the next quake uncovers it again.

One evening in January 2007, Carole-Anne ushered us out the door, so Danni and I went together to Mario's Drop-In for a hit — Drop-In 2.0, that is — the former one had been raided, fortunately not when we were there, and he'd begun renting an apartment on a different floor. I lined up my works. Again, Danni asked me if I could teach her to slam. Though it would've made stuff simpler because we could've cooked together, I'd been discouraging her for some time.

"You should be proud you resisted it all these years, Danni. Why d'ya wanna go messing with needles? Look at my fucking arm." I extended it, palm up. A nest of wasps would've done less damage.

And my leg was one carelessly prepared injection away from developing another abscess. "I'm not showing you how. There's all sorts of risks to worry about, including HIV. I'm not being responsible for that."

We were wedged into the corners of a sofa, the stench of smoke and spilled beer amplified by the cranked thermostat. Flo-Jo sat slouched between us, uncharacteristically stupefied, her head lolling, drooling onto her shirt. She must've been at the end of a run, crashed from exhaustion or from tranqs. The TV burbled, the volume down low, but a news item about an abortion doctor receiving death threats caught our attention. The reporter mentioned a surge in pro-life activity.

A sheen of sweat glistened on Danni's brow. "Crazy assholes." She grabbed the fabric at her belly and peeled it from her skin. I wasn't in favour of abortion, but people should live and let live. I couldn't argue with her. Death threats were crazy.

Crumbs crunched under my legs as I shifted. The filthiness we'd come to tolerate was astonishing. An upside-down wedge of pizza lay on the floor, an arrow pointing to Grumplepuss, who was in the kitchen and hadn't noticed it slipping off his plate. He was muttering to no one in particular. A dozen or so cockroaches brazenly circled, indifferent to the fact that the lights were on. Drop-In 2.0 clearly had the same bugs as the previous version.

Grumplepuss emerged from the kitchen, still muttering, stepped over the mess and slumped into a ratty wingback beside the couch. He stared ahead, his hands gripping and releasing the chair's threadbare armrests.

The news item on TV had shifted to a story about a man who'd fallen on hard times, lost his fortune, and started over. He was launching a charity that offered free and impartial debt avoidance and investment advice.

Danni shifted on the sofa. "You hafta show me, Paulie. Your highs last longer than mine. I'm throwing money away. Plus, my lungs are reaching their limits with the smoking. I don't even know what they're cutting that shit with anymore. Epoxy resin or something, I swear to God, it wouldn't surprise me."

"At least you don't smoke cigarettes."

"When you met me, I sounded like Jennifer Tilly. Listen to me — now I'm freakin' Angelica Huston —"

"Shut up!"

"— with a chest cold." Danni fake coughed.

"Okay, maybe Angela Bassett. A much paler, less fine version of her."

"Paulette." I refused to move even though she'd used my proper name, which she did when she was dead serious or upset with me. "Paulette!"

I squinted, craned my head around Flo-Jo. Danni pointed at her own eyes with her index and second finger. "See this face?"

"Ugly as shit. Yeah?"

"Fuck you. This is the face of your best friend in the whole world, right?"

"Shhh!" It was Grumplepuss, who'd been monitoring the door. He got up, opened it, and stuck his head into the hall.

"I swear, Paulette, if you don't show me how, I'll get Nervous Nellie over there to help me, and then you'll be sorry."

"No, you won't."

"Okay. I'll do it myself." She produced a syringe.

"Jesus, Danni, put that away, will ya?" I was exhausted. She was ruining this rare moment when we didn't have to worry about Aaron.

"If I die, it'll be on your hands. Remember our pact?"

This was sheer manipulation. The pact had been my idea, and Danni was about as committed to it as she was to the snowman we'd built the day before, the one now melting outside in a mid-January thaw.

"Remember? We live, we get off drugs, Aaron grows up to be a Supreme Court judge, and his Auntie Danni spoils him like shit."

"This is the way you're gonna get clean? Seems like you're kinda moving in the opposite direction."

Danni fiddled with the empty syringe. "This is how I stay alive, baby. Now, is it lots of air bubbles you want, or none? I can never remember."

"Oh, for fuck's sake."

Danni's smile dissolved. She stood, scooted Flo-Jo over, which provoked a brief grumble, and sat next to me. She took my hand and whispered, "I've got HIV, Paulie."

Thunder between my ears. I stood. "No. No, that's not ..." Danni pulled me back to the sofa and held my hand. I fumbled for something to say.

"Hey, it's okay. I found out almost a year ago. Last February. You were, you know, busy rehabbing."

"If I'd known —"

"What could you have done? There was nothing to be done. Remember, my stepdad's a doctor, so I know a thing or two about health care and how to get what I need. I got hooked up with treatment, and I'm fine."

Tears came to my eyes. "I'm sorry." I wiped my cheeks. I leaned in and hugged her again.

She fiddled with her syringe. "So, you know... there isn't that reason for me not to use. We just have to be sure not to share works."

"Jesus, girl. Is this how your people do guilt? 'Cause I thought Jamaicans were good at it."

My throat was scratchy and raw, my tongue thick with regret. I left my arm around her for a long while. It made sense: Danni's more ferocious drug use, her frightening skinniness when I'd run into her during my abstinence, the bad cough she'd had, always there if I ran into her in the elevator when I was working at the fish store. I took in her appearance. She'd gained some of the weight back, but not much.

Then a question formed, and against my better judgment, I asked what she was doing about tricks now that she was HIV-positive.

"Well, obviously, I can't tell them outright or the transaction would go south, right?"

"I know, but ... you know."

"Relax, I use condoms now. At least most of the time."

"And the other times?" I must've frowned, even though I'd tried not to.

She told me not to give her that look, and reminded me that she'd gotten HIV from a trick. When I said that didn't make it okay, she made her hand into a yapping mouth and said, "Yeah, yeah, two wrongs don't make a right." She got that, but I wasn't quite understanding the situation. It was only a couple of guys, she said, and they were aggressively insistent. She'd given them three warnings. I use condoms, she'd said. There's HIV and other shit out there, it's not safe. Etcetera, etcetera. And still they begged her and paid the additional fee. So at that point, she'd said fuck it and took their money.

"But, Danni, that's still not right. You lied about something really important. What if one of them gets infected? What if he comes back to find you?"

"You're still not getting it." She shook her head and stuck her hands out, gathering her words. "The way I said it, they should've considered I might be worried they're gonna infect me. So what does it mean, if they're still pushing? It means, if they're HIV-positive, they don't give a flying fuck about me, like, I may add, the guy who actually did give me HIV! If they're HIV-negative, they don't care I might be worried about other STDS. My worry, my health, my emotions mean nothing to these guys. You know that. Because we're not human beings to them. How many tricks have ever cared if they gave us something or got us pregnant? The guy you slept with when you ended up with Aaron sure as hell didn't."

"True enough," I said, nodding. I'd always had more disdain, more wariness for our tricks than Danni had, probably because I'd been punched, kicked, and slapped about and she hadn't.

"So, then there's the possibility they're HIV-positive and assume I might be too," she continued, "and if so, fine, no muss, no fuss."

"But what if they're negative, don't have any STDS," I said, "and think they're safe because you lied to them."

"So then they'd be just as stupid as I was when I got infected. I gave them three clear reminders about condoms. Are we their fucking mothers? Are we the fucking health department?"

I thought of how mad I'd been about Cleavon, Chantelle's daddy, how nobody made him step up. Danni leaned back; she'd rested her defence, and I sat next to her choking on it. I'd listened to a speech or two during our friendship, but this one, I'd deserved. Mostly. It didn't make what she'd done right; she could've turned those guys away. That would've been the most ethical path short of telling the truth, which I knew was too hard to do. Besides, how did I know what her situation had been then? I'd been off trying to get my shit together. And failing. She'd been on her own. Money might've been extra tight.

Maybe it wasn't my place to ask in the first place, to guilt-trip her. It definitely wasn't the time or the place. All things considered, she could've been a lot angrier. Besides, she made one very good point. Why are we the ones always having to take responsibility? Danni at least reminded those guys they should care, if not about themselves, then about her. What did it say if, after that, they still wanted to fuck without a condom? Too many of our tricks thought their shitty little fee was enough compensation to treat our bodies like candy wrappers to discard.

Danni fiddled with the syringe, tapped it, and held it up, waiting for me, getting us back to the original point of the conversation. The air in that room, already close, moved in tighter and pressed down. Danni's becoming HIV-positive hadn't led to anything actually positive. It hadn't given Danni the shove she needed to stop drugging. Now, if she ever did go into recovery, what would carry her through? What would stiffen her resolve during those long, hard early months? If a baby hadn't been enough to keep me on track, how would a virus help her? Her flicking that syringe told me she knew it wouldn't.

I relented. I showed her how to slam safely. Maybe because I felt sorry, or guilty about the conversation. Maybe it was to feel less pathetic. We mixed the crystals with citric acid in a spoon, and I gave her the lowdown. Vinegar would do in a pinch, but in the veins, it could cause abscesses. Never, ever use lemon juice: it causes infections, the most serious of all from a fungus that gets behind the iris and causes blindness. I showed her the best spots for when every vein was spent. How to avoid track marks and bruising by rotating the site and applying arnica cream. How to prepare the syringe so there were no air bubbles.

And later, alone in my room with Aaron, I cried again.

Hooers

WITHIN WEEKS, DANNI WAS SLAMMING LIKE A PRO, BUT WE CON-
vinced ourselves we were each of us scheduling our drug use for the
times Aaron didn't need our full attention. The problem was, at nine
months, he was becoming an expert crawler, meaning things were
getting harder in that he was no longer, as Danni called him, a potted
plant. One Monday late in March, I was standing on River Street
about to call it a night. The morning sun was showing its faint glow
through cloud cover. The air was cold but calm, the snow melted,
and an occasional breeze carried the scent of newly exposed leaf
mulch from the autumn, earthy and fresh.

Carole-Anne walked by, whistling. She'd received a raise and
was on her way to her own early shift at Domestic Despot. "I left
Aaron with Danni. I'm happy to take him again after work if you
and Danni want to go out together this evening."

I wasn't in a position to refuse. I went to collect Danni and
Aaron — he was scooching across the floor when I arrived, and I got
a nice smile when I entered the room. We went back to our place,
and I gave Aaron a jar of applesauce and a bottle. I caught sleep as I
could while Danni watched him. When I woke, she was passed out.
I needed a fix, but I spelled her off while she went to Mario's Drop-In.

When she returned and popped a Xanax, I took Aaron down to Carole-Anne's, waited until he went down for a nap, and did a needle myself.

By the end of that afternoon, all three of us back in our apartment and wide awake, we opened the vertical blinds. The clouds had relaxed, exhausted from their own day's work, and had descended into the streets and alleys. It was the first time either of us could remember fog in Toronto. We hadn't been pulling in much, working on River Street, so, since Carole-Anne had offered to take Aaron in the early evening, Danni convinced me to try our old stroll. She'd stay when Carole-Anne went to sleep and I had to retrieve Aaron.

On the way to Jarvis, we caught up to Olive, who was trying to hide a slight limp. She hugged Danni and gave me a friendlier wave than normal.

I flailed my arms at the fog, which blew at us like soot from a building demolition. "Can you believe this shit?"

"Best weather for turning tricks," said Olive. "Hey, if you guys want, you can work across from me tonight." She meant on the east side of Jarvis facing Hooker Harvey's. "But only tonight," she said, straightening a finger. Kindness was exploding everywhere.

When she trundled on ahead as if to beat us to her corner, I said, "What's with her, all lollipops and candy apples?"

"I spotted her a quarter of an eight ball last month. I guess I'm in her good books."

During our walk to Jarvis Street, the thermometer had dipped lower, to thirteen degrees, a reminder that winter hadn't released its hold just yet. For a half-hour, a cold, penetrating drizzle darkened the sky. Fortunately, the rain dried up, and, indeed, tricks emerged like zombies from the mist. Muffled sounds gave the night a hint of mystery. Danni wondered aloud if the hazy air made them feel invisible. She hoped the lack of visibility would also conceal the acne that'd bloomed on her face that morning and that she'd tried to cover with a thick slathering of foundation.

She still sucked at dolling herself up. How could she, naturally girly, be so bad at this, and yet I could turn my faux femme on and off like the flick of a switch? Tonight, she'd unenthusiastically squeezed into a tight-fitting low-cut crop top and a miniskirt. At the last minute she'd pulled on a hot pink fake angora sweater, which turned out to be the only thing standing between her and hypothermia. I had a thicker wrap with me, and I was glad of it, not only for the warmth but because since the baby, I had a slight paunch that I couldn't get rid of. No more exposed midriff.

Danni had teased her hair into a lion's mane, imitating my Tina Turner wig. Since the night I'd pulled it off to rock my flat-top, over a year earlier, there'd been no going back. I'd femme it up, but no more fake hair. Her two-inch heels were not Tina-worthy, but Danni refused to go higher.

I surveyed the whole ensemble. "Yeah. A for effort, but white chicks cannot pull off that look." She slapped my arm.

We landed at the church across from the Harvey's and watched Olive — a five-inch-stiletto expert — flash a smile to a potential customer she couldn't yet see through the window of a slowing car and teeter over to it.

Danni said, "Is that woman wearing, like, a gallon of mascara? When she bats her eyelashes, it's like a gull caught in an oil slick."

Olive took off her own faux fur wrap, braving the cold for the sake of business, and threw it over her shoulder, bending at the waist. While appearing casual and relaxed, she was trying to move things along.

The man rolled his passenger-side window down. Olive's painted nails curled over the windowsill, her nipples fighting captivity inside her tangerine bustier. Olive was hard-core, but she also needed to work harder at it. She was older. Danni pegged her for over forty, which after a life on the street looked more like fifty. Selling her physical attributes took more effort, but tonight she succeeded. Olive hopped in the car, which continued down Jarvis.

Danni got a bit of business early in the evening, but things were slowing. Danni'd been right all along: it was boring waiting for the next trick to come along — it almost made you wish for a nosy cop to come by, just to break things up. I watched her deal with it in her own way. She was hyper-focused on a wad of chewing gum crushed into the pavement near her foot. "Too bad it's Saturday. We could've at least passed time with Sam." She was referring to one of the workers from Street Outreach Services who came by to give us condoms or exchange needles if anyone needed it. To talk to us about what they referred to as "harm reduction."

"Hey," she added, "do you ever stop to consider, shit, we're real, live whores?"

"Non-sequitur, much?" Danni did that sometimes, voiced an inner conversation you weren't sure you wanted to join.

"Well, isn't it weird? Being a real whore and not just a woman being called one as an insult? It's funny."

"Mm-hmm. Hilarious."

"What a strange word: *whore*." She nudged a bottle cap off the side-walk. "It has so many variations. The American hoar. The African-American ho. The rolling r-ed hoorr of the Scottish. And, of course, there's the ultra-Canadian hooer."

I tried it out: "Hooer."

"You've gotta add the crack, though. Craaack hooer. That's what we are now! Crazy crack hooers." She threw her shoulders back and thrust her tits forward. I shook my head.

At around ten o'clock, a tan station wagon pulled up and Danni got in. The man leered, his face crooked from the effort. He had a dumpy body, but his thinning hair was washed and neatly combed. He was dressed casually but respectably. As typical as the three I'd blown earlier on, and he didn't hassle Danni about paying up front. Most of the guys who picked us up were decent enough in looks and behaviour, but the outliers stood out: unexpectedly handsome, mildly disgusting but harmless, or creepy and possibly dangerous. Except the ones who proved to be dangerous cut across all categories; it wasn't always possible to make an accurate prediction.

I turned a trick myself in the same time. After, when we were both dropped off, we counted the night's haul: a hundred bucks between us. Jittery for our next fix, I stuffed a bill in Danni's hand and went off with another trick while Danni sought out Ülle, never far away, and made a purchase in the lot beside the Harvey's.

When I finished up, we walked north, elbows locked, to find one of the side streets where Danni knew of another open-air but hidden-from-view parking garage stairwell where we could shoot up. I was wary of my old spot, since I'd been arrested there. We passed Carlton Street, continued north. The sidewalk on Jarvis was wide, the street wider. Stately mansions mingled with ugly and squat apartment blocks.

A crowd spilled from one of the old buildings. A herd of theatre-goers, Danni decided, based on the way they were dressed. Colliding with them was going to be awkward, but it was also the sort of thing Danni relished. Causing other people discomfort was always the best way to overcome your own, she'd once said.

I pointed with my chin to the other side of the street, but Danni tightened her lock on my arm. Our heels clip-clopped against the pavement. A breeze blew gooseflesh up our backs. Danni rubbed her hands against the sleeves of her fuzzy sweater and breathed in. Did the air smell of steel and cotton? Did those things have a scent?

People filled the sidewalk in small clumps. They talked, while some moved to the curb to hail cabs. Danni and I weaved our way through, Danni straightening her back and grinning. The theatre patrons smiled back for a tiny fraction of a second.

We were almost on the other side of the crowd when Danni's grin dissolved like sugar in warm water. There in front of us stood a petite woman, decked out in a lime-green suit, talking to a friend who towered over her.

The shorter woman was in mid-sentence when she spotted Danni and stopped cold.

Danni stopped too, but said nothing.

"Ah, hello?" I waited for her to explain.

"What are you doing down here?" Danni asked the woman.

"The ballet school had a show," she said, and I recognized in her Danni's nose, the full lower lip, the cheeks. "I mean, there was one. It's over." Danni's mom pulled her suit jacket closed. Pulled tight like that, it showed how thin she was.

Her mom's friend chimed in, "We're donors, so they invited us." She pointed to the red brick building.

Her mom, remembering she wasn't alone, said, "You remember Karen."

"Hi."

Karen nodded, arms crossed.

Danni glanced my way, maybe considered introducing me, but didn't.

"I'm Paulette." I extended a hand, but her mom left me hanging, reached an arm out to Danni instead.

"How... how are you?" Her voice had lost all propulsion.

Danni gestured sweepingly to her attire, and posed. "Fantastic! As you can see ..."

"You look dreadful, Danni." Her mom's voice had regained its force, and the words came out sharp and brittle.

"You look great too, Mom. That Chanel jacket David bought you has really held up. He always did have a great eye for fashion."

"It's been three and a half years of this, darling. I never know if you're alive or dead, or how to reach you."

Three and a half years. Had it been that long since I'd met Danni? Sure, a lot had happened — jail, recovery, Aaron, relapse — but we were in the same spot, doing the same old things. I'd imagined my life as a line on a paper, drawn in a forward path, even if that line forked from time to time by choice or bad luck. But that paper had become crumpled, each sharp turn leading nowhere at all.

"If I die, someone will call you." Danni's jaw was set, and the spite in her eyes frightened me. The mention of death reminded me of Danni's HIV. Would she tell her mom then and there?

"Lower your voice," her mom said in a strained whisper. "You can always come home again. We'll get through this together."

"Barbara?" her friend Karen interjected. "What about the stealing? Last time —"

"Karen, please stay out of this." Karen took a step back.

I turned to Danni, "What does she mean, 'last time'?" And it struck me how much I didn't know about what Danni'd done during those eight months I was in jail, and later when I'd been working at Bo Hai and Mei Zhen's store. So she'd gone home, tried to make a go of it.

She stared off in the distance. Was she thinking of that house? 'Cause I sure was. She'd described its soft carpets and plush micro-fibre sofa. The Jacuzzi. If longing for that comfort had momentarily softened her face, she quickly hardened it.

"Can I turn tricks from your house?"

Her mom's eyes welled up, but Danni stood her ground, impassive, relishing the reaction. Karen reached around her friend's back and gave her a sideways hug. Perhaps it gave Danni's mom the fortification she needed, because she snatched her tears back before they had a chance to escape. She stood taller. "I don't understand how you turned out this way. You were such a sweet little girl. The meanness, I understand — that's the drugs talking — but the rest?"

Danni stepped back. "You don't understand it?" She turned to me and, in a much louder, exaggerated tone, said, "She doesn't understand it! Wants to know how I turned out this way!" I narrowed my eyes, hoping to convey that I questioned her intentions. Undeterred, Danni turned to a cluster of gawkers. "My mother wants to know how I turned out this way! Has nooooo idea whatsoever what happened to me."

Her mom put a hand to her chest. "It's all my fault," she said, also louder. "Of course it is. It's always the mother's fault."

"Not always."

"Oh, for Pete's sake. You're almost twenty-seven. When are you going to take responsibility for your life, Danni? We all make choices. You chose drugs. You chose them over me, remember? You chose to leave grad school. Which would have been fine, but ... for this?" She wagged a finger at Danni's getup, and at me. I was part of the trash she'd accumulated. "You chose this. So don't you dare —" The anger was so fierce that the fog surrounding her could have been mistaken for steam.

"Barbara." Karen leaned in close. "It's time to go."

Danni took a step in her mom's direction. "Mom, don't go," she called out. "I'm sorry."

Her mom turned.

"Could you lend me some money? Just a hundred bucks to help us make rent."

A pitying look. "I only have thirty, and we need it for taxi fare." She turned her back.

Danni was about to yell something nasty, but didn't. She'd drop the HIV bomb another time. She swallowed and squeezed her eyelids together. I hadn't once seen Danni cry, and still, she kept it corked. By the time she opened her eyes, Karen was pushing her mom into the cab.

The patrons who'd been watching us had moved away. There was silence. The cab drove away, and Danni stood motionless, me behind her. The haze was close. Her shame was there all around us, ghostly and haunting.

"Well, fuck." She turned. "That was a whole ten minutes that I've wasted. And now I'd sell a baby for a fix."

"Don't get any ideas; you're not getting mine." I pulled her onwards.

We walked until we reached the stairwell where we'd planned to shoot up, and Danni immediately sat. "How does she do that? How does she always do that?"

I wasn't sure what she meant, but I had a feeling. I took a small package of citric acid from my purse and the baggie of crack from Ülle. I crushed a tiny bit of rock in my spoon, using the blunt edge of the syringe, and watched it bubble and foam as my lighter tickled it from underneath. "Danni ..." I was unsure how my question would be received. "You went back home while I was in rehab?"

"It was a stupid idea."

"Families. You don't have to tell me."

"We're better off without them. Anyway, we have a kind of family here ourselves, don't we?"

"True." I drew liquid into my syringe, leaving some for Danni. "But from where I'm sitting, you've got a warm bed waiting for you, in a nice house, and someone who's willing to take you back. By now, my mama's probably in a locked Alzheimer's ward, and the apartment's been given up. I'm not trying to get rid of you, but are you sure you don't wanna go?"

"Things are always better from a distance." She pulled the rest of the liquid into her syringe. "My mom and I ..." She drifted off, holding her needle clutched in her fist. She craned her neck at the open sky, where the clouds were once again dark and roiling, maybe fixing to rain. "We don't know how to come back from what we did to one another."

I squeezed her knee. We tore open two small packets of wipes and cleaned the skin where we were going to inject. Danni slipped the needle into her vein and pushed the plunger. She closed her eyes a while, and whether or not the drug helped, she talked.

Boystown

FOR DANNI'S FIRST DEGREE AT TRENT UNIVERSITY, SHE'D MANAGED
to pull decent marks, but they dropped as the years progressed. She
got As at first, then A minuses, and by the time she graduated, it
was Bs. Hard partying during the summer hiatus carried on in Peterborough through the fall and winter. And yet she managed to keep it
together, relied on her intellect to get her through and into a graduate
program in Women's Studies. Her mom and stepdad worried, but
they didn't know the extent of it. She finished the first term of her
graduate courses with a whimper — scraping by in all but one course,
which she nearly failed.

She came home to Toronto and partied over the Christmas break,
sometimes pausing for a roaring argument with her mom. The next
term was more of the same — but she left Trent before the marks
were posted in the spring. Striking pre-emptively, she withdrew from
her program. She never called to see how she'd done. Her parents
were not amused, and when her mom asked what she'd do next,
she said she'd figure it out.

On a Friday night in late July 2003, Danni left the house and
promised she wouldn't be home too late — a brittle olive branch.
At The Big Bop on Queen Street West, Danni chatted with strangers

and watched the bands perform. At half-past midnight, the people with whom she'd spent the night invited her to party at an after-hours club near Dundas and Church. They did lines of coke until four o'clock in the morning, when one of the guys came out with something racist about one of the musicians. Danni described it as unexpected, as the bird-shit-on-head-during-nice-sunny-day version of racism, which happens when it's white people talking amongst themselves. La-la-la-la-la ... splat! If you're Black, that does happen, though I'd say it's unpredictable, not unexpected, and it's more a bucket of sewage dumped on you from an open window. Or sometimes a steady acid rain that deniers claim doesn't exist, while it's clearly eating away at your skin.

Annoyed with the guy, Danni made an excuse and left. She'd intended to take a taxi once she located a bank machine. Unlike many of her classmates, she hadn't needed summer jobs, so she hadn't bothered and had zero job experience. Her stepdad, David, was supporting her through deposits to a joint account, though he'd made noises about cutting her off when she began to do poorly at school. Now that she'd dropped out, the threats had escalated, but he was bluffing; David wouldn't dare cut her off, not from the pills and not from living expenses — at least not before she was on her own two feet — not with the cards she held. At least that's what she assumed until she hit the bank machine and discovered the zero balance: not a penny left. "Fucker," she spat, slapping her hand on the screen. He wasn't gonna get away with this.

She had fifteen dollars left, but it might not be enough for a taxi, and she couldn't call for a ride home. She had four tokens in her pocket, but the subway didn't run until six o'clock. She decided she'd go as far as she could on foot. She walked up Church Street and by the time she passed College, a blister was forming on her left heel. She leaned on a lamppost and took off her shoe, rubbed her ankle.

She needed to make it all the way to Forest Hill, over four kilometres away.

Two kids turned the corner at Maitland and walked by; they were seventeen years old, tops. They'd done a slapdash job of cross-dressing; their clothing was probably from Value Village, their makeup, tasteless. Their wigs were nests for crazed weasels. The description came from Danni, so I couldn't even imagine.

"Girl, you are in the wrooong place. This is the trannie stroll. Real girls are that way." This still makes me laugh. Despite their pointer, Danni'd still gotten her ass chased off the wrong stroll three nights later.

"How do you know I'm a real girl?" Danni quipped, rubbing her heel.

"The small hands, the hips, the tits ... plus no trannie'd ever work in shoes that hurt that bad." They had tiny hips and huge hands, and their breasts were too firm to be real, even for teenagers. They were so skinny she wished she could buy them a hamburger, the thought of which made her ravenous.

"Don't talk shit," said the other one. "You remember Shay? Her heels were bleeding last summer after she went shopping all fucked up and got the wrong size."

They'd mistaken her for a ho. Amused, she examined her outfit: short skirt; tight, low-cut blouse with a crazy floral pattern. Her torture-device, open-toed heels must've been another sign, though they were only two inches high.

"Well, I didn't mean to crowd your turf," she said.

"Honey, did you just roll off the bus from Timmins? We're not worried about the *compétition*," said the first one, the French pronunciation atrocious. "We're sayin' you won't get any business."

"Not unless it's dark and you use a strap-on," the other one added. They laughed, locked arms, and moved on.

Danni decided she wouldn't go home after all, not even in the morning. She couldn't walk in her shoes and was sick at the prospect of challenging David about the bank account. Instead, she set off for Hart House Circle, where she lay on the grass and fell asleep until the athletic centre opened at nine. She talked her way past the girl at the front desk by claiming she'd forgotten her membership card at home. She showered, remembering the kids she'd spoken to. They were resourceful. They had a way to make quick cash in a pinch. Would she have the nerve to do what they did? How bad could it be?

At this point in her story, Danni brought up the women's studies course where they'd discussed hooking. I rolled my eyes so far they almost got stuck in the back of my head. The class had dissected it from many angles, discussing power, sexual freedom, cultural taboos and norms. She'd sided with the camp that believed that, apart from the obvious dangers, there wasn't anything wrong with selling sex for money. She'd been curious about what it'd feel like to turn a trick, and — sweet Jesus — the professor had made them imagine it as part of an exercise.

After her spa morning at Hart House, Danni grabbed a *Now* magazine and scoped out free things to do for the day that didn't involve walking too far, or that she could get to by transit. She used part of her fifteen dollars to buy a pair of flip-flops in a dollar store, joined a street fair at Nathan Phillips Square that had free food samples, walked along Queen West, and decided, because she was close by, that Ontario Place would be a good site to spend the rest of the day. She jumped the turnstile, settled into a shady spot, and read a discarded newspaper. Later, she used more of her cash to buy a burger, watched a show at The Forum, and headed back to The Big Bop early enough that she wouldn't have to pay the cover.

Only one girl from the night before had come back, and she

introduced Danni to a different group: two guys and another girl. Danni told them she'd had a fight with her mom and hadn't been home yet, so they took pity, bought her whisky sodas. Together, they listened to a local band that'd shown up impromptu to jam on the stage.

One of the girls had brought coke. They did lines in the washroom, but this time, despite Danni's hints, nobody invited her to party elsewhere. When last call came and went, her bar buddies dispersed and, because she still had no money for a cab and the subway'd closed, she walked the nearly six kilometres back to Russell Hill Road.

It was two days since she'd been home, and past three in the morning. She didn't want to wake David and her mom, but she stumbled on the top step and her hip hit the deck, hard. She trapped a "f——" between her bottom teeth and her upper lip, though it tried to free itself.

She picked herself up, plunked herself into the teak chair, and stared at the tree in the front yard. The way the large oak tilted on a central axis told her she wasn't yet sober. The air was still, and rivulets of sweat snaked down her back from the trudge up Spadina.

She rubbed her sore hip and collected herself before getting ready to go in. Pushing herself up from the chair, she considered the empty driveway. Either her stepdad had been called in on an emergency or he was screwing another colleague. Danni turned the key in the lock and crept inside. She tiptoed through the front hall. A noisy floor was the trade-off for a beautiful old home, and she cringed at its creaking. A shape moved in the living room. Ice clinked in a glass.

"You're drunk again." Her mom's words were slurred. She sat in her bathrobe in an oversized wingback that exaggerated her smallness. Light from a streetlamp filtered through the window. Her mom's face was in the oak tree's shadow.

"So are you," said Danni.

Her mom's elbow rested on the armrest; her wrist was limp, and her hand struggled to grip her empty glass. "You've been gone for two days. This afternoon I reported you missing."

"I've been —"

"No, wait." Her mom put up her hand. "I don't care."

Danni'd been prepared for a lecture, for tears, for anger, but not for indifference.

Her mom asked, "Do you want to know where David is?"

"I don't know, at the hospital?"

"I followed him and caught him with one of his interns. His male interns."

"Oh."

"He admitted everything. I assumed he was cheating on me with a nurse, that's how stupid I've been. All this time, the late nights, the shifts in the ER. Turns out it's been years since he did a night shift in the emerg."

She brought the glass to her lap and worried it with her thumbs, looked into it like she was reading tea leaves. "I'm such a fool. But you knew that, didn't you?"

"What?"

"You knew." The statement was equal parts question and accusation. "You knew, and you let me make a fool of myself. He said you've known since you were fifteen. That you were blackmailing him."

Danni sat on the stairs.

Her mom's words were barely a squeak. "Is it true?"

The question exhausted Danni. Her mom's voice was threadbare from its search for answers. Danni was tempted to sew a patch over things, to deny it all, to lie, to further demonize David, in whom her mom's trust was already shattered.

But, despite everything, she didn't have it in her. She leaned forward and put her head between her knees.

"I see," said her mom. "So you hate me that much."

Danni knew, maybe for the first time, that she didn't hate her mom. Not the way she used to, at least not all the time. Since Stan Abel, perhaps since her dad's death, the two of them had been trapped in a home shaken apart by emotional tremors. Fear, betrayal, and lies had fallen in slabs on top of them. She considered their demolished shelter. If her mom couldn't dig herself out, what hope did Danni have that adulthood would rescue her?

Her feelings for her mom normally ranged from embarrassment to disgust. Tonight, Danni felt an embryonic form of empathy, but her inclination was to abort it before it tricked her and developed into love.

"No, Mom, I don't —"

"David's left. I want you out, too. By sunrise."

"Mom, I —"

"I'll write a cheque to get you started, but then you'll be on your own." Her mom stood and, as she passed Danni on the stairs, added, "Like me."

Jenga

KNOWING HOW DANNI ENDED UP ON MAITLAND STREET, BEATING A hasty retreat from angry trannie hos, gave me pause. I didn't have a riches-to-rags story like hers, and my journey to the strolls had been more roundabout. After I gave up Chantelle for adoption, a sadness settled in me, a disappointment that stayed like a gritty residue. Frankly, I don't know if I've ever flushed it out. I hadn't been ready to be a mother, but giving my daughter up left me shaky. I'd always taken pride in my body's strength, but after the adoption people left with her, I was a load-bearing pillar weakened beyond repair. Minor trials made my knees buckle, and I'd land in a heap, sobbing. Dread welled in me and made things scary; decisions, impossible. I couldn't go on the way I had. I stopped talking, except when necessary. I went to my bedroom and shut the door. At night, if I slept, it was a blessing. In the morning, the worst time of all, when I dragged myself from my bed, I calculated the hours left until I could sleep again.

Six months later, when I didn't feel any different, but the school year was upon us, my mama made me go. I tried hard because it was my last year, but my mind wandered and my marks plunged. The teachers mistook my silence for anger and hostility. Maybe I did bark out a curt answer or two, but I wasn't mad at them. I stopped showing up, went to a park instead, or to the library, or hung out in the City Centre Mall. My mama didn't know any of it until a favourite teacher, Mr. Sandoval, came to visit me, to convince me to come back. The fury in my mama's face when she learned I'd been playing hooky. The spices she was using to prepare a chicken dinner hung in the air and coated my throat.

I was too smart to give it all up, said Mr. Sandoval. I had real potential. How could I go from top of the class to this, he said. I was one of the bright lights.

I couldn't listen. I didn't believe him, and I didn't care. I needed a break, a fresh beginning. "I know I'm smart," I said, to make him stop. "But I can always get my diploma part-time, later. When I'm settled somewhere else."

My mama snapped, "Settled somewhere else? You talk like that and it might be sooner rather than later! Enough now with the self-pity. You're a James. We don't give up."

I shook my head in disbelief, stared at the wall. The radiator rattled and clicked. Had it never occurred to her that I might be like her? That was my first time retreating to my bedroom in despair and gloom, but she'd done the same thing so many times.

"You need to fight harder for yourself," said Mr. Sandoval. But I couldn't. I was too stubborn, but not in aid of the right objective. And it felt like wet cement had replaced my insides. My mama's hard, ungenerous nature didn't help. Unless I got one hundred percent, it was never enough. I was being lazy, squandering God's blessings. Never listening. Spending too much time with my brother. My mama glared, sharp enough to cut, the flash of a knife you had to dodge. It nicked me anyway; it always did. And, as with any fine cut, there was a delay to the sting.

Did she think I'd planned any of it? That I'd wanted to fuck that horrible friend of my brother's? Would any girl plan to get pregnant at sixteen? If only I hadn't gone to that party. If only I hadn't smoked too much pot and flirted with that girl Tanisha who was always making eyes at me in English class. She showed up in a red dress. A red dress, for Chrissake!

Her jasmine-scented perfume — White Musk — the lavender hair oil, smoking that clove cigarette like she was in Paris instead of a shitty apartment in Hamilton. My best friend, Jaleesa, glancing at us, occupied with a guy who'd cornered her by the cheese dip. Tanisha and me slipping away to the bathroom to freshen up. Tanisha's hand under my top. My hand between her legs. A long kiss. My first.

The door bursting open, fucking stupid, crappy lock.

And my brother's friend Cleavon, still grinning after Tanisha bolted from the bathroom and out of the apartment. I'm still wiping her lipstick off my mouth, and Cleavon's shutting the door behind him, leaning against it, blocking my exit. Saying he'd suspected for a while. He'll tell my brother and my mama I'm like that.

Unless.

People were talking about it, he said. This is all it'd take to confirm it. For everyone.

Unless.

When I got pregnant, my mama's judgments made me fume, all the more so because although she never knew how it happened, it came out that the baby was Cleavon's, and she never said one word — not a single word — to Cleavon, to his mama who went to our church, or even to Eddy. I wasn't the only one responsible, but the way she acted it was all my fault.

It became too much. I told my mama I was moving to Toronto. My friend Jaleesa and I got jobs at the Eaton Centre, selling jeans and cheap shirts with designer logos. My mama told me I'd better not come crawling back expecting to be taken in when things turned sour.

Jaleesa and I shared a basement apartment in a rundown house at the south end of Parkdale. I only got up for work, then we took the streetcar home, not talking, and I went back to my room. For months, she pushed me to get out there, to explore Toronto with her, but I couldn't. Then July came, and with the heat, the heaviness lifted. Once it did, I embraced our big adventure. Two girls in the big city. With my sadness gone, I re-emerged, possibilities and hope blinking awake in the sunlight.

There were two icky but harmless guys upstairs from us who were always flirting, and Jaleesa joked that we were Black Laverne and Shirley, and they, Tamil Lenny and Squiggy. Jaleesa made me laugh a hundred times a day, and with each laugh, a window cracked open. We hung out occasionally with those guys, and when they brought out a baggie of coke and placed it beside the beer bottles, we didn't say no. It wasn't the first time we'd tried it; someone at one of my brother's parties had once given us some.

Lenny, after a few snorts, tried to make a move on Jaleesa, right in front of his friend and me, but Jaleesa shoved him away, a foot to his chest, and laughed as he fell back onto the sofa. He smiled sheepishly, but didn't try again. There was a girl at work, Francine, and she was mostly into pot. We hung out with her a fair bit. One night, when we didn't have work the next day, Francine, Jaleesa, and I went back to Francine's place in Scarborough, and she brought out some crack to smoke. I was wary, but when Jaleesa took that spoon, the way she held the lighter under it made a soft light flicker over her beautiful face, and my chest tightened. I took the spoon after she was done and felt some of my new hopefulness dissolve away along with the liquefying rock. High, wired, too lost in crazy conversation to sleep, we stayed late and eventually slept on Francine's floor. In the morning, Jaleesa's arm was draped over top of me. I couldn't breathe, and not just from the weight of it. I wriggled free to use the toilet.

She and I got into drugs too fast, but it was crystalline courage, and I, for one, needed it. Two months in, one night in our apartment, fuelled by snorting coke and feeling electric, invincible, sexier than I ever had in my life, much sexier than with Tanisha, I leaned in and kissed her. Jaleesa kissed me back. Our lips parted, and Jaleesa's eyes dropped. She was as scared as I was, but I kissed her again anyway. I pulled her to my bed, and we were complete, one whole woman, inside one another, beside each other, hands pressed and melted together, full to the brim. Afterwards, her head on my chest, I marvelled that she was able to get to sleep, given the rise and fall of my ribcage.

The feelings for her, which I'd kept in check for so long, poured from me. They overwhelmed poor Jaleesa. I wanted her to stay every night in my bed, and for a while she did, but in the morning, when I woke, she'd be back in her room. She said that what we were doing was wrong, that she needed to quit the drugs because they made her do things that weren't her, weren't who she wanted to be. Once, after she'd spent a half-hour in her bedroom talking on the phone with her mama, I heard her crying behind the door. I asked if she was okay, but she didn't want to talk about it. I kept asking until she got angry and stormed out. I don't know where she slept that night.

Did I accuse that other girl on the stroll, Tammi, of glomming on? I guess I have those tendencies in me too, which can't have helped. One day, four months later, Jaleesa announced she was recommitting herself to Jesus and was moving to Oro Township to stay with an auntie. I was stunned. I'd been planning to hold hands in the gay parade, imagining romantic dinners, Jaleesa in a tight-fitting lemon-coloured dress to bring out the Brazil nut of her skin. My dream had wobbled and disappeared as I'd tried to grasp it. When she left, I struggled. I could barely make rent, but I was still stinging from the slap of my mama's words. Jameses never give up. My pride kept me from calling for help.

It isn't important to go into how I lost my job and apartment, moved into Yen Mah's extra bedroom, and started turning tricks. It didn't happen suddenly; it took nearly three years. You could imagine it if you substituted the details for a game of Jenga, where you try to pull wooden blocks from a tower until it crashes down. Once I started hooking, I lived like that for another three years. Until I met Danni and her friendship helped me re-stack some of those blocks. And, much as she irritated me from time to time, her risk-taking brought out a protective instinct, a strength — which was weakening again from the relentless wrecking ball of streets and drugs. That and the sameness of our days, a backhoe clawing, tearing away.

Then, though I hadn't expected it, Danni'd become my support, too.

Backup

THERE ARE MANY DEFINITIONS OF FAMILY, AND THOUGH I WAS NEVER in love with Danni, or even attracted to her, we banded together in coexistence, mothering my son as best as we could. On we went, spelling each other off in child care, slipping up but avoiding disaster, with Carole-Anne pitching in like a surrogate grandmother when she could. I bought Danni a cheap wristwatch with a timer that we set to beep when she was supposed to take her HIV meds, because although she was pretty good about it, it was easy to forget. And Danni's hippie days in university came in handy in saving on groceries. We cooked a ton of lentils, rice, beans, and ramen noodles, though I couldn't live without my roast chicken or stew from Mr. Jerk.

I truly believed we were doing well. Or at least well enough. Aaron didn't go hungry, and we never left him alone for more than a half-hour. But that didn't make our plan or routine more sustainable. If we'd been heroin users or pot smokers, we might've been able to make it work. The thing is, crack is not conducive to planning. It was difficult at that point in our dependence — almost impossible — to take two hits and call it a night. Two hours could become ten or twenty-four. With hindsight, the reality is so obvious as to be darkly comical, but I was a desperate mother deep into my addiction. Danni was my well-intentioned but similarly screwed-up friend.

More times than either of us cared to admit, the following scenario played itself out: Two hours of drugging would pass. The one taking care of Aaron in the apartment would get jumpy and desperate, counting each minute over the two-hour mark. We were still semi-serious about not doing drugs in our living space. Whoever was in charge would bring Aaron downstairs to the streets, or to Mario's Drop-In, in search of the other. That person, instead of taking Aaron and going back to our apartment, would bring him to Carole-Anne's to do another hit. Carole-Anne didn't love the idea of our shooting up in her apartment, but she agreed to it so she could spend time with my son.

If we were lucky enough to get Aaron to sleep, we'd put him on Carole-Anne's bed. If not, we placed him on blankets on the floor with a stuffed animal. We'd watch him motor around the room on hands and knees. If he cried, someone would hold him, feed him, or change his diaper. Needles were never left out; but once, I admit, when I'd still had the foolish notion that I could maintain a breastfeeding schedule, I'd smoked a pipe while he nursed. Danni and Carole-Anne weren't around. When I'd told Danni, she'd congratulated me on multi-tasking. It was the kind of praise you give someone to make them feel better. I hated smoking; I'd lit up because I'd badly needed a fix. I'd told myself that it was the more responsible decision to feed him and my habit at the same time when, in that state, the only alternative I could fathom was ignoring his hunger because mine was screaming more fiercely.

I knew it wasn't good. Had the drug gone straight from lung to breast milk and into him? Other times I smoked a pipe while he took his bottle. Was that better than doing it while breastfeeding? We honestly didn't have a clue. The drug might affect Aaron, stunting his growth or making him an addict in the first year of his life.

The plan was laughable for other reasons, too. Money to buy drugs didn't appear by magic. One of us had to work the streets, and though we had cellphones with prepaid time, we were often out of minutes, which meant that we weren't easily locatable if we didn't reappear when expected. If business was slow, and it often was, two hours needed to be four or five, as we changed location to try our luck on Gerrard or Jarvis. On many occasions, Danni's babysitting shift was up with no sign of me whatsoever. When that happened, she'd grab a piece of rock she'd stashed away — and which it had taken all of her willpower not to smoke or inject while I was out — and take Aaron down to Carole-Anne's place. With Carole-Anne often asleep or gone, she'd satisfy her craving and watch the clock until I returned.

When this happened to me, I feared Danni'd never show again, that something had happened to her on the streets. Maybe she'd been picked up by the police or had picked up a bad trick. In those dark moments, it was hard not to resent the child on the floor in front of me, for his helplessness, for his expectation that he be taken care of. For his irritating innocence.

Despite all these worries, we carried on, and after eight months of living together, when nothing terrible'd happened, I got cocky. It was early June 2007, just after Aaron's first birthday. Spring had been a tease: one day warmish, the next damp and cold, unreliable. This was the kind of hot June night that lets you know that summer is going to be different, that she's a working girl, ready to make the deal. It was Danni's turn to go out. We needed drugs and were nearly out of food, and I couldn't get Aaron to settle, so I decided I'd go for a walk with him at around ten o'clock. Danni wasn't planning to go far to find tricks; she'd stick to River Street.

She was taking forever to select her work outfit, something she should've been able to slap together in ten seconds, and Aaron snivelled and stretched in his stroller — a new find we'd scored, abandoned behind our building — so I gave him a sippy cup and he grasped it, sucked at it, and threw it on the ground. He squirmed at the straps holding him into his stroller. I wasn't gonna let him spend another hour crawling all over the apartment. By the time Danni dressed, she lost steam and sat in front of the TV, where the news was running. A program was on about the Tiananmen Square massacre. On the screen was the iconic image of that lone man standing in front of the tank. The effects of Danni's last fix had worn off, and she fidgeted more than Aaron, drumming her fingers on the remote.

"Are we going out or not?" I stood at the door and pulled at my jean jacket, which was bunching near my shoulders because I'd wriggled into it too hastily.

"Sorry." She switched off the television.

Danni stood, and Aaron quieted himself. "Naturally. We're ready to go and now he stops fussing."

"Do you want to stay?" she asked.

"Nah. He'll likely start up again in the elevator."

"Well, standing beside me with your baby carriage isn't exactly going to help lure tricks. What are you gonna do, hide in a shrub?"

I laughed. "Maybe."

"Okay, but if he starts whimpering, put a pillow over his face."

"Danni!"

She grabbed her keys to lock the door, glancing behind her, for what, I don't know. "It's just that it was your turn to stay in."

If Danni was gonna point out how late it was, that we should've had Aaron down hours ago, she wisely didn't. I pushed the stroller down the hallway. "Yeah, but I need to get some air."

The elevator took forever to reach our floor. While we waited, I said, "Danni do you think Aaron's okay? He's not walking yet.

Carole-Anne says he should be walking by now, but he's only just pulled himself upright and he's already a year old. I'm worried he might be delayed."

"He's going to be fine. You also worried he'd never say 'mama,' but he did, didn't he?"

"Yeah, he said it to Carole-Anne."

"He was asking for you."

"Was he?" The way Carole-Anne had smiled, I'd wanted to murder her. "And anyway, he didn't say it until two weeks ago."

"You're worrying too much. He'll get to it all, in his own time."

In the lobby, we walked past Mario, who was camped in his usual spot. "Hey, girls, can I interest you?" He waved a baggie full of crystals.

"Later," said Danni.

"Shouldn't that kid be sleeping?" he shouted as we headed towards the street.

"Fuck off and mind your own business," I shouted back, raising my middle finger without turning. "And if anyone asks, you didn't see us."

"Hey — you got nothing to worry about here!"

I turned and gave a reinforcing glare.

We pushed the stroller to T.O. Fine Foods, the convenience store at the corner of River and Oak, which we'd dubbed "Revolto Foods" because it was a more apt description of what they sold. You were lucky if you could find two-year-old Jos Louis cakes or a crinkly package of shrivelled Fig Newtons. Maybe pocked fruit and nearly expired milk. Danni checked her reflection in the storefront window. She considered whether she was slutty enough. She'd pulled on a miniskirt, sneakers, knee-high socks, and the only decent top she could find, which was, unfortunately, an oversized T-shirt. She'd tucked in its extra fabric at the back to make it more form-fitting, but she changed her mind and tied a knot in front instead.

The change worked. It showcased her tits while the knot covered her stomach, about which she was self-conscious, and hinted at a waistline. She pulled her hair into pigtails — she'd go for "school-girl" tonight. The small purse she carried was more for show than for storing anything of value.

"Can you watch him a second?" I asked, and went inside to buy a can of Coca-Cola.

The effort Danni'd put into getting ready was minimal compared to the elaborate prep she and I'd done for a night over on Jarvis Street. These days it was all about convenience, making enough money for drugs, food, diapers, tampons, and rent and staying close enough to home to make sure one of us was back in time to spell the other one off with Aaron. We'd settled for quickies from guys trolling in and around Regent. Less competition meant less effort but also less cash.

I returned with my pop.

"You know, that kind of Coke isn't gonna help you sleep either."

"Whatever. I'm gonna take the little guy for a walk while you do your thing."

"Sounds good." Danni adjusted her shirt again and walked along the sidewalk, taking up a position at the curb. Her body language struck the delicate balance between suggestive and inconspicuous; we had to be more careful than usual not to attract attention because this area was well policed.

Aaron had been quiet in the elevator and while I was in the store, but now that I was moving he fidgeted. I tightened the strap in his stroller, and he did not like that. I shushed him and scanned for police. Seeing nothing, I pushed him down the street.

"Do you have your key and cellphone?" Danni called after me. She'd already taken her position at the curb.

"Got 'em," I called back, holding up my new clamshell Samsung.

I set off north for a good, full tour. Maybe I'd cross to west of Parliament once I'd done a complete lap of the east side. Well-to-do Cabbagetown, north of the depressed area in which we lived, was especially pretty at this hour. Porch lamps cast soft light on red brick, and the Riverdale Farm, when I reached it, was still, the animals asleep in their pens. Residents passed me, out to give their dogs late-night relief. I sat on a park bench when the coast was clear and prepared a needle to inject, pausing to rock Aaron's stroller forward and back. I pretended I had a better, calmer, more sophisticated life.

Only seven blocks away, a car was pulling up in front of Danni, where I'd left her on the curb. The man she greeted was pushing sixty, and they negotiated a quick blow job. As they drove to Cornwall — a short, quiet elbow of a street running off of River — Danni dabbed Vicks VapoRub on her upper lip by way of preparation. It was to mask any foul smell, but when she took him into her mouth, he tasted mildly astringent: he'd put cologne on his cock. Not much surprised us anymore, but this was new.

After he dropped her off, she waited twenty minutes without any other business, fretting that she might not earn enough that evening. A silver Chrysler pulled up and rolled down the window. This one was younger, perhaps in his early thirties, with a full head of hair and a tan jacket over a collared sports shirt. She leaned into the car, and he adjusted himself in his jeans. He looked her in the eye when they negotiated, so she knew he'd done this before.

There was a creepiness about him, but Danni couldn't say why. I'd told her to trust her gut, but she'd often gone with guys who gave her a bad feeling and usually it'd been fine. There were also the occasions when she'd been robbed and spat on.

She negotiated twenty dollars for a blow job to be given in his car, an extra ten dollars so he could finger her while she went down on him, and another ten to let him come in her mouth. She made him give her half up front. She must've wished I'd been around, even if I'd been standing down the block. Danni still relied on me for my advice, and I'd gained a reputation as someone who'd brief new girls on the stroll. Maggie's, the local hookers' collective, had tried to recruit me, but I wasn't interested and referred them instead to Olive, who'd been at it longer and had seen it all.

Danni'd paid close attention to most of my street safety tips, spotty condom use aside. Don't wear dangly or hoop earrings, because they might get pulled, accidentally or intentionally. Tight pants and nylon underwear and pantyhose could cause vaginal infections, so it was crotchless underwear, stockings, or nothing at all. Although she hadn't put it on tonight, she fought me on wearing her favourite jean jacket. I relented, but insisted that when she wore it, she not button it up. I'd once worn mine to work buttoned to the bust line, the same jacket I wore that night to walk Aaron in Cabbagetown, and a bad date had pulled it down over my shoulders when he was done with me, pinning my arms. For a laugh, the guy'd pushed me out of his car to watch me hit the pavement without being able to brace my fall. I'd injured my shoulder and had bruises all the way up my right arm.

Remembering my advice, Danni circled the car and pretended to take mental note of the licence plate. She flipped open her phone and pretended to make a short call to me. "Uh-huh, yeah," she said to the dead air, "I'm in front of Revolto Foods about to get in with a guy in a silver Chrysler." She had a terrible memory and couldn't remember a licence plate to save her life, but it was important to make a show of it, to demonstrate to the trick that she was taking precautions. Still, she couldn't say too much on her fake phone call or the guy'd get spooked and drive off.

She hopped into the passenger seat and put her purse on the floor, where she could find it if she needed to.

"Zach." He extended his hand.

"Delilah," she replied.

She directed him to the same side street, and as soon as they were parked, Zach unzipped. He was already hard, and he cupped his hand to the back of Danni's head to pull her down.

She resisted. "I can get a better angle if I do you from outside the car, with your door open."

"Yeah, but I can't get my hand up your skirt as easily if you do that."

"Suit yourself." She tried to sound indifferent, but twisting her torso and leaning over him in this way was awkward. More dangerous. Nobody could see her, which was good for avoiding cops but not great if something went wrong. At least he didn't have a huge pickup or a van with room in the foot well. Crouching between a guy's legs was the worst position of all; you could get trapped.

Zach pushed her head down, and she took him into her mouth. He called her a skanky whore, his nasty baby girl, his fucking come-slut, and when he slipped his fingers between her legs she tensed up. "Uh-huh," he said, "you like it when Daddy does that to you, don't you?"

She was grateful her mouth was too full for him to expect a real answer. She finished the job, counting the ways she might kill him. He came in her mouth and jabbed his middle finger deep into her, his nail cutting her. She made a muffled cry, spit his come into a tissue she fished from her purse. "Jesus Christ! Trim your nails next time!"

He chuckled.

She was ready to leave, but he made no effort to get his wallet.

"I guess we should settle up," she said.

"Nuh-uh, you didn't swallow. You spit it out."

"So what? I told you you could come in my mouth. You never said anything about swallowing."

"What, you're too good to swallow my come? You think I got

AIDS or something? I'm not the one who's a fucking low-life whore opening her snatch to strangers."

"Zach, c'mon." She used his name, like I'd taught her, hoping its intimacy would defuse the situation. "I don't think I'm better than you. But we had a deal, didn't we?"

"Get the fuck out of my car."

"Not until you give me my money." She didn't know where this daring came from, this stupid boldness. Given the bad feeling he'd given her, not to mention the jabbing fingernail, it was foolhardy to insist. But she was pissed off and jonesing. We needed money soon.

Zach's eyes narrowed. He got out and strode around the front of the car. Danni tried to open her door, but her purse became entangled on the drive shaft. He opened it from the outside, grabbed her near the shoulder, and yanked her out, slamming the door behind her. She fell on the ground.

I'd made my long loop into Cabbagetown and back, had tacked on a loop down Sumach to Dundas and across to River. I was walking up River past Cornwall Street as Danni's body was hitting the sidewalk.

"Hey! What the fuck?" she shouted.

He kicked her in the ribs, and she screamed.

"Hey!" I called out, but neither of them reacted.

He pulled her up by her jacket and pushed her away from the vehicle. She stumbled. He started back around the front of the car, to the driver's-side door.

"Give me my purse, you goddamned piece of shit!" He got into his car, threw her purse out the window into her face. "And my money."

"Just walk away, ya fucking cunt."

"Don't you call her a cunt!" I shouted, louder, speeding up and marshalling my toughest stance.

The man shook his head and laughed. Stuck his head out the window and shouted, "Coming to defend your girlfriend?" He revved the engine.

Danni stood in front of his headlights. The Tiananmen Square hero. "Paulette, stand behind the car." The man turned his wheels and tried to pull away from the curb, but Danni moved to block him.

They locked gazes. His hand moved to the gearshift, and his eyes flickered to the rear-view mirror. By the time she understood his intent.it was too late.

Danni shouted a warning. He gunned into reverse. I dove, but not fast enough. The car clipped my leg, and I shrieked, fell on the pavement.

As the trick drove off, Danni ran to me. I moaned, the pain shooting straight up to my hip. Aaron was crying off in the distance by the intersection. I'd left him there. The bleating of a police horn from the end of the street startled us, and was followed in counterpoint by another cry from Aaron, off in the distance.

I was on my back, clutching at my leg while Danni's hand added pressure. There was blood on our fingers. An officer emerged from her car and walked towards us. Her partner went to the unattended stroller. We knew these cops; they were the ones who'd arrested me in the stairwell and sent me to jail. The female one approached us, but turned back to her partner, now removing Aaron from his stroller.

"It's gonna be okay," she lied. "Stay still while we call for help."

Giant's Arm

THE UNATTENDED STROLLER NEAR THE INTERSECTION, FAR AWAY AND in the dark, couldn't have been a better visual representation of neglect. I was high and had a record. We were well known to the police. Children's Aid night duty met us at the hospital. The social worker took Aaron into custody. I wailed, my fingertips losing contact with his waist. Aaron's eyes bugged huge, staring back, puffy and red. His head bobbed over the worker's shoulder. I forgot the pain of my broken tibia until I tried to run after them and my legs gave way in the hall.

I don't remember how I got home, or if Danni came with me. My life had cracked open again, and another enormous chunk had dislodged and crashed at my feet, kicking up a cloud of dust. It made it impossible to see anything or anyone. Days passed like that, weeks, maybe, shapes forming in the filthy air, shapes that blew apart when another chunk dislodged, kicking up a new cloud of dust.

One day I caught sight of myself in the mirror, and it wasn't the uncombed hair or the dull ash of my skin tone or the lines under my eyes that unsettled me — it was my mouth hanging open. I was lobotomized. I'd been limping about our apartment in a wordless stupor, from bed to toilet and toilet to bed, drooling without knowing it. Sometimes I made it into the shower. Protecting the cast with a plastic bag was more effort than I could muster. I barely ate, and the sadness was blinding enough that sometimes its haze dulled the most clawing urges — only for a minute or so, but that was something. Then I'd shoot up again.

And what can I say of hope? I don't know how others experience it, what it feels like when they have it or when it's lost. For me, hope had been a delicate web I'd spun from false promises and foolishness to catch bits of someone else's better life — all of which would be torn down by the thoughtless swing of a giant's arm. I was out of thread. I crawled into the shadows and stayed there, folding my arms around myself.

I couldn't talk to Danni. I couldn't look her dead-on. Her eyes were glassy with sadness, her outstretched arms lined with track marks of self-reproach. Her apologies thudded between us, her words lead weights she'd dropped at my feet. I didn't have strength for my own regrets; how could I possibly lift hers?

Aaron had been taken into foster care, and Children's Aid gave me times when I could visit. Unbelievably, while we awaited my court date, they wanted us to work together so Aaron could come back to live with me. My social worker, Donna, said Aaron's foster mother was experienced and that she'd be "part of the conversation," whatever that meant. The date of my first visit arrived, and I tried to pull myself upright, to choose good clothes. I put on a skirt because with the cast on my leg, I couldn't fit into jeans. Track pants were too casual.

I went to the mirror before leaving the apartment, and the room quivered. Everything about me was fake. I was untrustworthy, trying to pull the wool over their eyes. The cast gave me up for sure, but also the clothes were too drab and businesslike. I was some kind of pathetic, novice drag queen. Certainly not a mother. I sat on my bed and stared at the wall until I made myself late. When the hour's visit was up, I called Donna and lied, said that my leg had been throbbing, that I'd been worried about flesh-eating disease because another girl I knew had it, so I'd gone to the hospital and had left my phone at the apartment. Donna's voice, flat, unmoved, meant she didn't believe me, but she gave me options to reschedule.

By the next date, I'd figured something more comfortable to wear, a simple long-sleeved shirt and loose-fitting slacks Danni'd left on my bed without saying a word. They fit over the cast. I grabbed my crutches and was about to set off when shocks of panic coursed through me again. What would I say to Aaron? Who was this family he was with, and what did they think of me? I tried my best to ignore the urge, but it was too strong. I shot up, pulled my shirt-sleeve down over the red mark, and tried to pull myself together. Hoped I could fake it.

When I turned up at the house, Donna was waiting. She was a chipmunk of a woman, all compact sinew packed into a five-foot-nothing frame. She introduced me to Mrs. Tremaine, the foster mother, a white lady with two children of her own and with the highest cheekbones ever known to womankind. Mrs. Tremaine wiped her hands on a dishcloth and shook my hand. She smiled, raising her ridiculous, punchable cheeks higher. The house smelled of brewed coffee and bacon. A caged budgie chirped in the living room, and the dog, outside chained to a tether, yapped at unseen rivals.

I caught sight of my outfit in the hall mirror. It was too manly, and that could be used against me. Aaron wobbled my way and into my arms. He'd taken his first steps. Here. I burst into tears but quickly pulled myself together. Donna and Mrs. Tremaine — she tried to get me to call her Janet, but I couldn't — were steering the conversation to practical matters of child care strategies, like I was a moron. They didn't have a goddamned clue. As if I didn't know what I needed to do. I tried to stay cheerful and talked too much. The drugs, the tension, the stakes. The budgie! Why wouldn't it shut up! I was going to do better, I knew I could do better, I said, and "Jesus, that bird!" I shouted.

It made Aaron cry. I was flying. All I wanted to do was grab Aaron, unlatch the birdcage, run into the yard, unchain the dog, and tear into the streets, screaming, until the four of us were out of earshot.

The bird never let up. Mrs. Tremaine said, "Sorry. Beejay's a talker." She held back from taking Aaron, probably scared of me, but Aaron's hand slipped from mine.

It was Donna. She said, "Paulette, let's go to the porch for a minute and get some air. Aaron can stay with Janet." She handed him off.

My face went hot. Mrs. Tremaine pitied me. She led Aaron away, bribing him with a toy I could never've afforded. He followed without turning back, and I took it as a sign that he was happier with her. How could he not be?

On the porch, Donna's eyes were huge, bright interrogation bulbs, and my skin crackled under their gaze. "You're high. I know this is a lot of pressure, but this isn't good." Her perfume coated my throat and made me gag. The dog had stopped barking and was whimpering. The yard smelled foul.

My body crumpled, shrank back, packed itself up, trying to hide my unsheltered failure from her withering judgment. My arms crossed themselves, and the tips of my fingers dug into my ribs, my thumbs pressed in and up, hiding themselves under my breasts.

I tried to apologize. My voice was a thin wisp of dust. Donna said, "Sorry?" but not because she was repeating my words. When I tried to project more regret into the air between us, it came out in small puffs of soot. "I'll do better!" I wheezed. "I promise." My voice was once more losing its force.

I pray I'll never again know anything so horrible. Aaron being taken from me in the hospital? That was raw terror and searing pain, but grief blinds and blocks sound and smell. That, there on that foster mother's porch, was something worse. I saw, heard, smelled everything.

Donna forced a smile, her cheeks tightening, and waited for my grimy apology to settle between us. She took two deep breaths before she spoke. Did I physically reek? Was she trying to quell her nausea? She confirmed the next appointment and stated the obvious: that I couldn't show up high. She repeated that it wasn't helping. Did I understand?

The condescending way that she addressed me ignited a spark. Instead of saying yes, I denied that I'd been using. I'd had too much coffee that morning and I was nervous, I claimed. She frowned, as if to say, *Do you take me for an idiot. You're embarrassing us both.* She let me say goodbye to Aaron and ushered me off.

The next day, I called Donna and told her that they could have Crown wardship without access. She asked if I was sure, but didn't talk me out of it. She explained, to make extra sure I got it, that this meant my court date would be cancelled and Aaron would be adopted quickly into a new family. The court date. I wouldn't've stood a chance. I was known to the police, they'd bring up my prior convictions and the fact that I was a hooker.

"Find him a good family. Promise me."

"We don't have open adoptions in Ontario yet, Paulette. You won't be able to visit."

"I know," I said, thinking of Chantelle.

I was allowed a final visit, as if I were being executed. I told Donna I didn't want to go back to the Tremaines', so Donna arranged it for the CAS office. I was allowed to give Aaron a small gift that he'd be able to keep, that he'd be told was from me, and a letter that'd be kept sealed by Children's Aid for when he was an adult. I agonized over what toy to bring, whether it should have special meaning. Maybe he'd be adopted into a white family and grow up adrift in that world. If I could find the right thing, it might anchor him, but we hadn't had any special toys growing up that were different from anyone else's. I didn't want it to be one of the toys from our apartment; they were too shabby. I settled on a new, plush stuffed elephant and focused my efforts on my letter. It took me a dozen discarded drafts, but I settled on something short:

August 10, 2007

My beloved Aaron Clifton James,

I hope you haven't been angry all these years that I gave you up or that I didn't fight harder to keep you. I loved you as much as humanly possible, but I had too many struggles and there wasn't enough help. One thing is that I have depression sometimes, and it paralyzes you. Your Gram-Ma has it too. A doctor told me a while back that it wasn't my fault — it's in the genes. I hope you didn't inherit that part. I hope you got the feisty part, the part that doesn't take any shit from anybody, pardon my language.

I don't want to get into what else happened, because I don't want you to be any more ashamed of me than you probably already are, but my problems got the better of me and things fell apart. I'm not the kind of mama that you need right now, someone who can give you a good home, a stable home — where there's happiness and there's always food on the table, proper toys and an education. But someday, I'd love it if you came to find me. By then, I hope I'll be in a different place. I want to see the man that you're going to be. Maybe you'll also look for your sister, Chantelle.

Love, your mama — your real mama — Paulette James.

The visit was predictably horrific. I don't remember much of it; the blindness was back. Donna snapped a photo of the two of us, which she promised to send me. There was no smell except the sweetness of the top of his head. There was no sound except my breathing, and then my wailing. When Aaron joined in, I hugged him too long, and Donna had to bring the visit to a close sooner than was planned. When he left the room, and the door clicked shut, a wheeze left me from a hollow place, a part of me I'd never fill again.

Hopeless Crazy

I WENT BACK TO THE APARTMENT, SHUT THE DOOR TO MY ROOM, and turned on the radio. I rotated the dial trying to find something good. It landed on a news station, and there was an item about a woman who'd been arrested after lunging at an abortion doctor somewhere downtown. She'd screamed that he'd killed innocent babies. The woman was clearly crackers, but I could relate to the anger, the desire for revenge. I blasted a reggae program on CKLN until the neighbours pounded on the wall. If I'd had earphones I'd have put them in, but I didn't, so I turned the volume up to drown out the pounding.

Without Aaron to consider, Danni worked nearly every night. For the first couple of weeks, she turned tricks for the both of us. She tried hard, staying later, after there was little hope of getting business. She kept food in the fridge and bought drugs for me. Any addict will know that buying drugs with your own money and handing over half of it to a friend is a monumental feat of self-control. In this case, although it wasn't in my best interest, it was also generosity. I'll stand by that, even though it's not conventional twelve-step wisdom. What is true generosity if not giving up something you badly need?

I met Danni's kindness with indifference. With ingratitude. I barely left the apartment. I slept until I developed a sore back. One day, a faint sobbing in the other room woke me. I opened the door a sliver. The first time Danni'd ever cried in front of me.

She lifted her head. "I can't do it. I can't pull in enough." Our rent was due, and she begged me — apologized, but still pleaded with me — to get up and out to work or we wouldn't be able to pay. She'd already gone to a food bank.

I shut the door and went back to sleep.

Christopher, our so-called landlord in that illegal sublet, harassed us with phone calls, and made one unpleasant visit. Unpleasant for Danni; I never left my room. He didn't want to get in trouble, he said, but he also wasn't gonna put up with any shit. He threatened to have the locks changed. He left, and Danni opened my bedroom door.

"That's it, Paulie. This is it. I don't have a choice. I'm scared to stay in a place that we can't even fucking lock up behind us."

I shook my head, as if to say, Where's your backbone?

"For fuck's sake, say something!" she screamed.

I lay back on my bed.

"I'm sorry, but this is no way to live. Not being able to leave our home in case we can't get back in? It's not a life; it's a prison."

I chuckled. Of all the things that could've scared her about our lives, this was the thing she couldn't tolerate — it was comical. She threw up her hands, as if to say I'd gone insane. Maybe I had. She closed my door.

She moved out immediately, said she was going back to Carole-Anne's. When the front door shut behind her, I went to her empty bedroom. She'd left the polystyrene remnants of a takeout meal and a pile of magazines. I went to the containers, lying on a grease-stained newspaper — maybe she'd left food in them — but they were empty. An article in the newspaper mentioned another abortion doctor, this one in British Columbia, who'd been stabbed on the way to work. The attacker was doing God's work, he said, "to save the voiceless murdered children."

Did Donna consider me stupid and irresponsible not to have aborted Aaron when I'd had the chance? Is that what I should've done? Or was abortion a greater sin than damaging a child for life? Maybe they'd taken Aaron in time. I imagined the foster mother, Mrs. Tremaine, trying to undo what I'd done. I wished she'd screw up, hurt Aaron — not seriously, but enough that they'd take him from her and she'd understand the humiliation. A new wave of self-disgust: that I was imagining him hurt so that some other lady could feel what I did.

I scanned the rest of the apartment. It hadn't been cleaned in weeks. Bits of food lay scattered on the floor. Dust motes all around. An odour of rotting meat fought with air freshener, and was winning. I went to the bathroom and looked in the mirror. This time, there was no drool. The corners of my mouth were cracked. I hardly recognized myself. My cheeks were cavernous, my skin pocked and sallow. The cold sore that had been throbbing at the edge of my bottom lip had erupted and was huge, stop sign red. I went to the kitchen, got garbage bags and a pair of scissors. With squares of black plastic, I covered the mirrors.

If I could only end it. It wasn't the first time I'd considered it. I made a mental list of the bridges I might jump from, now that there was a suicide barrier on the Bloor Street Viaduct, but I didn't have the guts. I suppose somewhere deep down there was still a scratching attempt to survive.

I had to get myself out of the apartment. I made it down the elevator and went to Mario. I asked if he could hook me up with a better, quicker way to earn cash. Based on my reflection, I wouldn't have much luck pulling in business on the stroll, and while I needed something to get me through the night, I also needed fast money and a lot of it, for rent, for food, to get myself back on track. Maybe if I could do it, it wouldn't be too late. Maybe they'd give Aaron back to me.

Mario hooked me up with friends who were operating a mortgage and money transfer scam. Gullible people would respond to an ad these guys put in the paper, using my name but another address, one in Uxbridge or Maple or somewhere like that. The person would send five thousand dollars to a Cash Money branch downtown, money they expected would get them a mortgage within twenty-four hours.

Later that week, two young guys with Eastern European accents, not much older than I was, met me in a Chrysler LeBaron that had been painted sloppily all over, failing to hide a bubbling of rust at the wheel wells. A sickly pine freshener dangled from the rear-view mirror, a man swinging in a hangman's noose. They drove me to the Cash Money location on Overlea Boulevard and told me I was to go in, pick up the five thousand bucks, and bring it to them. They'd be waiting in the parking lot.

I swung up to the counter on my crutches, gave them the fake ID the guys had prepared in advance, and the employee handed over an envelope of money. I couldn't believe it'd worked. In the parking lot, I got into their car, and the guys counted the bills. A fly buzzed past in the car. I shifted my weight, and a pretzel crunched under my legs. They passed three hundred dollars into the back seat. It'd been so simple, but they couldn't do it too often or we'd be caught. Three hundred wasn't enough to cover back rent and food, and I spent half of it on drugs, so after we did it a second time and I still wasn't able to put enough aside, I needed another scam. One I could do as a straight trade for drugs, which might help me put my earnings from the Cash Money scam aside for my other needs. I remembered something told to me by a guy I'd met in that crack house on Jones, and went to propose it to Mario.

"I'll help you," he said, "but only because you've been a long-standing and loyal customer. If I catch the slightest whiff of a cop, I will leave you without a second thought and say we never met. And," he added, "not until you get that fucking cast off and can wear decent clothes."

"Lucky for all of us, my appointment is in a couple of days."

The day after they took it off, I went to Canadian Tire and bought a small safe. I put my remaining money from the second Cash Money scam in there. I went to Carole-Anne and asked her to keep the key and not give it back to me until the first of the month. She refused. "No way I'm getting between an addict and her money, sweetie, no offence but that is not happening." I went to Mario, and he kept it for me.

We got in Mario's car and went to the Zellers in Thorncliffe Park. I walked down the aisle where they kept two-hundred-dollar ink cartridges and picked up two boxes. I went to the cash. Maybe I'd been recorded on their cameras? Was I followed by store security? Surely they could tell I was not the kind of person who bought such things.

When I reached the checkout, I avoided the cashier's eyes. My sweaty hands had left stains on the boxes. I pretended to peruse the items for sale next to the register. "I'd like to return these." I pushed the cartridges forward. "I thought I'd need them, but I didn't after all."

"Paulette? Is that you?"

Panic pressed in. "Jaleesa? What are you ... didn't you move up north?" I held tight to the counter.

"For a while. But now I live nearby. I've been working here for about a year. You ..." She'd begun to say that I looked good, but reconsidered telling an outright lie — or was hyper-concerned about saying anything that smacked of being gay. She settled on a simple, "How are you?"

"Oh, good, good." I glanced at the ink cartridges, and so did she. Did she know what I was doing? "I'm working in Riverdale at a fish store. Writing on the side, a lot of journaling on a laptop. I got a bunch of these cartridges for my printer, but they're freakin' expensive, and I overestimated how many I'd need. Can you believe how much they cost? That's how the printer companies make their money. First they get you to ..." My words cascaded, landing here, there, a random scattering of hopeless crazy. The muzak got louder and louder. The customer behind me fidgeted and checked her watch.

Jaleesa nodded. She was more beautiful than I remembered. Healthier and darker. Was this what finding God had done for her, or had she simply kicked drugs? I wished God could give me that much comfort. That I could lose myself in the certainty she had. Jaleesa didn't believe my story, and it was a scalding cloth thrown on my face. I steadied my breathing. Tears would overwhelm me if I didn't hold them in check.

"Well, I'll just take care of this." She pecked at her cash register. "But unfortunately, I can only give you a gift card. We had a person try to scam us a few weeks back. I'm guessing soon they won't even let us give out these cards." A pause. More pecking at the register. "Just so you know."

So she was warning me. She placed the card in my palm and squeezed. I felt the sweet familiar touch, the pads of her fingers firing electricity straight to my sluggish heart. I said, "You made the right choice leaving," and before I lost my shit in front of her, I grabbed the card. "Thank you. For this, I mean. I gotta run, but I'll be in touch, I promise."

"You take care!" she called after me.

In the parking lot, Mario was waiting with his hands on the steering wheel, eyes darting about. I handed him the card, and he shoved it in his pocket. "Well, it's not cash, but I can use it anyway." He handed me a bag of rock.

I opened my palm. Jaleesa had placed a small piece of paper with the name of her church together with the gift card. It read, *Leaside Bible Chapel. Engaging God, Engaging People*, with the church's address and phone number on the flip side.

Cracked Wide Open

I BOUGHT CHEESY SNACKS AND WENT HOME, ITCHING TO START MY run. I was fixing up my works in the bedroom when Christopher thumped at the door. "I'm here to change the locks!" he shouted when I didn't answer. Had he come with the police? I wished we'd had Carole-Anne's paranoia and had also installed padlocks. I pressed my ear to my closed bedroom door. He came in, told the superintendent we'd been roommates. "I had to move out temporarily," he said. "This one and her friend are squatting now. No rent for months." He yelled obscenities at me through the door.

When they were finished, the super advised him to wait me out, if he could; if I wasn't gone in a week, he'd come back with the police. I shot up when they left, turned on the radio and played air guitar and air drums in my room until the fix wore off and I did another. I repeated this for three days. Only once did I leave — to get more snacks and to buy a baseball bat in case someone broke into the apartment I'd no longer be able to lock. I knocked on a neighbour's door and asked if I could borrow a measure of duct tape. Her eyes were wide, and she held a small dog to her chest. It yapped at me protectively. She went to get some and said, "Please go away and don't come back." She held her dog closer and shut her door. I hadn't meant to scare her.

I taped the bolt on my front door so it'd stay open and went to the store. Who'd wanna rifle through my meagre possessions, I didn't know, but the apartment was untouched when I returned.

Late at night on the third day, when the drug was used up, I went to Mario and asked him for the key to my safe.

"No way, girl, you made me promise. I don't want you to be on the street." He didn't know I was four days from homelessness anyway.

"You're an asshole."

It was three-thirty in the morning. Back in my apartment, Jaleesa's image flashed, standing at the Zellers checkout. Aaron's face, smaller and smaller down the hospital hallway. In the foster mother's home. Mei Zhen's face, frightened on the floor of the fish store. And Danni's. On the stroll, the day I met her, scared to death by scrappy trannies. In Mario's Drop-In, as I taught her to slam.

I swept them all aside and focused on the safe, which I'd placed in the middle of the living room. I took my baseball bat, imagined it was our landlord, Christopher, and swung high. I brought it down, causing the safe to bounce and make a neat dent. The door didn't open. Once, twice, twenty times, I bashed at that sucker. Nothing. The neighbours banged on the walls and yelled for me to shut the fuck up, but I paid no attention. I kept swinging and swinging until I lost count and was damp with sweat. The goddamned thing might as well've been run over by a tank but hadn't cracked open the slightest. I sat on my sofa, out of breath. This puzzle wouldn't get the better of me.

The simplest idea is often the best one. I lifted it onto the balcony railing. Nobody was passing by below. The apartment was on the tenth floor, on the backside of the building, but there was a patch of pavement before the grass lawn began. A cool wind blew and sent a shiver down to the tips of my fingers. The lights from the Don Valley Parkway glistened in the distance. The smell of decomposing leaves from a pile on the lawn drifted up, strong and musty. The pavement below was clear. I pushed the safe, and when my fingers lost contact, there was a brief rush, a mere second when I myself was dropping, battered and dented but enjoying the adrenaline of the fall. I started for the elevator, leaving the apartment door ajar, my leg still complaining despite the cast being off. The crash and clatter the safe made when it hit the pavement reached me. I flinched, but I envied that safe: cracked wide open, I hoped, by a massive impact. Freed of its burden by a force bigger than itself.

The elevator took an eternity to reach the lobby. I exited the building and noted that off in the distance, next door, Mario was distracted by a deal in progress. Did the man ever sleep? I ran around to the back, where the safe had hit the pavement and rolled onto the grass. A neighbour was on his balcony three floors up. "Jesus, was it you who dropped that thing?" I ignored him. The safe's door was open, finally, but only two inches. It was cruelly bent and stuck in that position — my own fault from the crazed pounding I'd given it in the apartment — so that I had to use all my strength to pull at it to widen the opening. Enough to push my hand through, scraping my knuckles, and ... bingo.

"Get it together, or I'm calling the cops," said the man on the balcony. I reached up and gave him the finger. "Crazy crack whore," he cursed, and went inside.

I'd heard it so many times. I remembered Danni poking fun, trying to reclaim the term for ourselves. This time it was true. This was what'd become of me: bashing at a safe with a baseball bat in the middle of the night and dropping it from a tenth-storey window to get at three hundred dollars that I didn't have the willpower to use to prevent my own homelessness.

I pocketed the money, shoved the safe onto the lawn, and went on another crack run that I stretched out, made last until the dawn of day seven of my countdown. When it was done, when I knew the police were coming to evict me and there was nothing left except a crushing ache deep, deep in my bones, I pulled the garbage bag off my bedroom mirror and stared. I pressed the talk button on my cell, but there was no juice. I'd used up the prepaid time anyway. I scrounged for change, packed my belongings into a garbage bag, and dropped coins into a payphone on Parliament Street. A groggy voice picked up.

"Gwen, it's Paulette. I'm sorry it's so early, but I didn't know who to call."

Teardown

I WAS ABLE AT LAST TO MOVE INTO A NEW PHASE OF RECOVERY, A more honest one. It wasn't about telling a lie or telling the truth. Getting to real honesty was like stripping floorboards: a difficult process that may or may not uncover something beautiful, but that'll at least get rid of the layers of crap.

In approaching my twelve steps, I was humbler. I'd listened last time, but maybe not as carefully. I'd had Aaron with me. I was more demanding this time, too, if that doesn't sound contradictory to humility. I wanted more from people and was told, twice, not to cross-talk. I asked more of myself, too. I thanked Gwen for getting me through that jagged first month, for referring me to a shelter and getting me hooked up with social work and welfare and a room in an apartment with an older couple. With a doctor who prescribed anti-depressants, the first time I'd been willing to take them. But I decided NA was too rough a place for me to land, the people too transient. Too many of them had only hours or weeks of sobriety and too few were celebrating years. Maybe too many of them were like me. There were exceptions, like Gwen, but it didn't feel hopeful enough.

When I switched to the AA group at The 519 community centre in the heart of the LGBT village, I knew I'd come home. Three months in, I met my new sponsor, Rosalie. She came up to me after I shared about Jaleesa, about what she'd meant to me, what I'd done to push her away. She took me for coffee and said, "Paulette, lots of us have stories of first lovers running back to the closet, drugs or no drugs. And we Black women have all sorts of other challenges to face when we try to make it in the world. That — and lots of what happened afterwards — was not all your fault. The challenges are huge. We can't do it alone."

"But I wasn't alone," I protested. "I had a good friend with me. We tried to make it work."

"Paulette, we have to give ourselves over to our Higher Power. Lean on one another. Speak the truth and be generous. I'm sure whoever it was was a good friend. But when you look back on your friendship, was she in a place to give you the help you needed?"

I was grateful for Rosalie's wisdom, for shoring up my instincts. For reflecting back to me my life, which was a teardown on a wiggly footing — ugly, dangerous, but one that was worth reconstructing. For Danni, too, though she'd have to save herself. Rosalie helped me sort through it all, to distinguish between the chunks that had fallen off me, that were mine to own and make amends for, and the mess of cracked concrete and girders that were part of a substructure stacked against people of colour and immigrants. Against lesbians, and women in general. A foundation whose unsteadiness I couldn't be held responsible for. It was a strange relief to learn that history and its cruel legacy had been there all along, promising me solidity but in reality weakening, making things unsound and unreliable.

Four months into my recovery, in January 2008, I got a job at Timothy's, down the street from our meetings. It paid shit — I'd forgotten how little people made in retail — but it was a decent place to rebuild myself. I missed Danni like hell but resisted the urge to tell anyone what'd become of me until I was sure what that was.

My co-workers were nice enough. My boss, Gregor Romanz, hugged his staff in crushing, awkward attempts at team building, but the next moment would draw his arms up into a terrifying flamenco-like pose, his face twisted from pent-up frustration with us, before throwing his arms down at his sides as though preparing to snap invisible castanets. We'd freeze in our spots and wait until he'd tapped out his instructions or rebukes with his heels. These fits of imperiousness wouldn't last long before he returned to hugging and gossiping about who'd hooked up on the weekend, and with whom. If a customer was cruising us, he'd nudge us forward, reminding me of the pimps I'd been so careful to avoid, except that Gregor only wanted people to find love. Sure, flirting with customers was good for business, but it was harmless, and we could slough off his encouragement if we weren't interested in the people batting their eyes at us.

The staff called Gregor "The Minister of Romanz," or Minister for short. Most of the Timothy's customers were big bears — hairy middle-aged gay men — but women came in too; I flashed them my slyest smile. I was nowhere near ready for any follow-up, but the attention I received was cocoa butter to my rough, parched skin.

Minister smiled when girls flirted with me. One day, he nudged me forward in the direction of a particularly attractive one. "That, there, is your emotional bailout package." The sub-prime mortgage crisis in the u.s. was all over the news, and he was trying to be clever. "You need that, girl — part of your recovery stimulus." Minister knew all about my recovery; he was a twelve-stepper too. "Remember, this job has all the benefits of bartending without the temptation of booze."

"Or the tips," I quipped.

At night, I'd go back to my room in St. James Town and close my door, try to block out the sounds of the hallways, the clatter of people caught up in the life I'd left, the sweet but intrusive attention of Letty and Brian, who'd rented the room to me, by turning on my radio or my small TV set and figuring out a way to make it through to the next day. I wished someone would lock me inside, take away the temptation to leave.

Once or twice during a work shift at Timothy's, the door would open, and from the corner of my eye, for a flickering moment, I'd see Danni coming to say hello. But it was someone else, another girl with a similar haircut or swing of the shoulders. Disappointment and relief would squeeze my insides, one-two. I'd smile through it, help my customer, wait for the feeling to pass. At a lull, I'd organize the stockroom, mop the floor, count supplies for Minister, do more than he asked of me.

Seeing Danni wouldn't've been good for either of us, not when I knew she was still on her way down. The thing about reaching the bottom is that for some it's a free fall, and for others, like Danni and me, we land on deceptive ledges along the way. Those ledges fooled me into thinking I was at my lowest point, but my footing gave way, the ledge crumbled, and I fell further until I hit the real bottom.

I'd crawled back into a twelve-step meeting, sure this time that it couldn't be any worse for me. One day, I realized I still had more humility to embrace. My tale did not trump everyone else's. When I listened hard, there were a thousand versions of the fall. Some made me think, That's nothing, that deep pit you say you've tumbled into is barely a divot! A pawned wedding ring? An embarrassing hospital stay? Pfff! You're heading for a relapse. Then I'd hear one to cut me down to size. An arrest for drunk driving that killed a father of three. A beaten and traumatized child. A girlfriend repeatedly raped and humiliated.

Where Danni'd come from was a long way up from where she was, but she still had one or two more ledges to hit before she'd be lying in that rubble, staring up at the clear night sky.

Shake It

SITTING ON THE LEDGE WHERE I'D LEFT HER LOOKING DOWN AT MY fall, Danni could only see me flaming out into a smoking pit of sadness until she couldn't look at me anymore. If she hadn't done something, she said, we would've both ended up on the streets. From her perspective, she owed me lots; hell, she's still talking about how she'll always owe me, and I don't correct her, but back then, Danni was angry and, to quote Minister, she needed a fucking debt holiday.

When she left me in the apartment, she told herself that I wouldn't hold it against her forever, and she was right. A person can't give more than she's got, and I was a wreck. After Aaron was taken away, I didn't mean to, but I was pulling chunks off her, one fistful at a time.

She didn't want to move back in with Carole-Anne, God knows that was a trying situation to begin with, and it wasn't going to be much better, but what options were there? The hallway outside Carole-Anne's smelled its usual mix of curry, rancid deep-fry oil, and what Danni'd once described as decomposing bedbug poo. The door creaked open, and Carole-Anne considered Danni standing there, pathetic with a plastic bag of belongings at her feet. Carole-Anne's craggy face, jutting forward into the gap, was slack and unreadable. She rested her cheek against the doorframe and waited. Two of her many door chains jangled above and below her head, and she made no move to unlatch them.

Danni shoved her hands into the muff of her sweatshirt and told her what was happening, what'd happened. The horrible mess in which we'd ended up, emphasis more on my mess, I'd bet. She was, after all, trying to sell herself as a new and improved charity case. Still expressionless, Carole-Anne shook her head, but when there was a gap in the talking, she said, "I'm not taking in the both a ya." She unhooked the chains and stood aside. Maybe she wanted to avoid the drama between me and Danni. Or it was possible she was still miffed from the Christmas incident, how I'd blasted her about the crib.

She re-latched and deadbolted the door behind them, leaned against it, and stared at Danni with arms crossed. Danni dropped her bag and flopped on the sofa. She'd gone from an apartment with no locks back to that place, which Carole-Anne kept barricaded as if she were harbouring a terrorist cell.

Sir Purrsalot emerged from the kitchen, still completely anti-purr, and waddled over to Danni's feet to say hello.

"Paulie and I are not going to be spending any time together."

"She gonna be okay?"

"Oh, yeah." She stroked Sir Purrsalot. "It's Paulie. She always lands on her feet," she said, though I wonder if she believed it. Carole-Anne's raised eyebrows made the point: neither of them could be certain of it. "I just need to be away from her. I don't know what to do for her anymore."

"You've done more than anyone could ask. Sometimes you can't help these people." These people. Danni was right about her — it was always there under the surface. Do I blame her for not taking it on, in that moment? Not really. She needed something; this time, she couldn't afford to screw it up with one of her political statements. "You have to think about yourself now," Carole-Anne added, as if making my point, and then, as an afterthought, "Jesus, you look like shit."

"Thanks a lot, Carole-Anne. And you are a picture of health and youthful glow."

Carole-Anne smirked and went into the kitchen to resume her interrupted meal. Danni went to the bathroom mirror. She was one hairbrush tease short of a fright wig. I'd been gruesome looking, but Danni was no vision either. Her face was puffy and pallid, like a saggy bag of cocaine. Maybe she was only realizing the extent of it because I'd been worse from the crying. Makeup would take care of some of it, or so she hoped. She had to get out there again, make money, and the scariness was not going to do.

She tells me that the idea of hitting the streets caused the knot in her gut — already there from an image of me all alone at the apartment — to twist tighter. She gave herself some self-talk. What does any girl who has a job she doesn't like say to herself? She tells herself, *This is life. This is what it means to be an adult, going out and earning a living. It's what else we do with our lives that matters, not what we do to make money.* But there it was. What the hell else was Danni doing? She and I'd had many a laugh together, but it'd been a long time since she could remember having fun, or doing something meaningful. Earning a night's haul and pumping it up her arm was all that was left, which on its own was bleak.

Danni was coming around to admitting her uneasiness about turning tricks, to shedding her bluster. She'd never let on with me, but it was harder for her. Maybe she was being competitive and thought I was putting on a show, but I wasn't. I was nervous about the physical danger, but the sex was no biggie. With Danni, it was the other way around. Even after that guy went after her on that fateful night, she still had an underdeveloped sense of fear.

Being gay helped me separate sex with men, put it in a box off to the side. Unlike Danni, I sloughed it off. It's like this: if you love fine art, but you're stuck for years on end working in an exhibit with nothing but Elvis paintings, your surroundings are gonna make you sad. But if you're like me and you prefer music to art, well, who cares about the fucking Elvis paintings? It's not like they're gonna make me wish for Rembrandt. You put on your earphones and close your eyes.

For Danni, turning tricks had been manageable, tolerable, but it was increasingly taxing. Before, the freedom of our lifestyle and the excitement of living on the margins had been enough payoff to make it worthwhile. We'd had the good kind of excitement, the kind that leaves you with an adrenaline rush, euphoria, and an awesome story. Okay, the euphoria was also drug-assisted. But we'd racked up enough tales for Danni to write the book I always assumed she'd write one day, probably called something like *My Life in Toronto's Sex Industry*.

When had it all changed? I'd asked myself some of the same questions, except that Danni'd started this out as a kind of adventure. Then, slowly, the rewards got smaller, fewer, and the flush of excitement had turned to flashes of dread. We led lives on the margins. Danni'd seen those as boundaries to push, but now they were a cliff she was nervous to approach. The cost of this kind of living crept up on her, and she hadn't seen it coming. It'd become a game of diminishing returns. And then there was the night Aaron was taken away.

What would her precious Professor Varghese say about all of this? The one who'd taught her Women's Studies course at Trent. She'd convinced Danni that turning a trick wasn't any better or worse than marriage when it came to economic security. I got her lecture by proxy one night from Danni when she must've mistook my contorted face for interest instead of disbelief. "The terms 'hooking' and 'prostitution' are stigmatizing," she'd said. She'd tried to get me to stop using those terms and instead to talk about "sex work," and I'd snorted and shook my head. "You and your hoity-toity mumbo-jumbo terms that only one percent of the world uses. Or understands," I'd added.

She'd argued that words mattered. That selling sex wouldn't be stigmatized if our society weren't so prudish; I'm sure she was paraphrasing her professor's lecture. She said that all over the world, women and men sold their bodies to make a living. That she could name half a dozen of her mom's friends who stayed in their marriages for economic security, all the while having no sexual or romantic interest in their husbands.

"A huge assumption," I'd said, giving her a stare of exasperation that she couldn't have mistaken, which meant she was patronizing me while simultaneously being profoundly full of shit.

It was never spoken, but this was the major challenge of our friendship: each of us viewed the other with an alternating mix of respect and condescension. Yes, I did respect Danni, even if I didn't say it, and I certainly didn't express it in that moment. We were caught in a trap, one of us lecturing the other but not meaning to, the other feeling judged, the naive product of our upbringing.

Danni was intellectually curious, and I didn't fault her for that. She wanted to challenge her mind — that desire being the one good thing that came from her fucked-up childhood — but her curiosity did sometimes float her high above the building tops, where she couldn't tell a crack house from a castle. So I'd called it: Professor Varghese's comparison — while provocative and maybe true for some girls — was indeed bullshit for women like us, who couldn't control our habit. How did the five nasty blow jobs it took to earn an eight ball contribute to our fucking economic security? Survival, yes, if it meant getting through the night and the next day, but planning for the long term?

I don't remember where we were when we had that argument. Probably downing a burger in Hooker Harvey's or mopping up egg yolk with toast in the diner on Dundas. "There's always some idiot on the streets who has that pipe dream," I'd said. "Don't be one of them." Our life was simple. Put out, check out. Cash in, trade in. Needle in, breathe in. Get busted, get out, and begin again.

But was I right about the last part? Was there always going to be an opportunity to start over? For my sake, and for Danni's, I hoped so. I'd had my own moments of thinking I could plan for the long term, but in my depressed state that day, I'd settled for that smaller wish: that there'd be fight enough in each of us to stand up again when we were beaten down.

Danni'd clung to her professor's theories, but staring in Carole-Anne's mirror, she longed to tell me that I'd been right, that I could relax, that Women's Studies had been fucked and slammed out of her.

But I'd made that impossible. Maybe our friendship was over for good, maybe it was on a long pause; neither of us knew. She tried, through other people, to keep tabs on me, but I was lying low. She pulled herself together and hit the stroll, but not every night. Like she'd done the first time they were roommates, she made sure to hand Carole-Anne cash as soon as she made it, so that her rent'd be secure, and she went back to the food bank because she didn't have enough once her drugs were taken care of.

She didn't mention the food bank. Carole-Anne held up a can of Chef Boyardee. "I thought you didn't eat this stuff."

She shrugged. "I'm rebelling against the salads and two-cooked-vegetable dinners of my childhood. Besides, I find it strangely delicious."

"Maybe it's the fact that it's ninety percent sugar," said Carole-Anne.

They didn't speak much. Carole-Anne eyed her, much like when she'd first moved in four years before. Danni was a new person, an unpredictable entity, on probation again. She opened the TV console and, sure enough, there was the list of questions Carole-Anne'd used to interview her, still waiting for the next roommate, should she prove unreliable. And why wouldn't she keep it? Danni'd already left once before.

Weeks later, Mario told her that I'd left our old apartment and disappeared. "She went freakin' postal, man!" Everyone was talking about how I'd gone berserk, whaled on a metal safe and hurled it through an open window. It must've frightened her. I'd never been the kind of person to lose it. Not like that. She wondered if her own drug use was headed down that road. She was placing the buy, the deal, the fix, before food. Her HIV meds were free or she'd have been fucked.

Despite the worry, my absence was causing her more concern; nobody knew where I'd gone. Of the possibilities, jail was first on the list, but since Mario had no news that meant that I'd either moved far away or was at least outside the scope of his intelligence gathering.

Danni visited Yen Mah's apartment the next night. A young Black guy answered the door wrapped in only a towel. She hadn't realized Yen Mah had ditched her other boyfriend. He tensed his already rippling abs to call Yen Mah, who sauntered from her bedroom tying up a bathrobe. The guy flopped on the sofa and, stretched out, leafed through a magazine.

"New roommate?" Danni teased.

She detected a slight blush. "Nope. No roommate since Paulette."

"In that case, good for you." She nodded in the direction of sofa guy. Her voice must've been flat, envious.

Yen Mah uncrossed her arms. "You okay?"

"Right as rain. Paulie, on the other hand ..." She told her the story, but Yen Mah hadn't heard any news either.

"You let me know if you hear anything," said Yen Mah. A pizza deliveryman arrived, and her boy toy jumped up from the sofa and grabbed cash to pay him. "Okay, see you later." Yen Mah's attention had shifted to pizza. It was a more abrupt goodbye than Danni expected, but she'd interrupted Yen Mah's post-sexcapade meal.

Danni went to work. Without me there, it was harder and harder to pass the time. The nights were so dull that she was grateful for a trick to come by, not only for the money but for the break in the sameness of the strut-and-pose. If she was bored, she'd walk up to Gerrard to chat with Olive, who tolerated her for short periods. It had taken a few years, but Olive trusted her; there wasn't the same hostility, the posturing that she was homing in on her business. She knew why Danni was coming by and was grateful for the company too, even if after a while her worry took over. "G'won now," she'd say. "You're missing the action down the street."

The nights were getting colder. Danni dreaded another winter spent battling the elements. Between October and early January, she tried hard to ease off the crack, doing what cigarette smokers do, cutting down one needle a day for one week, one more the next, and so on, in the hopes of weaning herself. Harm reduction, like the outreach workers urged us to do. She couldn't so much skip a fix as hold off longer in between them and try to stretch the intervals longer and longer until the withdrawal shifted from mental torture to physical pain and it became too much. Some weeks, she didn't stick to the plan, but she did cut down.

One day, in the second week of January, we had a freakish weather spike to 18°C. People emerged from hiding, hos and tricks alike. It lulled Danni into believing the winter might be merciful. On her way to the stroll, she bumped into Olive, who mentioned she'd seen me over on Church Street, going into Timothy's. That I'd started working there. I was in recovery and was gonna make it stick this time, no fooling around.

"How did she seem?" Danni asked.

"It was daylight," said Olive. "I'd never seen her in daylight."

"What does that mean?"

"It means she looked like a girl who hasn't seen a ray of sunshine in ten years. She was all squinty. Like she was a vampire about to catch fire." Olive was harsh. I'd gained weight. Didn't that count for something? Wasn't it worth mentioning? Danni made a face, to which Olive pushed her lips outwards in a pitying pout. "Oh, honey, do you think you and I look any better?" She reached out and actually petted her head — "So sweet" — and clomped off on her platform heels.

At her position on the curb, Danni was preoccupied with the news that I'd pulled myself together again. Without a pregnancy and an infant to worry about, she gave me better odds, but the thought made her ashamed: she was blaming poor Aaron for my relapse and justifying his removal, a tragedy for which she held herself mostly responsible.

The one-day January thaw gave her false hope. The next day, the thermometer dropped twenty-seven degrees. Up until minus ten, we could pretend to be oblivious to the cold and still be sexually provocative. There was bravado on the strolls, a kind of *Survivor: Arctic Circle* competition that plays itself out in Toronto's sex trade. Babs and Serena, the ladies who had nearly made Danni's first night her last — but whom she'd later made peace with through glazed Timbits — strode by her one night on their way to Church Street.

Her teeth were chattering. Babs said, "C'mon, girl, this is balmy!"

"Balmy my ass. It's fucking minus nine."

"Your first problem is you're too skinny. You're gonna have to jiggle that skinny ass harder to stay warm."

"Shake it, girlfriend." Serena gave a pump of the hips. "Shake it, shake it! Shake it like a Po-la-roid *pic-shah!*" She showed her how, jiggling and thrusting in ways that Danni's body was incapable of emulating, even without the binding effects of too-tight clothing.

"There's only so much shaking a girl can do. And guys who are into epileptics are a small niche market."

"It helps to have grown up in the north. This is like a spring day in Geraldton," said Serena.

Babs added, "Plus, you see these stockings? Pure silk. My sugar daddy bought them for me. He's going to pay for my operation too."

She came closer and extended her endless leg, hiking up a skirt that needed no hiking. The smell of her sickening strawberry perfume was a visceral reminder of that initial catfight. It reminded Danni of how I'd taken her under my wing that night and nurtured a friendship the likes of which neither of us had ever known. A friendship I'd had to walk away from, but that Danni still saw as being salvageable, on the brink of collapse unless she did something about it.

"I would kill for a pair," she said to Babs.

"Of tits? Oh, honey, yours are … cute enough."

She slapped Babs's arm. "Stockings, you cow."

"Dream on." They trotted off, snickering.

She made it through the night, a decent haul, given the weather, but not terrific: three blow jobs in cars straining to pump out heat, a quick fuck in the new Econo Lodge at Jarvis and Gerrard, and only one hit to get her through until morning. Back at Carole-Anne's apartment, two downers and three blankets helped her shake off the chill of the night and find sleep. She emerged from her cocoon at one o'clock, showered, made herself presentable, bundled into the warmest things she had, and walked over to Church Street to find my coffee shop. The windows were steamed and frosted, with silhouettes of men clustered around tables.

Inside, music pumped through speakers, a pop song that may or may not have been new; we didn't know because we hadn't kept up. The scent of roasted beans permeated the air. She didn't spot me;

I wasn't behind the counter. She stopped before she got to the cash, exhaled, slumped her shoulders. A man stood before her, attracting attention because he had an iPhone, which, because it wasn't available yet in Canada, pegged him as American. More than the phone itself, she envied his having enough to do in a day that he'd need one.

I emerged from the chilly stockroom where I'd been unpacking and stacking and pulled off my woollen mittens but left on my thin toque as I approached the register.

When I caught sight of Danni, I nodded but didn't smile. Why had she come? Didn't she know how hard this was? How easy it was to fall back into old patterns? She could at least respect the distance I was putting between us, respect that this was my workplace. Things hadn't been left amicably between us, and I didn't need any drama now, with my boss watching. Still, I couldn't deny that it was nice to see her. I gave the man with the iPhone his change, and Danni approached the counter.

"You look good," she said.

"I guess Olive spilled the beans?" She nodded. "What can I get you? You still double-double?" Sure, it was all business, but a line was forming behind her. Did she expect we'd hug and start a long conversation? Her smile disappeared. She'd only wanted to see me. Maybe I could be nicer. Minister had been eavesdropping. He glanced at me, then Danni, and smiled. "Paulette, if you want to take a break, it's almost time."

"It's okay."

"No, go, I insist. I had you stuck in that freezing storeroom for an hour. Grab a coffee and warm up with your friend. We've got it."

I untied my apron, poured myself a coffee, and came out from behind the counter. We took a seat far from the cash, near the window. I avoided her gaze, stared at my ceramic mug, at the cream still roiling in the coffee, lightening its shade to about the colour of my skin, which still hadn't seen much daylight and probably wouldn't until springtime.

As if remembering Olive's jab, Danni closed her eyes. "I miss sunshine." The rays through the window were comforting. They soaked deep into our necks, our arms. Danni's face was so serene that I thought maybe she'd gone into recovery, too. But she was tapping her foot.

When she opened her eyes, I was making a whirlpool in my mug with a plastic swizzle stick.

"So, how's the job?" she asked.

"It's okay. The people are nice. The smell of beans stays on my clothes worse than crack smoke, but I can deal with that."

Mentioning crack wasn't fair. It'd disturbed the brief calming effect of the sun and revved up the drumming of her foot. She gulped her coffee. "It's nice here. A change of pace, I guess."

"It's pretty relaxed. And I need that."

"Where are you living?"

"Rose Ave. I'm renting a second bedroom from an older Caribbean couple."

"Wow. So what's that like?"

"A little hard, I guess. Good, because they keep me in line." I thought of the two clicks in rapid succession that Letty made if I told them I wouldn't be joining them for dinner. It simultaneously irked me and made me smile. I'd shared just enough with them to encourage the concern that they showed. "It's probably the best thing. I'm on the wait-list for subsidized housing, you know, so I can live on my own, but in the meantime …" I folded my arms, tucked my hands into my armpits. "They treat me like their daughter. Which is nice, but also has its challenges." I didn't say that I'd lost confidence in my ability to be an adult, which is why I put up with it.

"And this job? You're making enough?"

"Eight seventy-five an hour before deductions. Plus my share of the tips."

She apologized for not leaving anything in the jar, and I said I didn't need anything from her. She drew in her breath. My comment hung in the air between us. "I mean, I'm clean now, so, you know, I don't need as much."

"Stop using that word, Paulie." She scratched at the table.

I'd intended to soften the first part of my statement, to keep the cloud from bursting. "What word?"

"You were never dirty."

"Will you freakin' let it go, Danni? For ten goddamned seconds? Jesus." I stirred my coffee in jerky circles.

"I'm sorry." But then she stiffened. "It's only that it's ... it's offensive. Do you know how many tricks have asked me if I'm clean? Meaning if I had HIV?" Her voice was rising; she wasn't sorry. She didn't think her condescending comments were anything to apologize for, ever.

"It's an expression, Danni. You can't take it personally."

"It's bad enough when tricks say it, but when it comes from you? Are you just parroting what the twelve-steppers told you back when you were first ..." She searched for her words. Had she almost said *clean* herself? "... when you were first off drugs?"

"I'm one of those twelve-steppers now." I pointed to my chest, to the deepest part of me, where I hoped to hell those steps would settle and take hold.

She sat back in her chair, perplexed. I'd vented to her about my first experience in recovery, how my group had done sweet fuck all to help me stick to meetings while caring for Aaron. She couldn't understand why I'd go back.

"This whole idea of dirty bodies, dirty blood. *Dirty*," she spat, showing no sign of shutting up, "is how you feel when someone jabs a finger up inside you when you're ten years old. But no amount of abstinence or twelve-step jibber-jabber is gonna help with that. You tell me what those people can possibly know about truly feeling dirty, because it certainly has nothing to do with what we smoke, or inject, or this virus running through my veins."

I looked away, shaking my head. She gripped the seat of her chair, and there was a long pause during which we both breathed through our noses. "They know," I said, trying hard to mellow my voice. "You'd see that if you came to group."

"I'm good." She held up a palm. Outside, a couple pulled themselves closer and braced against a stiff wind. "I've cut down since I moved out." As if her body was contradicting her, she winced, sucked air through her teeth, and grabbed her right arm above the elbow, rubbed her bicep with her thumb.

She was deluding herself, and I couldn't help her. We were only pissing each other off.

Her chair scraped backwards as she stood. "Okay, I'm gonna go." She pushed her coffee across the table.

"Danni —"

"And you can take that back to the counter, 'cause apparently I'm just another customer here."

Sharp Stabbing Needle

THE TEMPERATURE DROPPED MORE. COLD LIKE WE HAVE ONLY IN February gripped the city. Minus twenty-three. Minus twenty-five. A reprieve meant minus fifteen. At that temperature, even the likes of Serena and Babs complained, or more often stayed indoors, taking the night off. Danni couldn't handle the cold the way she had when I'd met her, and she no longer had the insulating shield that our friendship had provided. She was exposed. She wasn't working more than two nights a week. It wasn't enough. Carole-Anne was ruthless when Danni told her she wouldn't make rent for March.

"You're seriously gonna kick me out in the middle of February?"

"I'm not sending you to sleep in a snowbank, but you'd better look for another place." She'd almost left the room but paused. "You know, nobody's made you go do what you do, Danni. And it isn't as if this is your first winter."

"No, it's my fourth. That's the problem."

"It's your fifth, and it's not my problem. Find somewhere to go or get a real job. Oh, that's right, you can't, because you're as bad a crackhead as Paulette."

"Fuck you."

Carole-Anne crossed her arms. "You have until the end of the week." She retreated to her bedroom. She'd started on methadone, and her smugness couldn't be contained. Carole-Anne had always been stuck-up when it came to crack users. Although this was the first time she'd let her guard down, we knew. Had she forgotten how hard it was for people who didn't have a legal, publicly funded equivalent?

Danni's best option was to go to Yen Mah. This time, she called and asked when she could come by; she didn't want to risk walking in on her again. Yen Mah had her over that evening after she got off her shift at the grocery store, which she was now managing. She sat Danni on the sofa and brought her green tea in a beautiful porcelain pot with matching cups. They were decorated in light blue swirls in the shape of ribbons and dragons.

"Yen Mah," said Danni, getting to the point, "things aren't going well over at Carole-Anne's. I can't make next month's rent because it's been too cold to work."

"Fucking cold winter."

She tried to hide her surprise; Yen Mah had never sworn in front of us. "Last time I came by, you didn't have a roommate, and —"

"You want to move in."

"I wouldn't ask if I didn't need to. I'll work more now that winter is coming to an end, but I want to be honest; I can't pay what Paulette was paying you. Not at the moment."

"Sure," she said. "You can move next week. Five hundred a month, don't pay until April. My manager's job is better pay."

Danni could hardly believe it. Why was Yen Mah always so easy-going, so kind? She got up and hugged her. Yen Mah stiffened, but maybe Danni'd taken her by surprise. She relaxed into it. "I don't know how to thank you."

"Stay healthy. Stay out of the fucking jail."

"Yen Mah, I'm sorry that we haven't been better friends to you."

"It's okay." She searched for the words, and came up with the following: "Drugs are a nagging child. Always interrupting. It's not your fault."

That nagging child had awoken, the next needle pestering to be stabbed into Danni's arm. She had to go. She didn't know how she'd be a better friend to Yen Mah, but for the moment, the apology would have to stand on its own. She thanked and hugged her once again, and left.

The clock ran out on her last week at Carole-Anne's. Despite the bitter coffee we'd had at my work, Danni ached to tell me about Yen Mah's new potty mouth. Nobody else would've appreciated the story as much. The next day, she wrote it down on a piece of paper, stole an envelope that she hoped Carole-Anne wouldn't miss, and dropped it off at the coffee shop, late, when she guessed that I wouldn't be working.

She wrote her email address on the note, but I resisted writing back, though it would not have taken much effort to reactivate my email account at the library. Still, this was a new beginning. I couldn't jeopardize it.

When Danni accepted that she'd get no reply, she resolved not to come back to my coffee shop. The first visit hadn't gone well, and she wasn't a glutton for punishment. She moved into Yen Mah's in March, put her head down, and tried to get back to a routine. Having a month's free rent, and having to pay only five hundred a month made it easier, but it also made it easier to work less. The March snowmelt dragged on for weeks. She worked the stroll at night and, in her downtime, tried mostly in vain to come up with ways to busy herself, something that didn't involve shooting up. She was prepared to deal with the monumental throbbing of her limbs that came when she delayed her next high — a sensation I knew all too well — if it meant doing something, anything other than what'd become an unbearable routine.

Halfway through March, she went to the library again to check her emails. Still no message. While there, she got a library card and went to the Alice Munro section. One of the titles, *Runaway*, drew her in, even though after the first few pages, she discovered it had nothing to do with her situation. She remembered having read *The Lives of Girls and Women* in high school. In her situation, I would've chosen something more escapist. Since being in recovery, I'd started reading again for the first time since high school, picking up books lying around Brian and Letty's apartment and devouring them in my room at night before bed.

At home, after waking up and having coffee, Danni worked her way into *Runaway*, but to sit still while those urges pulled at her, tugged at each limb, fingertips and toes, as if — to go with Yen Mah's analogy — a freakin' orphanage of attention-seeking children were annoyed that she was ignoring them, was nearly impossible. The number of times she reread a page two, three times ... she eventually gave up.

Worldly Possessions

ONE DAY NEAR THE END OF MARCH, ANXIOUS AND JUMPING OUT OF her skin because it was only mid-afternoon, Danni went for a walk. She had enough cash for one hit before she'd need to earn more for the next one, and she'd need that one hit when she got to Jarvis Street. So she headed west to Allen Gardens, looping north up Sherbourne to Bloor, east to Parliament, and back down through Cabbagetown into Riverdale Park West. On the footbridge that connected with the eastern side of the park, she took the stairs that descended to the path beside the river. The current was fast from the snowmelt, churning up the peaty scent of early spring. The days tipped above zero, but the nights refroze the ground cover into a slippery crust. She hopscotched from one patch of exposed pavement to the next to avoid the icy snow.

She followed the path north, at first, and went as far as Pottery Road, then doubled back, past Riverdale Park, until it reached another staircase at Queen Street, which took her up to one of the other bridges that cross the Don. She walked back, westwards to our side of the river, where the Humane Society's head offices stood. At that intersection, King Street angled north and merged with Queen before reaching the bridge at her back. Just before that merge,

River Street intersected the other two, forming a small triangle of land, a tiny arrowhead of a park that pointed east. The words *This River I Step In Is Not The River I Stand In* were written in iron latticework arching over the bridge.

A group of four people congregated in the triangular park in the snow and mucky grass: an elderly couple sitting on milk crates and a young man and middle-aged woman holding signs. They were all wrapped in layers of ratty but colourful clothing. A United Nations of scarves and shawls and bulky sweaters: hippie tie-dye, black and white Middle Eastern, Indian, South American — one part funky Kensington Market thrift shop, one part Goodwill.

One of the signs being thrust up and down read, *City of Toronto: Shame*, and another read, *Evicting homeless people: Your taxes at work*.

Danni went to say hello. The woman who held the *Shame* sign introduced herself to Danni as Borka. She had an Eastern European accent that Danni later learned was Montenegrin. White lace netting held her thick brown hair loosely at her neck, and she wore a stiff pill-shaped cap, black around the sides, with a red pattern on top. Its velvet was worn and slightly soiled. Her face was leathery, the skin ruddy at the cheeks.

When Danni asked what the protest was about, Borka said they lived in a makeshift settlement that was being threatened with eviction. Originally, they'd been part of an encampment at Cherry and Lakeshore but were evicted from there in 2000.

"A handful of us," she said, gesturing to her friends, "moved to a smaller camp down on Rosedale Valley Road. In the spring to fall," she added. "Otherwise, we are in shelters. He goes out to Vancouver."

"The city is threatening us again," said the young man to whom she'd pointed.

"Not exactly," said Borka, holding her palm up. "The outreach workers come by, trying to convince us to stay in the shelters all year long, but they don't know where we live. We decided to organize pickets to resist an eviction before it happens. Not my idea, but I help anyway." She shrugged.

"It's only a matter of time, Borka," said the older woman. "We have to send those workers a message. A show of strength."

Borka ignored them and turned to Danni to explain. "Those workers, they don't give shit. You see, they are only doing their job, but," she raised a finger into the air, "doing their job also means informing their superior about where we are. You never know when suddenly political situation changes or developers want land we are on, and then bulldozers will be back. Maybe if they don't know where we live, we will be okay."

Danni felt the money in her pockets, fingered the bills that'd be exchanged for her next high. She knew there was extra, so she offered to get them all coffees. Borka accepted.

She returned with a tray of cups, and the elderly couple opened up flasks from which they poured a measure of whisky. The man sniffed at the spiked coffee and exhaled a deep, satisfied sigh before taking a large gulp. At Borka's invitation, Danni sat with them on an extra milk crate. Borka introduced her to the others. The older couple, Sara and Philip from Owen Sound, sported messy grey dread-locks, hers more arranged than his. Before WMDs became "weapons of mass destruction," we used to call men like Philip "White Men with Dreadlocks."

Danni called them Trustafarians, which I liked even better; we'd encountered one shooting up in Mario's Drop-In, and she'd pegged him for a kid from North Toronto or Forest Hill, like her. Danni doubted this old couple sitting on milk crates had trust funds; if they once had, they had long been depleted. The last of the group was the young man, Wayne. He had pasty skin except for red cheekbones, and his dyed jet-black hair hung about his acne-covered face.

She told them that she lived nearby, just up the street. Life synopses fell out of their mouths in about two minutes flat. They sounded rehearsed; they were eager to build allies, and this was the way to do it. Borka had divorced her husband and had been called to a life of activism in which she also was compelled to give up her worldly possessions. Sara and Philip had worked odd jobs as kitchen staff in diners until Philip's joints gave out and Sara's hands couldn't hold the pots. More importantly, their drinking had gotten the better of them. They didn't hide this. "We are who we are," said Sara.

Wayne wasn't sharing his story with anyone.

The group got by with social assistance, panhandling, visits to soup kitchens, and the odd dropped-off gift from the Ontario Coalition Against Poverty, members of which, Danni was told, sometimes also joined the picket.

Wayne handed her his sign, saying she could make herself useful. She and Borka passed the time together until Danni went home to warm herself up for the stroll. But she went back again days later, and again after that. She was getting involved in her local community, supporting a real and tangible cause, one that was outside of herself. She hadn't understood the extent of her navel-gazing until she'd run into them. I understood that sentiment because I myself had begun volunteering at Maggie's, the local prostitutes' collective. Olive had been organizing a demo, trying to get people to take notice of the alarming number of Native girls missing from Canadian streets.

Danni was finding her own purpose with that motley group of street picketers. She chanted with them, sipped whisky from their flasks, and learned more about their lives. She grew fond of Borka, Sara, and Philip. As for Wayne, she reserved judgment. He didn't talk much, and his chants were often too angry, his foot-stomping aggressive. He yelled back at rude drivers, guys who lowered their windows to tell him to get a job.

Because of the name of the street where they gathered, Danni dubbed them The River Gang. When she mentioned it to them, Philip glanced at his friends, as if sharing a private joke, and beamed. "I love it. Makes us sound like badass rum-runners."

The River Gang weren't crack users; they were solid alcoholics, all except Borka, who didn't touch anything mind-altering. Danni hadn't shied away from liquor, but she'd drunk less of it since moving on to the harder stuff. Now she mixed her vices.

One afternoon in April, sitting on the milk crates, the sweet smell of grass and earth rose up from the patch of lawn. The sky was a hopeful postcard blue. Danni stretched her back. Wayne had been staring for some time.

"Anything wrong?"

He spoke to the others. "How do we know this one isn't a police plant? An *agent provocatooer.*"

"Are you serious? Do I look like I'm provacat*ooring* anything?" said Danni.

"How do we know what your game is?"

"What? You think I've been liquoring you up to get you to talk? I can stop bringing bottles of vodka by. Believe me, it's cutting into my budget."

Sara and Philip poured vodka into their flasks. Wayne snatched the bottle for himself. "You can keep these coming, irregardless." He drank openly, tipping the bottle high in the air. "If you're not on the up and up, I don't mind having the police or the city pay for our booze." He chuckled.

"It's *regardless,*" said Sara. "*Irregardless* is a double negative. And you're a knucklehead. She's not a police plant."

"I swear I'm not," said Danni. "I wanna support you. The city shouldn't have taken away your home."

Wayne passed the bottle to Philip. "I'm just saying, if it turns out you're a rat ..."

Borka gave him a gentle swat. "Sara is right. Don't be idiot. If the police want us gone, they will come take us away, like last time."

Danni passed the rest of that afternoon picketing with the gang and surreptitiously swigging from a flask, which dulled the pain in her limbs. When the sun waned, she set off to do a hit, and, late at night, when she should've been working, she went back to Yen Mah's, took a downer, and found sleep.

Retaining Walls

BY MID-APRIL, DANNI'S VISITS TO THE RIVER GANG HAD BECOME
daily events, the better weather making it easier and more pleasant.
A friendship was growing with Borka. She'd lived in Sarajevo with
her husband and young child through the siege in the early 1990s.
She was a professor of mathematics. Her husband taught classics. As
faculty left the university, class enrolment declined, and students
and professors lost their lives, they barely made ends meet. One day,
their seven-year-old son Dobrilo's school was bombed. It took two
days to find his body.

In the aftermath of the war, her husband got a job teaching in
Ottawa and they were able to emigrate, but once in Canada, Borka
left him and moved to Toronto. "My marriage collapsed, like that
building that fell on our son," she said. "It fell apart two years before
I knew it was over. Borka the Wife was underneath that pile of
rocks. I was hoping to find her alive, but she died along with poor
Dobrilo."

Her candour shocked Danni. "After the war, I realized all those
material things, they were ways to soothe. I was sad and scared because
bombs are still going off, every time reminding me of Dobrilo. So I
scraped together my dinars and bought television. Turned it up loud.

I missed my son, so I bought new dress. Nothing worked. Stupid to think it would."

"But you were only trying to give yourself some comfort."

"Yes, but that is point. These material things are another kind of drug."

"I guess so …"

"No guessing. It is so. We must search inside." She poked Danni's chest.

Borka had no job when she packed up and left Ottawa, but the need to leave her life behind was powerful, compelling. She glossed over the events between her arrival in Toronto and joining the encampment. "You can see now I decided I will not hide behind false comfort."

Her world was viewed through a grimy smear of trauma, but Danni accepted as sound the reasoning behind her life of poverty. A person would have to have superhuman inner strength to shun any of the regular creature comforts, but it didn't mean she was nuts. Not normal, but wise and tough. Danni knew what solace crack and alcohol had become to her; she hadn't needed a poke in the chest to figure that out. She ruminated on Borka's story, on the determination it might take to be like her. Danni had been making her own choice to give up a life of material comforts when she'd joined me in a life on the streets, but we hadn't gone as far as Borka had, with her stark rejection of self-soothing and her self-imposed hardship. Besides, thought Danni, nobody lives without any comfort whatsoever. Borka gained comfort from friendship and from the satisfaction of her resilience.

As an influence, Borka's abstinence was no match for the regular guzzling of the others. Danni's drinking spiked. She was doing crack less often, though her body didn't feel any better for it. Maybe, she thought, this was the so-called harm reduction that worker had told her about. The intestinal distress, the headaches, the fuzzy brain that went with drinking were all things she'd been glad to avoid when she'd embraced crack. She didn't like them any better, but the downer effects were a nice antidote when Xanax or Ativan was scarce.

Less and less, she turned tricks. Extricating herself from bed, she rubbed her forehead to massage away the headache and got into the shower. She started it off hot, but made it colder to wake herself up, tilting her face into the spray to shrink the puffiness — an unsuccessful strategy. The stroll was uglier under the effects of a hangover, and Danni probably was too. The concrete on the curb was more chipped, the car horns louder, more dying goat than bleating lamb. The johns were angrier, more insistent, breathing more from their mouths than she remembered.

Her body, when she forced it into a pose, moved in a thicker, doughier, clumsier way. If she was bird-like, as Borka had once described her, she was more waddling duck than graceful swan. A new HIV medication was messing with the fat distribution on her body, so that her arms were thin and her face gaunt, but her bra and skirt were soon-to-burst retaining walls preventing a full-on collapse of new breast and belly fat. She was twenty-eight and hadn't expected to feel this way until her forties. Grumplepuss, back in Mario's Drop-In, had complained about his weight gain while using crack. In Danni's case, it was mostly the medication, but that wasn't helped by the drinking and a move to a diet of donuts and pizza.

As the weeks passed, she'd sleep too long from drinking too much and would awaken confused. She'd get up to pee and blink at the "3:00 a.m." flashing on Yen Mah's electronic wall clock. In the washroom, she'd stare at her Medusa's mane, which I'd tried and failed to help her permanently tame, and consider dressing to earn some income. She'd given up on the blonde dye, and her roots were a wide band of brown. She'd need to find a wig. She passed a hand through her hair once and it caught on a corn chip, which fell into the sink. She stared at it, pressed her finger into the chip, crushing it into pieces that would fit down the drain. She turned on the tap until it had disappeared, then crawled back into bed.

Another night, after her three o'clock pee, she grabbed the bottle of vodka she'd bought to drink with the gang the next day and parked herself in front of the TV with a plastic cup full. She turned it down low so as not to bother Yen Mah and changed channels until a telethon on the Buffalo PBS station hypnotized her. A woman with a bowl cut and a nearly Amish dress yammered on about a new box set of *Gone with the Wind*. Danni dozed in and out while that PBS lady attempted new ways to convince her to pick up the phone and pledge. She fell asleep and was awakened by Yen Mah sitting down next to her with a bowl of congee. Light streamed through the living room window.

"Good morning," she said, and changed the TV channel to CITY to watch the morning news. Danni rubbed a crust from her eyelid, went to her bedroom, and went back to bed until noon.

When the first of May came around, Danni couldn't pay Yen Mah her full rent. She gave her what she had and told her she'd work all the next week until she had enough. But she didn't, not one day. The next Saturday, after spending all afternoon with the River Gang, she went home resolved to do a night's work. She got into work clothes and headed west along Gerrard. The sun squatted low but still pulsed at her, making her eyes squint. The leaves were sprouting on tree branches, but we couldn't smell them for the stench of tar from a street repair crew.

I say *we* because that afternoon was the demonstration we'd been planning, and I was standing with Olive and our fellow demonstrators, gathering in front of the Maggie's offices on the north side of Gerrard as Danni approached Parliament. The regular anti-abortion protesters — five middle-aged women and two younger men — were on the south side, where they always were, prohibited by law from getting too close to the clinic.

Olive and I struggled to hold a banner with the Maggie's logo that said *Sex Work Is Work*. A group of Native women held an even bigger one from their organization, and still another group held signs from the University of Toronto Women's Centre: *No More Missing Women!* and *Sex Work Is Work*. Four of them opened red umbrellas, though there was no sign of rain; it was a symbol of sex workers' rights. This world of activism was new to me, and I had adopted their terminology, wondering how infuriatingly pleased Danni'd be that I'd done so. These were the same terms she'd tried to get me to use, but I had ignored her, mocked her for it, rolled my eyes enough to give myself a headache: *sex work* instead of *prostitution* or *hooking*, *racialized people* instead of *minorities* or some long list of different ethnic groups who weren't white. I still wasn't sure what to call the Native women. Some used that word, others *Aboriginal*, *Indigenous*, or the name of their specific community.

Danni and I spotted each other. She walked towards me from the east.

"I didn't know you were coming." I looked to Olive, as though Olive might've known and had the decency to warn me. Not that I wouldn't've come, but at least I'd've been prepared.

"Actually, I was just heading over to the stroll."

Olive said, "We're organizing a protest," as if that hadn't been glaringly obvious. "The number of hos going missing is getting scary — especially the Native ones. We've got to do something." She was like a broken record with that line; she said it to anyone who'd listen. I needed to be more comfortable in helping to spread the word, but I hadn't found a way to do it without sounding robotic, like Olive, or taking on that preachy tone that I hated when it came from Danni.

"Um, yeah. No, that's great. I wish I could join you." Danni was disoriented, seeing me and Olive in this new light while she was stuck in the shadow of our former lives. In university, she'd been the one organizing demonstrations. She'd railed against people who didn't know a thing. about the issues affecting them, how they lived their lives oblivious. I took those slags as subtle jabs at me. Had it dawned on her now that she, too, had become one of those people? That we had both been stuck in our own little world with no clue about this alarming problem? I'm not proud of it, but I enjoyed the role reversal.

A megaphone barked, "Where's Colleen? Is she joining us? Does anyone have her phone number?"

"Olive and I are volunteering with Maggie's now," I said, consciously pouring salt in her wound. "There's a whole bunch of groups coming together around this one."

"So this is Maggie's." She looked up at the row of buildings, scanning up and down the street. She still wasn't sure which door it was. That block was freakin' Stigma Central — next door was the Cabbagetown Women's Clinic, which performed abortions, hence the protesters across the street, and next to that was a Christian homeless mission, and next to that, a second-hand clothing store.

The woman with the megaphone ordered me to take a stack of flyers. I ignored her. How was I going to carry them, in my teeth? Plus, she could ask me like a real person, not a drill sergeant. I asked Olive when we should set off. Danni lingered as we discussed it. Was she wondering if she should join? Waiting for me to suggest it?

When barky megaphone chick quieted down, Danni said, "Are you ... does this mean you're back working the streets?" What she was really asking was if my involvement with Maggie's meant I'd relapsed, and it hadn't occurred to me that she might've thought this. If I'd gone back to working the streets and still hadn't contacted her, it'd mean I'd gone out of my way to work in an area far from where we used to be, to avoid running into her.

"No, I'm still clean. Still at Timothy's. Olive's been pestering me about Maggie's since forever. I guess when you dropped off that letter, it got me thinking, what could I do about the fucking stabbing needle of society?" We smiled, and for a moment, there was a thaw.

"Yen Mah, right?

I nodded. "Always keeping us guessing."

I continued to nod, but the frost crackled back in from the edges, and there we stood, shifting on our feet, neither of us knowing how to melt it.

"We're about to march to police headquarters," I said. "I don't know if you —"

"No," she interrupted, "I have to go. Have a good demo. I'll see you soon."

She hurried away, ducking under our banner and through the crowd of women. The street tar smell wafted back. A lump solidified in my throat.

Now she knew: I'd gotten her letter but hadn't had the kindness, or even the courtesy, to send a message back. As if through a hole punched into a brick wall, I saw myself as Danni must've: I was getting closer to Olive, who was herself an actively using drug addict, same as Danni. Why couldn't I have Danni near me in my recovery, if it was all right to spend time with Olive? But Olive and I had never really hung out socially; being with her didn't send memories tumbling down onto me, memories of good times spent shooting up, laughing, of Danni and me against the world. Olive and I didn't have the same history. Besides, mess that she was, there was a feeling that, while she might not get any better, she also wasn't going to get any worse. As long as I'd known her, she'd been the same Olive. Was she wired differently? Drugs, for her, didn't seem to pull her lower and lower, like they had with us.

I didn't know yet about Danni's involvement with The River Gang, but it must've made things worse to know that this project, Olive's and mine, might be more pressing, more serious a cause than the one Danni'd chosen. The River Gang said they were persecuted by the city, but Borka had made her doubt that. Danni hadn't met or spotted a single city worker.

When she arrived at the stroll, it was barely dusk, and she stood far too long waiting for her first trick. When a man stopped for a twenty-dollar blow job, she got into his car, but as they drove in silence to the place she told him to go, the place she always had them go, her breathing became laboured. Ants crawled beneath her skin. This man was no less attractive or more repulsive than most of the guys she'd tricked with, but he made her recoil. Sweat bubbled on his forehead and around his collar. His muskiness turned her stomach. She rolled down the window. His pants were dirty, and she shuddered at what hygienic horror might await. He gripped the steering wheel and released it in time to a song playing on the radio, a kind of full-body pumping motion that churned her guts more.

"Stop the car, please." She tried to quell a rising panic. "I ... I can't do this."

He was shaken, maybe even worried for her. "I'm sorry, I —"

"Stop the fucking car!"

He pulled over at the first opportunity, and she jumped out.

"Crazy bitch," he muttered, and drove off. She should've been angry, but he was right. She didn't know why, but she couldn't do it, with him or with anyone else.

She'd been dropped off farther away than she'd hoped to be, and she resigned herself to a long walk back to the apartment. By the time she reached the building, the panic had subsided, but she was out of breath when she shut the door.

Yen Mah was in the kitchenette doing dishes and putting away leftovers from dinner. "You okay?" she asked, when a wheezing escaped Danni's lips. She collapsed on the sofa.

"Fine. Just ... I'm not feeling well." Yen Mah cocked her head as if to say she hadn't expected her to tell the truth. Danni stood. "I tried to work tonight, I did. But I can't, I'm sorry." She went into her room and shut the door.

The next night she tried to work again, and the same panic overtook her. When the man, an older gentleman this time, drove away terrified by her erratic behaviour, she sat on the curb and fought back tears while she laboured to catch her breath. She walked over to Church Street, sat across from my coffee shop, on the steps to a hair salon.

Danni'd never wanted to work in a coffee shop, but how she envied the normalcy of it all. She wasn't like Borka and never would be. How could she ever get back to that? How would she explain a five-year gap on her resume? Amnesia? Witness protection? Jail or the loony bin were the conclusions anyone would draw.

More immediately, she was concerned about how she'd pay Yen Mah her rent. She'd resented Carole-Anne when she'd pressed her for it because of how nasty, how stuck-up she'd been. But Yen Mah's kindness and flexibility made her ashamed to linger in her apartment putting off paying her, begging for credit and forgiveness. It made it worse to know that she'd give her both.

Danni considered her options. She could've gone to a shelter, but maybe there was a better choice. She went to a dollar store and bought a thimble for Yen Mah, then painted it with red nail polish. She wrote her a note, leaving twenty of the ninety dollars she had left, and bundled her clothes into a garbage bag. When she got to River and Gerrard, Wayne was missing; he might've gone to get pizza slices or to find a washroom.

"What is this?" Borka made a circular pointing motion. "What has happened?" When Danni told her about her housing situation, without hesitation, she said, "Well, okay. You come stay with us."

"Are you sure?"

"Do you have tent?" She shook her head, and Borka patted her arm. "We will make room."

Make room? We? She hadn't thought this through. Would she be sandwiched between Borka and Wayne in a tight space? "Borka, is your tent big enough for three people? Maybe I should find my own."

"Three?" She held up fingers. "Oh, *sonche*, you didn't think Wayne and I ..." She leaned in close. "Wayne is disgusting child still learning manners. We make him sleep in his own tent." Danni thanked her, and assured her it'd only be until she knew her next move.

Creatures Circling

DANNI HADN'T MISUNDERSTOOD WHERE THE RIVER GANG KEPT THEIR camp. Borka had been purposefully misleading; she'd mentioned Rosedale Valley Road, and Danni'd pictured the area in the ravine to the east of Wellesley Park, where there were homeless people camped out from time to time. But The River Gang had never been there. They never mentioned their true location because they didn't want other homeless people to get wind and join them, which might lead to their discovery and removal by the city. Their camp was hidden about two hundred and fifty metres east of the Bayview Extension, through a clump of forest. Drivers heading down the Extension had no way to see it.

Danni walked with them a fair way north along the western edge of a busy stretch of the Extension, waited for a break in the traffic, and ran across the street where a small service road began on the east side, running parallel. They marched along that road, under the Bloor Street Viaduct, and farther north. Borka paused near a chain-link fence and examined a growing weed nonchalantly until there was a break in the traffic. Then she crouched through a hole cut in the fence. The rest followed suit. A narrow path led through a grassy field into the trees.

"Take." Borka reached into her knapsack and handed Danni a head-lamp. "This is extra one." The sun hadn't set, but she must've read Danni's mind: how the hell would a person find her way in the dark?

The path opened up into a clearing, and their camp came into view, messy, pots strewn about, clothing hanging on a line, three tents in a triangle, firepit in the middle. It was near the water's edge, on the bank of the Don. In a place where there would never be condo development, so it made her doubt even more that their worry about bulldozers was justified.

"Welcome to The River Gang." Philip tossed his grey dreads away from his face. "Now you know why I loved the name so much."

The setting was magical, despite the mess: a hidden oasis in the city. A bird took wing from a tree, and the water burbled steps to their left. Danni'd worked up a sweat walking there, so she went to the water, stood on a rock, and crouched to dip in her cupped hands. The icy cool she splashed made her cheeks tingle, the drips of water tickling like when, as a kid, friends held a dandelion to her chin to see if she liked butter. She hadn't taken a breath that deep and satisfying in years.

"Not bad, eh?" Sara plopped herself into a foldable canvas chair. She took off her shoes and massaged her cracked, bare feet with impressive flexibility. Philip pulled off his knapsack and unloaded food. So did Borka and Wayne: cans and vegetables, pasta, beans, coffee, a bag of cookies.

"I'm sorry, I didn't bring anything." It hadn't occurred to Danni to ask about food: how they afforded it, where they shopped, how they cooked when they weren't eating junk.

"You can chip in once you get your cheque," said Philip.

"But welfare takes off the housing portion; better warn her about that," added Sara. "Or are you on disability? Either way, same thing."

Danni told them she wasn't on any social assistance.

"Well, there's time to apply," said Borka. "We all get something or other. My ex still sends me support. Philip and Sara are on Ontario Disability Support Program. Wayne is on welfare. We pool our money and go shopping for groceries."

"I'll make an appointment." She took the can and the opener that Sara was gesturing at her to use on it. She'd visit the nurse at the clinic where she got her HIV meds; the nurse had mentioned that she could be eligible for ODSP, but she'd never applied. She hadn't needed to.

Without much discussion, Borka, Sara, Philip, and Wayne set about preparing a supper of spaghetti and meat sauce, cooked on a Coleman stove. Danni helped as she could. Borka took fresh vegetables and eggs that they weren't using, placed them into a large Tupperware container, and went down to the river. She submerged the container and lodged it under large rocks to keep the produce cold and safe from raccoons.

There was no extra chair for Danni, so she sat on a log that Wayne had dragged over. For dessert, Wayne cut up a pound cake. Sara boiled a pot of water for tea, and soon Philip made a fire. They sat around it, drinking the hot tea, some of them spiking it with rum. The honey locust wood fire crackled and warmed Danni's feet and shins. It released sweet smoke into the night air.

"So how long will you be with us?" asked Philip. Did Danni detect nervousness? Was he taking on Wayne's paranoia?

Borka interjected. "Long as she wants."

"She has a mouth, Borka. I was only asking a question."

"I don't know," said Danni. "I've been needing a change. I'm grateful you've let me join you."

"Make sure you don't tell anyone where we live," said Wayne. "The city still doesn't know about this place; it's hard to see us from the trail."

The same day she'd met them at River Street, Danni herself had missed their campsite on her walk up the Lower Don Trail, the bike path that wound along the far side of the river. In the spring and fall, before and after the leaves, there might be a glimpse, but it'd be easily missed.

Sara added, "Well, we think they don't know. If they do, the only reason they wouldn't have swooped in is we aren't a big threat. The city cares more about the environment than they do about us. If everyone and his dog comes down here wanting to stay, they'll say the ecosystem is threatened."

"Ain't that the truth," said Philip.

"That's why we try to be clean as we can," said Borka. "It's not ... what do you call it, Philip?"

"Zero-trace camping."

"Yes, not zero-trace. But low-trace."

Danni noted that they were hardly low-trace. As if to punctuate her observation, the piece of cellophane that had covered the pound cake blew by her feet. No one did a thing to pick it up, until she stood to snatch it before it sailed into the river.

Sara pointed to a nearby tree. "The garbage is in that bin over there. Make sure you put the bungee cords back on. The creatures are basically circling, waiting for us to let our guard down."

They drank into the night, and Danni fought off the strong urge for a needle. She hadn't planned to be so far from a dealer. The thing to do was to drink enough to fall asleep. When she could barely keep her eyes open, she followed Borka into her tent, a sizeable one. Borka passed her a sheet and a blanket and slipped into her own bedroll, pulling a patchwork quilt over herself, tucking it in on either side for warmth. She was a colourful caterpillar.

Danni's last thought before nodding off was of her mom. It'd been over a year since their run-in on Jarvis. Had her mom forgiven her? Did she still worry, or had Danni drifted beyond concern, beyond hope?

She fell asleep in her clothes, despite the tree root under her back.

Rotisserie Chicken

DANNI AWOKE IN THE LATE MORNING, SHIVERING. WHEN SHE STEPPED out of the tent, her shoe sank into a squishy mud slick. The outside world was dripping. Dark green and brown, mossy smelling. She'd been faintly aware of rain, its light drum roll on the tent rising and falling.

"Philip saved you porridge." Borka pointed behind her as she parked her ass just inside her tent, her feet still outside so she could yank off her mud-covered boots and leave them outside the flap. The rest of The River Gang had already retreated to their tents, presumably after eating and doing their morning whatever it was they did. Danni went to pee — it stank from dehydration — and to eat by herself. She went to sleep again for an hour while Borka read a tattered German paperback.

At noon, Danni gathered the oomph to push through a massive headache and get herself cleaned up, presentable, and out of the valley. Huffing her way into Wellesley Park, she removed her muddy shoes and rinsed their soles in the water fountain.

She set out to tick off the four things on her list. City camping was a good temporary solution, but it required planning. They were isolated; no way to run to a corner store if she forgot something. She went to Goodwill and bought a folding chair and a bedroll for under ten dollars. Score Number One. Then she walked to Oak Street, found Mario and Score Number Two, a quarter of an eight ball. If she'd given up on sex work, she might not be able to do drugs as often, but come nightfall she wasn't about to be trapped again in that valley with only booze. She needed more booze, so she bought a small bottle of Forty Creek Barrel Select whisky — not so select, since it was the cheapest one in the store. Score Number Three.

Last, she went to the Regent Park Community Health Centre and asked where she could apply for disability. The staff directed her to the welfare office at Wellesley and Jarvis to get emergency cash while the health centre started on the medical part of her ODSP application. She made it to the welfare office twenty minutes before closing, but there was no time to see a worker. She'd have to return the next day. She'd been told, when she first learned she was HIV-positive, that having the virus was qualification for getting the higher disability rate from a program that didn't carry with it the pestering pressure-to-get-a-job component of its sister workfare program, but since she'd been more or less symptom-free since being on antiretrovirals, she was doubtful they'd give it to her.

The day had been a more productive one than she'd had in years. The burst of efficiency buoyed her. She was competent. Possibilities might present themselves. She finished by buying a container of chilli with the last of her cash, her contribution to the gang's dinner.

When she drank that night, it felt like a reward, a celebration. But when she awoke in the middle of the night to pee and, upon emptying her bladder in the woods, was gripped by the powerful urge to shoot up, it drained her of any sense of accomplishment. She went back into the tent, groped around for her works, and re-emerged. In the spotlight of Borka's headlamp, which she aimed at the bend of her elbow, she tied the elastic under her bicep.

When the drug took effect, a surge of energy crackled through her body, and there was no outlet for it except to march around the forest floor. The needle had been a big mistake. If fumbling outside with her works in the light of a headlamp hadn't woken everyone, trampling the underbrush would surely do the trick. Staying in those woods wasn't an option.

Danni pulled on proper clothes and set off. A car nearly mowed her down on the Bayview Extension, no doubt startled that a pedestrian had popped out of nowhere in the dead of night. The honk of his horn faded ahead of her, and she followed it to Rosedale Valley Road. On her way up the stairs from the ravine into Wellesley Park, instinct sent her hand to find her keys, to shove in an attacker's eyes if need be. But she had no keys — the first time in her adult life. Instead, she stuck her hands in her pockets to seem purposeful and stormed down and up and down the streets of Cabbagetown until the spiders crawling under her skin had subsided to ants.

She returned to Wellesley Park, sat on a bench, and drummed her legs quietly on the ground, making sure not to attract attention. She had no defensive weapon, no mace. While there, a guy emerged from the top of the staircase from the ravine, probably one of the men who lived down there, the ones Borka had told her about. She made herself quiet until he left. After an hour or so, she returned to the camp, poured a drink, and pulled her blanket from the tent. She laid it out under the stars, wrapped one side over top of herself, and counted from one corner of the sky to the other and back again, until her eyelids were heavy.

Sara nudged her awake and passed her a mug. She'd prepared coffee. The sun winked through the trees on the far side of the river. Danni's blanket was soaked with dew. She was shivering. The coffee smelled rich and nutty. It warmed her enough to fortify her for more shivering at the edge of the stream. She gave her face and underarms a splash.

After eating a peanut butter sandwich, she went back to the welfare office to meet with a worker. The worker asked when she'd last showered. Her cheeks burned. Her ineffective bird bath. She must've looked frightening, too. The worker wasn't being unkind; she was only informing Danni about shelters where she could wash up. Danni thanked her for the information and left, but didn't want to go to a shelter, so she went to Hart House and snuck in the same way she had the first night she'd left home, five years before. The hot shower, her first in days, was luxurious. After scrubbing four times and shampooing twice, she was disappointed to have to pull on her smoky clothes.

The next four nights, she didn't slam. She was so proud of herself: harm reduction at last! Instead, she drank herself to droopy-eyed numbness. But that didn't always get her through until morning. On two of the nights, she awoke to use the facilities — a makeshift outhouse seat Wayne had fashioned and placed atop stones and logs he'd piled up on either side of a deep hole he'd dug in the ground. There was a shovel near it and a pile of earth they kept replenishing to cover the shit. After these nighttime pees, it took Danni a while to fall asleep again. Her life with The River Gang was supposed to be a good change, but she remembered she hated camping. Peeing in the darkness while the forest snapped, crackled, and popped. Her back was sore from the root on her side of the tent, which she kept rolling onto while asleep. A polka-dot pattern of mosquito bites decorated her belly; an early crop had descended upon her, so giddy that their first human meal was near their swampy birthplace that they hadn't bothered to go farther afield. It was harder to take her HIV meds without anyone noticing. She thanked the heavens that she'd already had her period, because who knew what that would be like. Simply getting to the out-of-the-way encampment felt to her like the opening scene of The Piano. She was Holly Hunter in the New

Zealand rainforest, hiking up her Victorian skirt to walk through the mud and into a life to which she was completely unsuited.

On her one-week camp-iversary, she got shit-faced, but not enough to fall sleep. It was a hot day in mid-May, and the evening hadn't cooled things down. A swarm of cars buzzed to the west, adding to the distant hiss of traffic on the Parkway to the east. Bulrushes and sweet grass from the river's edge honeyed the air. She didn't feel like going to bed, so she hiked out of the valley, walked a long way up and over into Riverdale, back across the Gerrard Street Bridge, and back north to find the bench in Wellesley Park she'd sat on earlier in the week.

Perspiration tickled her forehead. The bench was too illuminated for her liking. She lay atop a picnic table hidden behind the empty children's splash pad. She shut her eyes, tucked her whisky bottle under her back on the left side. If someone attacked her she could smash the bottle on his head. Twenty minutes or so later, she opened it and took another drink. A handful of stars twinkled from behind the clouds in the night sky. An animal rustled behind her in the forest. A breeze picked up, strumming the leaves in the trees.

Footsteps put her on guard, and she stood up. A man, not the one from the other night, was smoking a cigarette on the wooden platform at the top of the stairs, his back to Danni. He leaned against the wooden railing that ran from the platform down to Rosedale Valley Road. In the forest to her left, a dim light scratched its way through the dark. She stood and moved closer in the darkness. A second man appeared from the gloom of the staircase below. As he reached the first man, a streetlamp overhead cast shadows on his face. He was in his twenties, tall and thick, rough but handsome with a short, scruffy beard that framed his jaw. It might've been the man from the other night, but she couldn't be sure.

He nodded ever so slightly to first man, who smiled back.

The first man fished a pack of smokes from his pocket. "Want one?"

"No, thanks. Need to catch my breath first."

The younger man sat against the opposite railing, glancing over at the first. They were cruising each other. Watching this intimate ritual should've made her feel guilty, but she was having fun. She leaned against a tree. The night swayed and blurred, her last drink kicking in, adding to the effect of the others. The men's eyes met but bounced off in unison, ending up at their shoes. After another good long drag on his cigarette, the first man ground his toe onto the butt and raised an eyebrow, tilted his head at the woods. He led the way, stepping off the platform to walk along the edge of the park, where grass met shrubs, trees, and ravine. They disappeared into the shadows. There was a dull thud, a heavy object hitting the forest floor, and thrashing and grunting. Content to let them have their privacy, Danni walked back to the picnic table, but a cry of fear — not lust — emerged from the bushes. She ran over. One of them had pinned the other's chest and arms. The young man straddled the first but faced his legs, while he simultaneously reached an arm back to cover his victim's face with a jacket. He fumbled in the man's pockets while being bucked at every angle, but not strongly enough to throw him free. A muffled cry escaped the trapped man's lips, and he freed an arm to punch at his attacker's ribs.

"Fuck!" yelled the younger man, and he grabbed at a yellow flashlight that he'd had lying beside him, swung backwards, and hit a cheekbone. There was a muted pop as the flashlight connected. Deciding what to do, finding a plan in Danni's state was like lifting a pile of heavy rocks to see what lay underneath. The attacker sprang up, twisted, and slammed again onto his victim's chest like a pro wrestler, only this time facing him. Another thud when his fist hit skull.

Danni swayed again, feeling unwell.

His hands were around the man's throat, and he squeezed hard. The man gasped, wheezed. "You gonna give me your wallet, faggot? Or am I going to have to choke you to get it?" His knees restrained the man's arms. Danni's breath caught, and her legs gave out. She left her body briefly, a child's bedroom below, a man covering the child from view.

She stood again. Crept slowly. Steadily. Keeping her balance. Neighing sound from the man being choked. He bucked again, to little effect.

"Please," the man gasped. That word. Instantly, Danni was faster, steadier.

A loud cracking, louder than any of the previous ones. The assailant fell, crashed, and rolled. Downhill into leaves. Crumpled. Motionless. Danni's hands, heavy. An enormous branch, almost a log. She didn't remember picking it up.

She dropped it.

The branch fell on the man who'd been attacked. He yelled, retracted his leg. Coughed and gasped. Held his foot. Blinked, pushed himself to his elbows. Stared.

She stared back. Her breath was a series of rapid-fire explosions of terror. Upbeats of euphoria. Slowing to surges of horror. And, as it evened, injections of dread.

On her knees again, and she held her head. It, too, might've been struck. No. Just booze. Trees and ground tilted. Spinning sky. "Fucking guys." She pointed. At darkness. "Always pinning us. Fucking assholes."

She stumbled up. Balanced again. No sound from downhill. No sound from the other one. He was afraid of her. Stomach loop-de-looped until she burped. Loudly. A pair of fireflies up above them. One-two. One-two. She reached for them. They went dark.

Still no stirring from downhill. Possibly dead. Maybe unconscious.

She didn't care. She sort of cared. Down to him, nearly tripping. She reached into his pockets. Rank sweat from his body. A cellphone and a wad of bills. Maybe from the other guy. Looking uphill. "This yours?" He was sitting. Shook his head. "Well, now it's mine." Danni's first theft — from a stranger, at least. Was that worse or better than stealing from her mom?

She felt sick. Not here. Somewhere, and fast. The staircase. A sound behind her. *Please be the good one*, she thought.

"Wait!" he shouted, but Danni was on the steps. Stumbling into the wooden railing. Her left hand grabbing. The midpoint landing. She wouldn't reach the bottom. She heaved a leg up. Onto the railing. Mounted it. Bent forward and hugged. Rotisserie chicken.

"Wait," the man said again. "What's your name?"

Half rotation of her body, downwards. Into dirt and leaves. On hands and knees.

Sweet leaves, then dog shit. She heaved.

Clarity returning. The body's slap on the cheek. Shit smell still there. She heaved again. Her stomach muscles burned.

"Are you okay?"

Danni wiped the puke off her lips, pulled her hair back, and stood. "I should be asking you that question." She faced him, brushing herself off. Leaves clung to her top, which in the bright lamplight showed its grubbiness. Before he could answer, she said, "Don't tell the cops, okay?"

"I won't."

He stepped into the light. His face was bloody. Maybe from being bashed with the flashlight. "Thank you. I was sure I was a goner."

He might've been thirty, thirty-five, and was wild-eyed, scared. He was strikingly handsome. The shame on his face made him more so. She wanted to say, Buddy: of the both of us, tell me, who should be more ashamed?

Instead, Danni repeated herself. "Please don't tell the cops."
Needed to get back to the river. She turned and step-slid down the
hill towards the road. "You better get going," she called back. "There
might be a dead man in those woods, and you'll be the only one
around."

Luminous Veil

WHEN SHE AWOKE, SHE WAS STILL BUZZED. THE DELUSION THAT SHE'D dreamt it all didn't last. A full bladder forced her into the dark night, to the woods, behind a tree. She was too tired to find the forest throne. Off to the south, the Luminous Veil on the Bloor Street Viaduct — the politely named lighting they'd installed on the vertical wires of the new suicide barrier — dripped its coloured tears into the valley. It glowed the same eerie blue they use in club bathrooms to prevent people from finding a vein. Danni brushed her teeth at the river, washed her hands, and splashed water on her face.

Wayne sat in a chair at the riverbank, lit up by a trembling moon. Had he been there since she'd returned to the camp? He chucked a leaf into the stream. It twirled in an eddy and floated downriver, and he threw in another. He had a handful at the ready. Danni said hello and bent to cup more water in her hands. It smelled of moss and copper.

"Couldn't sleep either?" His voice was nearly a whisper.

She wiped water from her face and pulled up a chair. "Well, I had to pee."

"That'll do it."

He tossed more of his leaves into the river. How would he react if Danni said, sort of casually, Hey, did you know that I might've just murdered someone? That I robbed his maybe dead body? Would he freak out, worrying she'd bring police to rain down on their camp? Or maybe he'd say, Cool, and continue his leaf chucking. She wasn't sure which reaction would be more alarming, but it took a surprising amount of self-restraint not to tell him.

Wayne was hyper-focused on his task. In the quiet of the near dark, sitting, the anger and suspicion that usually twisted his expression were gone. He was at rest, and his features were almost inviting. The jet-black straight hair. The narrow face and gentle curve of his chin.

"What?" He touched his cheek self-consciously. Danni'd forgotten the acne, couldn't see it in the moonlight.

"Anyone ever tell you you look like Adrien Brody?" she said.

"Who?"

"The actor from that movie. Set in Nazi Germany. He won the Academy Award."

"You're saying I look like a Nazi?" He paused his activity. Was this a good thing, or was the anger back?

"No, he wasn't ... It was a compliment, ya *shmegege*."

"Oh." His face spasmed into a sort of grin. "Thanks." Then, "What's a *shmegege*?"

"It means 'damned fool.' Smiling looks good on you, by the way. I've never seen you smile."

He seized his chair and wrenched himself left, so that they were nearly facing each other. "Once, when I was in this foster home, where the mom drove me fuckin' insane with her rules and curfews and her fuckin' nagging ..." He made claws. "That woman? She was always telling me to smile."

"She sounds like a douche."

"When someone tells me to smile, I want to punch them in the face. It's like they're so high and mighty in their happiness, and they think they can command you to be happier. Like that's possible."

"Guys say that to women. All the time."

"We do?"

"Yeah. If we're not flirting with you. Heaven forbid we should be daydreaming."

"It made my foster mom think she was fixing me. Believe me, nobody's gonna fix me."

There was nothing Danni could say to that. It reminded her that Aaron was with a foster mother of his own. They sat still again, until Wayne said, "Well, anyway, I decided I wouldn't smile for her. Not ever."

"How long did you last there?"

"A year. Maybe my smiling muscles wasted away." He laughed and pointed at his face, feigning surprise. "Hey, I was wrong!"

"It's like riding a bicycle."

He leaned forward, paused, tipped himself out of his chair onto his knees in front of Danni, paused again. She pulled back and raised her hands, but he leaned in for a kiss, and she didn't resist. When their mouths separated, he took her hand, put one of her fingers to his lips, and they crept back to his tent. She proposed a condom, but he didn't have one, and neither did she. Her doctor had said that because the number of copies of virus in her blood was undetectable, it might mean she couldn't pass it on. They didn't know for sure, but she slept with him anyway, hoping it was true. Hating herself for wanting it so badly. It was her first non-transactional sex in over five years.

Wayne was clumsy but surprisingly gentle. The tent stank of cigarettes, campfire smoke, and musk, but she pulled him into her, needfully, crazily, desperately hoping that their stifled, frenzied tumble might roar loud enough in her mind to drown all of it out: the embarrassing moan of insincere lust expelled turning a trick; the pitched internal whining when a drug wore off and the baggie was empty of rock; the low sneer and dull thud of a man kicking her in the ribs and calling her a cunt; the explosive crack of a large branch hitting a man's skull. The mournful cry of a mother who lost her son forever.

It didn't last long enough, and it didn't work. She prayed they weren't overheard.

She stepped backwards, bum first, into the night air. She zipped the flap behind her, and, as a pair of accusatory crickets chirped, she crawled into Borka's tent, pulled the covers over herself, and tried to get another hour or two of sleep.

In the morning, pain shot through Danni so intensely that it seemed to be something else altogether. It radiated up from her fingertips, throbbed up her arm and down her spine until every muscle fibre and tendon felt like they were being crushed in a clamp. For the first time in five long years, the idea of rehab was less hopeless and more urgently necessary than her next fix or swig of whisky. She didn't know if it would make her feel better, but it might make her feel less horrible.

She sat up and ransacked her belongings. "Fuck," she muttered. Her fingers found the stolen wad of bills. She closed her fist around it and tucked it surreptitiously into her underwear. She opened the flip phone. It still had juice, so she powered it quickly off. All she needed was for someone to call it. She stuffed it under her bedroll.

Borka pushed herself onto her elbows, rolled towards her, and rubbed an eye.

She struggled with Borka's tent zipper and freed herself, gulped at the cool morning. A sole bird chirped. Wayne's tent was still zipped, thank God.

"Danni?" Borka called after her. "What is wrong?"

"Nothing. I thought I'd lost something." In a secluded spot on the river's edge, she crouched and counted the money. Three hundred and forty. Together with her emergency cash from welfare, it was a fortune in her present state of poverty. She tucked it away again, had a piss, washed in the river, and dragged all of her clothes out of the tent.

Borka had come outside and was sitting brushing her hair. Her cap sat on the ground beside her, and she watched Danni, frowning.

"What the hell is she doing?" asked Sara, who sat next to her, preparing the morning coffee. "What's gotten into her?"

"Yes, what is wrong, Danni?" echoed Borka. "You are acting like crazy person."

Danni halted her packing and sat near them. "I ... I can't stay."

"Something I said?" asked Philip, who'd emerged from their tent. Sara swatted his arm, but Danni smiled, grateful for his shot of humour. Wayne, too, stumbled into the morning. She couldn't let him catch her eye.

"I need to change my life, is all. Really change it, this time." She went to her things and handed Borka fifty dollars. "This is for what I ate last week, and for all of your trouble."

Borka made to refuse the money, but Sara snatched it. Borka said, "I'm sorry to hear it. We all like you. Even Wayne, though he won't admit it."

"I'll admit it."

Danni turned so only he'd see her and drew her lips into a wordless apology.

"You've all been amazing. But ... I need more than a tent. I need walls. A solid structure around me."

She finished gathering her things, stuffing them into the same garbage bag she'd used to bring them there. She left them her recently purchased chair and returned Borka's headlamp. The cellphone was tucked deep into her pocket to ditch later.

Philip said, "Wait," and came back with a large plastic shopping bag from The Gap. "Please take this for your stuff. You shouldn't walk through the city carrying a garbage bag over your shoulder. It attracts attention."

She hugged each one in turn, feeling like Dorothy — if her tornado had tossed her into a muskeg of drunkards instead of into Munchkinland. Wayne said, "I'm sorry I called you a *provocatoor*. I'm working on my paranoia." She was grateful he didn't make a scene, plead with her to stay; it would've made the others suspicious. As she came to Borka, she thought, *I'll miss you most of all*. When they let go of each other, Borka held one of Danni's hands and caressed her cheek. "We don't live in country where bombs fall, so a solid building is good thing. But make sure building is not so strong nothing gets in, or nothing comes out. That is a tomb."

"I hear you."

"You must come and visit us, Danni."

She released Danni's hand after she promised she would, and Danni walked down the path to the grassy field, across the railroad tracks, through the chain-link fence, and along the Extension. At Rosedale Valley Road, she took the staircase into Wellesley Park. Two police moved in the woods, where the other homeless camp was, on the edge of the ravine. Their bodies bent forwards, searching for clues. At the top of the stairs, yellow tape surrounded where she'd left that man. A clump of Cabbagetown residents exercising their dogs watched from a distance. A nearby chocolate Lab arched her back to relieve herself. "Good girl!" exclaimed her owner, drawing a plastic bag from his pocket. A woman craned her neck towards the ravine. Her snow-white Pomeranian was so poufy Danni was barely able to tell its bum from its snout.

"What happened?" she fished.

"Someone was attacked last night. Bashed on the head. They say the attacker might've been one of the homeless men who lives down there."

"How terrible. Is he okay?"

"He's alive, but we're not sure."

Above them, branches strained against a strong morning breeze and slackened, bracing themselves for the next gust.

Twelve-step Yoda

DANNI DITCHED THE STOLEN PHONE WAY OVER NEAR YONGE STREET and doubled back to the Regent Park Community Health Centre, where she asked if they could get her into detox. They sent her to the same one I'd been to, which was called Women's Own Withdrawal Management Centre. Naturally, Danni had her own distinct take on the place. First, she was amused by its name, which made it sound as if we should be proud of the place, like, "Right on, sisters, we fuckin' *own* this centre!" As if somehow we weren't all a bunch of fuck-ups going to the one place in the city that would take you if you had a vagina.

She had a shorter stay there than I'd had, because there'd been funding cuts and they could only keep people four weeks. She met Jacqueline and stifled a smile, remembering my description of her. Her hair was black with a streak of white, and as Jacqueline emphasized a point, she brought her hands up in front of her cheeks and made them into two claws facing each other. I'd called her Meerkat, but taking her in, Danni pictured her on her hind legs eating a cob of corn and decided Jacquie Raccoon fit better. She imagined the fake-serious debate we'd have about our duelling nicknames.

Jacquie told her the story of her living under a bridge in Paris.

Danni pictured her there in the dark, the way racoons hid behind a shed in the backyard of her stepfather's house. Being alone like that, exposed and in danger, was much worse than living in a tent on the edge of the Don River with friends next to you.

Her headache intensified, and Jacquie Racoon said, "Danni, are you okay?" She assured her it was the usual, nothing serious. The story of how Jacquie'd survived her ordeal in France gave Danni hope enough to push through that headache. At night, fever gripped her and she tossed in bed, soaking the sheets in a way she hadn't done since HIV first tore through her and her immune system tried in vain to fight it off. Pain rocked her body. Jacquie'd told them they might feel much worse before they felt any better, that it could get so bad that they'd simply have to trust her, it would pass. In those dark hours, the man in the ravine haunted her. She wished she could feel sorry for him, but she didn't. Would she feel remorse if he died? She had no name, no way to check anyway, unless it made the news.

Sometimes she'd go to the common room where people were rigid and rocking in chairs, either hands under bums or legs pulled up, arms around their knees but backs straight. Unable to relax. If she could've caught someone's gaze, they might've given her strength or distraction, but they were mostly riding their own wave, staring at their toes or at something on TV. So she drank tea. There was always plenty of tea, "To wash ze toxeens away," according to Jacqueline.

Drinking those teas, which came from Germany and Switzerland, helped get rid of the horrible pasty white coating on Danni's tongue. But it grew back with alarming speed. Other than that, she doubted the tea did much more than warmly re-stoke her resolve. Her body, on its own without its frequent infusions of crack and whisky, was oozing resistance and excuses. She took hot showers and scrubbed until she was raw, only to step onto the shower mat, still dripping screwed-up delusions. Her fingertips were no longer hardened and red from crack pipe burns since she'd switched to injecting, but her inner arms were riddled with healing abscesses and hardened lumps. Her face, puffier than it'd ever been, was still colourless. Her hair was becoming less stringy; they had decent conditioner in that detox centre, a luxury she hadn't permitted herself in years. When I was in there, I'd left it on my head and, turning off the tap, sat wrapped in a towel on the shower floor and enjoyed the buttery, almond-scented tingle. I imagined my hair, my scalp, my brain itself, soaking up its moisture like a starved plant.

The days tightened between dawn and dusk, a set of hands wringing Danni dry. Four weeks passed, each of them feeling less merciless. By the end of it, when she'd done her time, her disability benefits had been approved but her housing remained uncertain. In an appointment with Jacquie Raccoon, she told her she had no-where to go, that she'd lost everything. If anyone would sympathize, she would. She referred Danni to Nellie's shelter, where she stayed for two weeks while they got her on the subsidized housing list.

The women at Nellie's were a mixed bag: immigrant women who'd landed in Toronto unsupported, unprepared, carting around one, two, three children; a woman with cerebral palsy in her fifties whose parents were dead and who'd left an abusive boyfriend in her small town, taking a bus to Toronto without any plan whatsoever other than to come to that organization, which she'd read about on the internet. Their only commonality was living in that place, and Danni, compared to the others, discovered she was a fraud. Their website talked of helping women "who have and are experiencing oppressions such as violence, poverty, and homelessness." She'd never considered herself homeless, more temporarily unable to afford housing. She'd been without a place to live for all of five weeks, four of them spent in rehab. She didn't consider herself oppressed; she wasn't. Hell, if I wasn't, she sure as hell was not. Comparing herself to the women in that place, Danni's refusal to call her mom felt like childish pigheadedness, a prideful stomping about and holding of her breath. Unlike so many of them, she could've called her mom at any given moment and that woman would've taken her back to live with her. Especially now that she wasn't turning tricks and was in recovery. But, yes, there was a cost to that, and she wasn't ready to pay it, so she lied and told the staff there was no one.

Noreen, one of their workers, helped her find a furnished studio apartment the size of a matchbox on Sherbourne Street near Dundas. Danni described it as grim. Noreen took her to ODSP to make sure they knew to add on the rent supplement. She found Danni sheets, towels, and clothing. Ajax, laundry detergent, and dish soap. And, extra-thoughtful of her, thin patterned fabrics to liven the place up. The apartment was close to where we'd lived together, too close, which she'd mentioned to Noreen, but there weren't any other affordable options unless she wanted to move out to Jane and Finch, or Scarborough, or maybe Thorncliffe Park. I don't think snobbery held her back from moving out of the downtown; she'd've had a tough time of it. She'd have known nobody, stuck out in ways she wasn't used to. Most of all, it was harder to get to services and health care. A doctor that knew anything about HIV. One thing about the downtown is you can swing a dead cat and hit someone itching to help, if you're willing to accept it. Unless you're a drug-taking hooker, single mom, and then there's sweet fuck all.

Danni's new apartment was in the basement, had creaky plumbing, a chipped enamel bathroom sink and tub, filthy smoke-scented carpeting, and a kitchen that was visited by cockroaches nearly the size of Sir Purrsalot. It was worse than Mario's Drop-In, and much grimmer than the three apartments she'd lived in on Oak Street. Those buildings were not well-maintained, but she began to understand how bad Toronto housing could get. Still, this was her own place, not a tent on the edge of a mosquito-infested river, and after a good scrubbing and strategic draping of Noreen's textiles, presto, she'd lifted it from slum to student dorm.

Jacquie from Women's Own and Noreen from Nellie's had both urged her to find a Narcotics Anonymous group. She understood the need, but her skepticism of the twelve steps was deep-rooted. Giving over to God or your Higher Power? Danni was an atheist and a feminist, she told Noreen. The model chafed against her political views and apparently even her culture. She said to Noreen, "Women already have less power than men. Are we supposed to find giving up power a good strategy? Plus the 'no questioning, no crosstalk' part. It might work for some people, but Jews are even told to argue with God. Not that I believe in God, but I'm just saying, it's in our DNA. In a Jewish house, crosstalk is just another word for dinnertime. You might as well club me senseless."

Noreen smiled, put a hand on hers. "It's not that you can't question. You can do all of that with your sponsor. But arguing in meetings is frowned upon. Yes, you'd have to shut up and keep stuff to yourself. But you know what? You can do that. Because you know what else? You can't do this alone, and those groups are held every day somewhere in this city. You can go whenever you need strength. Give it a try?"

She wasn't sure which group she could attend, worried, at first, that she might run into me. She guessed that I attended one that met on Saturdays at The 519, so she crossed that one off her list, thinking I would have felt intruded upon.

The group she chose met in a church at Avenue Road and Bloor, not too far away, on Wednesday nights. I give her credit for going, because it was hard for Danni to entertain the possibility that she might be full of it. Achieving humility was going to be a work in progress, as she entered that room full of snideness and suspicion. She took in the room, lit like a séance, she thought, and the members sitting morosely in a circle, adding to the effect. When the meeting began, they listened to one another as if waiting for the person sharing to channel the Beyond. Maybe the Higher Power, she didn't know. That person would finish sharing, and in the murmuring of thanks that followed she heard an undercurrent of disappointment that no message from the Beyond had been received.

People were friendly enough, but she was going to loathe it; she could tell immediately. She'd hoped for that satisfying scab-picking feeling of penance, but it didn't feel self-imposed. It was more like a regular punishment, the kind doled out by someone else, and for sure it was nothing near the salvation that everyone promised. The Higher Power stuff, which was a way to avoid saying "God" because that would alienate some, sounded to Danni like New Age crap. One meeting's chair, whom she dubbed Yoda, clasped his hands together, prayer-like, when he spoke.

Not commenting on people's stories was as agonizing as abstinence itself. She searched the faces and listened for clues that there might be another Jewish person there to ask advice on how to make sense of it all. There wasn't anyone identifiable. After her first meeting, three people sidled up to tell her she'd be welcome back, and though she knew they meant well, their gesture smacked of a cult.

She went back anyway. She forced herself to hold on because, as a diversion from the urge to use, it was useful enough — Noreen had been right. The need for distraction is strong in any person newly in recovery, but in addition to trying not to use, there was the unsettling fact that she hadn't gotten her period for the second month in a row and was queasy in the mornings. She set that worry aside. This wasn't the first time she'd skipped a month or two; it'd happened before, especially in the last five years. Her body was in a state of shock from withdrawal, she reasoned, and her uterus was saying to the rest of her organs: I'll sit this one out until the rest of you have calmed the fuck down. On the whole, this could be written off as an adjustment to detox and recovery — and an upset stomach from Kaletra, the same HIV medication that was causing shifts in her body fat distribution. Weren't these normal responses of an unhealthy body stuck in its destructive ways, fighting against getting healthier?

Long ago, Danni had concluded that she was infertile. She'd only recently used protection — when tricks agreed to it. Her unwelcoming womb had been a rare lucky break; it wouldn't betray her. And, in spite of the fat redistribution, she was losing weight. Didn't women gain weight if they were pregnant? Passing through a drugstore, she spied a stack of home pregnancy tests but, after checking the price tag, had second thoughts.

Going to another meeting would help her refocus on the necessary but excruciating process of reintegrating into society, which, aside from this recent scare, was foremost on her mind. It was a strange and uncomfortable sensation to be in the world again, trying to be a normal citizen instead of an outsider. To turn tricks, Danni'd had to be loud and conspicuous, but somehow, moving through Toronto in her donated, unfashionable mom jeans and faded pastel-coloured T-shirt, she was more on display. To a degree, both situations invited unspoken questions, curiosity, and judgments. But now she cared. Wearing drab clothes from an out-of-favour decade, she couldn't pretend this was intentional, rebellious, or counterculture. She was no longer sexy and edgy; she was a source of mockery or pity. Even in her twelve-step group, she was drawing attention — by withholding her story. She was a fool everywhere: sad on the street, pouty and secretive in group, and, in spite of herself, drawing attention. Above all, she was embarrassed by her vanity; why did she care? More than likely people's interest was fleeting at best. Those strangers all around her in a circle of chairs, they were passersby.

They might stare, and they might've been sympathetic, but they'd move on and leave her be. Wasn't that a good thing?

Why, then, in public or sitting in that circle, did that passing interest give her the sensation of having been stripped naked and left in a busy intersection at rush hour? NA had promised her anonymity, but Danni longed for invisibility, too.

Cuchi-cuchi

JULY MELTED INTO AUGUST, AND AN EAGER GOVERNMENT DISABILITY worker helped Danni find a contract at a community centre. The job involved organizing an end-of-summer music street fair called Regent Park Rock and Reggae Fest. It was to take place on Labour Day weekend, in early September. Her boss was a hardbitten woman named Carlotta Mazzanti. When she walked in the first day, Carlotta harrumphed, possibly disapprovingly, but then nodded more ambiguously, neither surprised nor judgmental. She beckoned Danni to her workstation with a sinewy, tattooed arm.

Over the next week, Danni learned that she was backfilling the job of someone who'd made a complete mess of things. By comparison, Danni'd be great, right? "Passable," Carlotta'd grunt, or sometimes "Decent." It didn't matter; Danni received her boss's faint praise gratefully.

The fair was the perfect project. Danni enjoyed working up to a big, fun event that would end, with no lasting commitments. She lost herself in the details, the logistics, and was pleased by her knack for organizing things. She worked with staff and volunteers whose enthusiasm and excitement, in contrast to Carlotta's all-business approach, reminded her that there were people in this world who loved their work.

During that same period, at her NA group, a new guy named Brad joined them; he'd transferred jobs from Halifax. He was tall, muscular, and possibly Latino. Handsome, in his thirties. At his third meeting, he shared his story, and, as if not central to whatever had led to his addiction or resulted from it, he mentioned he was HIV-positive. Brad had been in recovery for ten years, nearly the longest of anyone in the group, but people frowned at the HIV disclosure. A woman folded her hands over her heart.

Thanks, Brad.

Danni still hadn't said a word, about that or anything else, but that pity would be a sticky puddle, a tar pit they'd both get caught in. When he was done, someone started in with his story, but she raised her hand, and the meeting's Yoda could barely contain her glee. "Mark, how about if we let Danni share first," she interrupted.

"I'm Danni ..." she hesitated "... and I guess I'm an addict."

"Hi, Danni," chimed in everyone. The unison was still creepy.

"And I'm also HIV-positive, like Brad," she added with more confidence. "It's not a big deal. People live full, productive lives now." She told an abbreviated version of her story. She ended up on the streets, she revealed, but didn't say she'd been turning tricks. Her drug and alcohol consumption had progressed over time, she said, and left it vague. She'd gotten quite sick two years back and discovered it was HIV. She didn't say that she'd ended up one night in St. Mike's after collapsing on the stroll, that she didn't remember how she got there, or that Olive had come with her and she'd made her swear not to tell me. How even now, more than two years into her diagnosis, she couldn't imagine ever dating again.

I still didn't know that story, how anxious she'd become over a period of months about her stubborn cough, her passing out on the street, any of it. How relieved she'd been it'd been HIV and not terminal lung cancer like her father had had. How, once diagnosed and on meds, she'd gone crawling back to her mom for two weeks until she'd stolen money for a fix and was caught and kicked out again. I'd been pregnant, working in Bo Hai and Mei Zhen's fish store. We weren't living together. Later, those details weren't important to her.

When Danni came to the part of her story about hitting bottom, she described losing her housing, omitting the coda about nearly killing someone in a drunken rage of unresolved trauma. When she'd finished sharing, the woman across from her, smug little scarecrow of a lady, sprouted a cornfield of clichés on her face: There it is, Everything in time, Everyone comes around, She's warming up to us, Without a struggle there's no progress. Others reacted the same way, but not Brad, who nodded in her direction, a kind of salute. As for the rest, she wanted to wipe those Stepford wives smiles off their faces. She wasn't warming up to them at all; she was only sharing because they were all such condescending, HIV-ignorant turds, and she was trying to be an ally to this poor newcomer.

Brad approached her after the meeting, and introduced himself. "Thanks for that."

"Hey, no problem. Strength in numbers."

His brown hair fell across his face, partially covering one eye. He swept it to the side, tucked it behind his ear, and said to his bangs, "Stay!"

After chatting for a while, Danni made an excuse to leave. She walked home absorbing the horror of all those people knowing things about her. How they might say something, tell someone, despite the oath of confidentiality. Who'd care, she didn't know. Why they'd care — why she herself should — she didn't know either.

At her next meeting, she had a longer conversation with Brad, and he suggested they grab coffee at a place on Cumberland Street, near where he lived. Danni searched for something to wear that wasn't unflattering and screaming of the nineties. She chose a beige peasant dress that she'd found at Goodwill, because it had colourful stitching and a high waist that concealed her out-of-shape body. She pulled her hair back into a ponytail after parting it in the middle and drew lipstick across her mouth, smacked her lips together, and, not wanting to fuss anymore, made her way to meet him.

The café was full of tourists, local office workers on break, and, worryingly, many upper-middle-class women of a certain age. She'd taken a seat without a direct view of the door, and so, even after Brad arrived and they'd ordered, she kept turning to check who was arriving. Brad asked if everything was okay.

"I'm sorry. All of these women are variations of my mother. I haven't seen her in a long time, and it wouldn't be good if she walked in."

"She lives nearby?"

"No. But she's been known to shop in Yorkville."

"Tell you what," he said. "Let's switch. That way you'll spot her coming and you can bolt through the back if she arrives. And if your eyes are wandering, I'll try not to assume you're bored with the conversation," he quipped.

She felt ridiculous. What were the chances? But she wouldn't relax otherwise. "Thanks." They exchanged spots.

"Hey, I get it." Brad tugged his shirt at his waist. "I'm two thousand kilometres from my father, and it's not far enough."

They settled into an easy conversation about family, the kind she hadn't had with a man in years: clever banter and amusing stories, skirting the edges of honesty and disclosure. Brad had moved to Toronto to become a manager at a large social services agency, but didn't mention which one. He was from Halifax, but had degrees from u of t and ubc. He'd been a cocaine snorter in the mid-1990s, in his twenties, but had somehow avoided career destruction before getting into recovery. His family relationships had suffered more.

"You never did needles?" she asked, trying to get at how Brad had acquired HIV, which he picked up on immediately.

"Once or twice, but the HIV probably came from a girlfriend who was a needle user." He quickly added that he wasn't blaming her; he'd been "a typical guy," as he put it, not wanting to use condoms. That in truth, he didn't know how he got it and probably never would.

"Mine was definitely from sex," Danni said, and left it at that.

They exchanged stories of medication side effects, weird dreams from Sustiva. One of hers involved being chased by a rabid, foaming-at-the-mouth cartoon SpongeBob SquarePants who spoke using Patrick Stewart's voice. His involved a skydiving trip with Charo, who had her guitar still strapped to her as she jumped from the airplane.

"The woman from the Geico commercial?

He chuckled. "I forget you're like ten years younger than me," he said. "She's a Spanish guitar player. She shook her tits a lot and said 'cuchi-cuchi.' In fact, she said it as we fell to the earth."

The staccato of Danni's laugh startled her, and Brad too. *Good God*, she thought, *am I flirting?* Horrified, she excused herself. At the washroom mirror, shoulders sloped, she saw her skin was whiter than Marilyn Manson's. Her lipstick wasn't smudged. But her ponytail had released short strands near her forehead. Unlike Brad's charming curls, Danni's, reflected back to her, said "sad Jane Austen protagonist." Especially when taken with her dress, which on second look was less peasant and more Elizabeth Bennet — if she'd had to shop at the Salvation Army. A Salvation Army in Ukraine. She wetted her curls and stuffed them back in, hoping they wouldn't spring free again.

She returned to the table. "I should get going."

Brad didn't disagree. He took the bill. Danni protested, but was grateful when he ignored her and went to pay at the cash.

On the sidewalk, there was an awkward moment, but she leaned in to snap-hug him goodbye. "This was fun," she said, too chirpily. "See you next week in group."

"Hey, do you have an email address?" he called after her.

Danni turned, still moving, now stepping backwards. "Unfortunately, my computer died," she lied. "So I'm afraid it's plain old texting." A laptop was way beyond her reach, but she hadn't yet conveyed to him just how poor she was.

"Oh, okay, sure." She guessed he didn't encounter people like her except as clients in his undefined social service job. Besides, she didn't want to get personal emails at work; she wasn't sure who had access to them.

She strode off and, once around the corner, let herself slow her pace. She walked home along Bloor, cutting south at Church Street so that she'd pass by my coffee shop. When she walked by, I was at the cash handing someone a big whipped cream-topped drink, but I didn't see her, and it took her a second to recognize me. In the three months since we'd seen each other, I'd grown my hair some, had woven in some short extensions. She almost came in. But as my head turned to the window, Danni lost her nerve.

The following morning at the community centre, Carlotta shouted, "Snap out of it, Wexler," from the other side of the room. "Tick-tock!"

She'd been zoning out at her computer screen, clutching a mug of coffee.

"Sorry, sorry. Rough night."

"Don't wanna know. Don't care. Your problems are not going to be my problems." She told Danni that they needed the stage and audio logistics nailed down by end of the next day and that Danni was acting like she'd snuggled up in front of her favourite soap with a cup of hot cocoa.

"I'm on it." She placed the mug on the desk and made her back a wooden plank. And, after a suitable interval, she asked, "Just wondering, is there any, by the way?"

Carlotta shrugged in exasperation, indicating she wasn't a mind reader.

"Cocoa, I mean. 'Cause this coffee —" Daggers. "Never mind. I'm on it."

She pulled her shit together, did a list up on a pad of foolscap, and got down to work. At lunch, there was a text from Brad, saying, *Good to get to know you a bit.* She waited until mid-afternoon and texted back, *Same. Thanks again for paying.*

The rest of the afternoon flew by, occupied by a minor crisis with the audio tech people, who'd misunderstood the order and who had to source more microphones and speakers on short notice. "My email was clear." She channelled Carlotta into the phone. "I don't care how you do it, but your problem is not going to be our problem. You're going to sort this out by ten o'clock tomorrow."

Carlotta leaned back in her chair. "Well done, Grasshopper."

"Are you sure? I feel like I could be fiercer if I got some tattoos up my arm ..."

Carlotta made her thumb and index finger into pincers. "Now you've cancelled out the tiny bit of goodwill you started to accumulate."

Danni put her head down and hammered at the keyboard, careful to hide her smile. Bullying that man had given her a gush of adrenaline, a brief release of a pressure valve. It was small, not enough to deal with the clawing urge to slam, but it did make her think that if she were a power suit-wearing Bay Street executrix bossing people around for a living, it wouldn't make for a bad drug management strategy.

Dinner tomorrow night? buzzed her phone as she walked home. *My treat again. I know you're working part-time.*

She didn't answer until well after dinner, and by that time, the delay had prompted a *Say yes, or I'm calling your mother and inviting her instead.* She composed five separate texts and deleted them before sending. She wrote, *I will save you from my mother. Money tight but you can't pay again. Happy to go to McDs!* and hit send.

Brad insisted on a Vietnamese place on Yonge Street, which wouldn't break the bank, he said, and he negotiated with Danni that he'd pay most of the bill and let her pay tax and tip. The next day, the audio-video guy called her back, sheepish. He'd sorted everything out, and they'd give them a slight discount for the mistake. When she told Carlotta, she said, "Nice work, Wex-a-matic. And no tattoos were needed." Danni's chest puffed as she turned back to her computer.

Fool's Gold

THE REST OF DANNI'S WORKDAY DIDN'T LIVE UP TO ITS BEGINNING. She checked tasks off her list, but her computer shut down with the blue screen of death and she lost unsaved changes to a file. Distraction got the better of her as she struggled to build momentum. On break, she leafed through a two-day-old *Globe and Mail*. More news about all the u.s. banks failing. Another news story about the air quality at the Beijing Olympics. And one about a foiled plot at the Brock abortion clinic downtown, a man caught trying to get in with a female decoy. They had guns on them, intent on shooting the staff in the name of Jesus.

She left at five o'clock, back and shoulders stiff. Would Carlotta be pissed that she hadn't reached their dub poet to confirm her time slot on the entertainment lineup? Would Brad make a declaration of interest before she could move them into the friend zone? What the hell would she wear? At her apartment, she dumped all of her clothes onto the single bed. A passable brown skirt and a nondescript blouse would have to do. She could belt the skirt and arrange the blouse in a way that was somewhere between sexy and frumpy. She dealt with her hair. She decided to wear it down and styled it modestly, with the tiniest bit of hairspray.

Brad was early this time, and when they took their seats, she said, "It's good to be making a new friend in the city."

"Yeah, same." He didn't hesitate. She exhaled her worries; he wouldn't make moves, she didn't need to say anything more.

When they'd finished their meal, they ordered green, gloopy Vietnamese desserts that reminded Danni of snot. She poked at hers with the tip of her spoon. Brad said, "I've tried nearly all of the sweets in this restaurant, but this may be the most off-putting yet."

"So you're a regular."

He tucked into his dessert, unafraid. "I work at the Children's Aid Society."

Danni absorbed the news. "I've never met anyone who's worked there before." She swallowed her gloop, which was not as sweet as she expected it to be. "Must be hard."

Brad explained that he was a manager, supporting caseworkers who were, as he put it, "on the front lines, making the hard decisions." She mentioned a friend who'd been on the other end of those decisions, keeping her voice somewhere between conversational and accusatory. He apologized, ate more of his dessert, eyes fixed on his green mess. "In group, I don't talk about where I work. There are lots of people — like your friend — whose children have been apprehended." Did his use of the word friend have quotation marks? Did he think she was talking about herself?

"Some of those people deserve a second chance, wouldn't you say?"

He deflected the question, instead talking about what drugs can do to your state of mind. He was speaking as though Danni weren't a drug addict, too. About how kids are often forgotten, neglected. Beaten. "And it depends on what drug the parent is taking. Crack, heroin, pot, they're all different."

She started and stopped what she was going to say. "You know ... maybe because you used to do lines of coke in a fancy nightclub and weren't slamming crack up your arm, you think you were a better class of drug user than the rest of us —"

"I don't —"

"— but those crack users with kids? They're really trying hard to make it work out there."

"Of course they are."

"I'm not saying they shouldn't be in recovery."

"Danni, you're misunderstanding —"

"— but I wish Children's Aid had a better way of trying to help people be the parents they want to be. Like maybe paying for child care, or finding child care at hours that they need it."

Danni's feistiness, her sticking up for me, warmed my heart when I later learned of it. Would I have had the guts to say those things myself? I wasn't sure they'd've made a difference.

"And what if kids are actually being abused and neglected?" said Brad.

Yes, what if, Danni thought. Her mom had been oblivious to what her boyfriend had done, and later wilfully blind. But would she have wanted to be taken away from her? "I'm not saying abused kids shouldn't be protected. What I'm saying —"

"— is that removal is absolutely the last resort. Yes."

"What I'm saying is that instead of only focusing on taking kids away, you could help parents keep it together. Especially the Black and Native parents, who seem particularly to be targeted by —"

"— but we are trying to help."

"Not enough, maybe."

He dropped his fork onto his plate, beside his unfinished dessert. "Danni, maybe we should pick up this conversation another time. Unfortunately, I need to finish some work tonight before bed."

She stared at her place setting. There was too much red on it, and the green dessert was turning her stomach. The restaurant had become small, quiet.

Brad hailed the server. "Look. I'm sorry for whatever happened to your friend. The system could be doing better, I know that. But it's not that easy with the resources we have." His voice was soothing, practised. He was no longer Danni's date, if he ever had been. She was a hysterical client, needing to be managed.

She willed herself to be calm. "I know." She pushed away her dessert. "I just ... It would be good to know you haven't given up. On finding a way."

Brad paid, she put down money for the tax and tip like they'd arranged, and they said goodbye on the street. "Now you know why I don't talk about work." He was quietly mad.

"Thanks for dinner," she said. "I guess I'll see you in group."

He smiled, but didn't answer. His polite refusal to acknowledge that they might happen to run into each other by necessity and not by intention said everything.

On the way home, Danni bought a pregnancy test. She read the stick in her apartment, leaning against her living room wall. It was positive. She slid to the floor and stared at the blank wall opposite her, contemplating how it could be possible for a person to so spectacularly screw up her life. She and I had made a disaster of things with Aaron; how could she be confident she'd be any more capable a mother, even off drugs? Her net income now, without the expense of crack, was less than when she'd been turning tricks regularly. We'd been two breadwinners then. It was one thing when she was chipping in to help provide for my son, but the notion of raising her own child in poverty slapped her in the face. She dreaded her paltry paycheque having to feed two mouths and was ashamed at her selfishness. If ever there was a sign that she was unfit to be a mother, this was it.

What she never admitted to me was that her expectations for a child of her own were higher than they'd been for mine. Being happy and loved in a life of poverty might've been enough for Aaron. But for her own child? Unacceptable.

She needed to find a meeting, stat, and luckily on Friday nights there was one called Night Owls that met at ten o'clock. She nearly ran there. With that new collection of strangers, she shared more than she had in her home group, revealing for the first time that she'd turned tricks and that she'd done so for five years. People nodded at the disclosure. What would Brad make of it, if he found out? Maybe he'd write her off, if he still cared at this point. Maybe he'd turn into a shithead with a saviour complex, excited to have a hooker with a heart of gold that he could sweep out of her sad life. She chuckled bitterly: when he discovered it was fool's gold, the joke'd be on him.

After group, she stayed up late watching an old movie, and slept in as long as she could. In the morning, still struggling, she looked up meetings in her area and, feeling lazy, chose an AA gathering at The 519 that met two hours before the NA group that she assumed I attended. She'd been curious about the differences between NA and AA. It was listed as LGBT-friendly; she'd be in the minority, but they wouldn't exclude her.

The clock behind reception registered 10:05. She was breathless by the time she reached the top floor. She crept in, conscious of not disturbing the group, and took a seat while a woman stuttered her way through a reading. The scent of fresh-brewed coffee and donuts filled the room. It wasn't until she settled that she noticed me sitting at the other end of her row and froze.

She took me in. I was wearing tan shorts and a blue sleeveless T-shirt. She wasn't sure if I'd seen her when she'd come by my coffee shop, so she worried I'd think she was stalking me, that I'd wonder what she was doing in this group, but all I could think of was how good it was to see her. How glad I was to know she'd taken that first step.

I grinned, gave her a small wave, which she returned. She clenched her fists and raised her shoulders in a pantomimed hug. I mimicked it back. Breaking away from Danni had been one of the hardest parts of my recovery. Waiting to talk to her made the meeting painful, and I hoped her fidgeting was a sign that it was the same for her. Danni hadn't changed; her eye-roll during one of the readings told me that. The chanting in unison was a bit robotic. I could see it all; I just didn't care because it was helping. I hoped it would help her, too.

Danni tried hard to focus on the meaning, the true meaning of what people were saying, to get past her usual grumpiness. This group was different, and not just because it was LBGT-friendly. It was AA, not NA, but I wasn't sure why that made such a difference. I'd been shocked at how aggressive NA people were about jumping in to share, despite the rotating chairs' attempts at a calming presence. Heaven help you if you were meek. No sooner was the last person finished — everyone still chanting, *Thanks, Bob* or *Thanks, Sue* or *Thanks, Edna* — than someone was already barging in, talking over the thank you to launch their own story. This was more civilized; it's why I'd switched. The chair kept an actual speakers' list. When I raised my hand, Danni shifted uneasily. The chair asked again if anybody wanted on the list, but Danni kept her hands firmly under her butt.

A sketchy twenty-something man named Kieran was the first to go. "I had three months clean, but last week I went and fucking blew it all. Fortunately, I ran into my sponsor on the street." He tipped his baseball cap to a man sitting a few rows in front of him. "We had a chat this morning over coffee. So here I am again."

After Kieran, a gaunt woman named Crystal spoke. "I know I've been away for a while. I've been off the wagon for years, but —" She paused, swallowed, and lifted her eyes, which were wet. "— I have cancer. I doubt I have more than six months. I came back because I didn't want to die drinking."

Danni and I both pulled ourselves from the edge of tears, but others weren't so successful.

A serene fifty-something woman was celebrating her seven-year anniversary. "It's hard to go after Crystal, especially when things are going well for me these days. Life keeps getting better and better," she said, "but that also brings new challenges. The good things fill my days, and it gets harder to find time for meetings. But I need to come. I was thirteen years clean and I got complacent. I went through a whole bottle of cough medicine and a bottle of sleeping pills in less than three days. Now I'm seven years clean again, struggling with the same thing. I've learned I need to get to meetings no matter what."

I was up next. I was self-conscious in front of Danni, so I shortened and sped up my intro, said, "Hi, Paulette, addict," with barely a punctuating pause.

Hi, Paulette.

"I want to start by welcoming my good friend over there." I nodded at her, and she waved back. "You and I went through a lot together, girl. It's good to see you here." She flashed me an encouraging smile. I mentioned I'd been working extremely hard on Step Four in the past month. Working it, not just working on it. How hard it'd been. Making a moral inventory of myself? I felt like I was writing a novel, and so far, it was a really bad one.

Danni was embarrassed by her own Step Four list, which she'd abandoned; it was pitiful. She'd moved too quickly through the first three steps and would have to go back to them, for sure, just as I had. My sponsor told me not to worry about how much I'd been writing, that I should let it flow, but there'd been days when I'd written one thing down and cried for two hours. Other days, I'd written boring stuff that I didn't want to bother her with. The week before, I'd written five pages of things about myself that I hated so much I could barely stand rereading them.

"The hardest part," I continued, "has been writing about my kids. My first one, Chantelle, I gave her up when I was a teenager, so I never got to spend any time with her. But my little boy, Aaron ..." Danni couldn't meet my eyes. "He's the one I think about more. The first time I got clean was when I had him. He was with me a year, but I relapsed. He turned two in May, and I miss him so much. I wish I could get him back so bad I can —"

I choked up, lowered my head, and put my hands up in the air in surrender. To God, to my Higher Power, or maybe just to my tears. I shifted in my chair until I composed myself.

"I know that owning up to my shit, pardon my language, means looking at how I did wrong by Aaron. I know I can do better. I'll probably never get that chance, though. He's a Crown ward now, on the adoption list — I didn't contest it. I have hope for him, even if I sometimes don't have it for myself. So, you know, I hope you'll all put him in your prayers."

I'm not sure how I'd found it in me to lay myself bare in that way, given how I was raised, though I hadn't had the guts to say exactly when I'd messed up, which was three months into that year we had Aaron, and I hoped Danni'd forgive the vagueness. Hadn't we done okay for a while, or had it all been a hopeless delusion? Also, it would've been more precise to say that Aaron was taken away because we'd both messed up, but it wasn't Danni's responsibility in the first place, and I wasn't gonna lay any more guilt on her than she already felt.

The meeting over, participants congregated to chat or offer one another support. One woman congratulated another on her progress. A huddle formed around the coffee urn. Danni and I hugged for a good long time.

I let her go first. "It's good to see you. I'm sorry about the last time —"

"No, I should apologize."

We talked about each of our groups, their pros and cons, the characters that showed up. I asked where she was living, if she was back with her mom.

"Are you kidding?" She raised her eyebrows as much as humanly possible. "Even if I'd been thinking about it, and okay, it may have crossed my mind a couple of times, I'll admit it, a woman in my group warned me about calling too soon, before I've worked through enough of the steps."

The advice that woman had given was right; it wasn't only about being abstinent, it was about doing all that other work: the stuff that'd help make a reunion successful or that'd prepare us in the event that it wasn't. Which outcome, I wondered, did Danni imagine? Did she fantasize a hug in the hallway of her mom's house? A hand on her face and then being led to the kitchen for almond cookies and hot tea? Or did she imagine the worst, as I did when I thought of meeting up with my brother: being subjected to humiliating questions and a major guilt trip about abandoning our mother? There was no reason to think Eddy'd changed, and Danni's mom still didn't know that she was HIV-positive. These meetings wouldn't be smooth.

The room had nearly emptied, so Danni suggested we sit on a bench in the park next to the community centre. She followed me downstairs, out the front and to the side of the centre, where there was a bench under a large tree. It was a hot day, and even in the shade my shirt clung to my back. The air carried a scent of mustard-covered hot dogs from a cart parked nearby.

As we sat, Danni told me about her pregnancy.

My lips parted, not much. "Three months? You said you couldn't get pregnant!"

"Apparently, the joke's on me."

I considered a mini Danni, an ankle-biter with wild hair and an attitude. I told her it might do her good and asked how long she'd been clean. "Sorry, sober," I corrected myself.

"Also about three months," she said. "I don't know what I'm gonna do yet, but it was a wake-up call."

Had she done something dumb and gotten herself a boyfriend? I asked, but she made fright hands and told me there was no need to panic. I gave her arm a gentle backhanded slap. "Isn't it good to know that recovery hasn't made me any less gay?"

"Or less nosy," she countered, with a slap of her own.

She fiddled with a new ring on her pinky, turned it around and around. A cyclist wove her way lazily along the path next to us, nearly clipping Danni's foot. "Let's just say the baby daddy is not in a position to be a father and leave it at that. He wasn't a trick. But, no. No boyfriend."

She wasn't ready to tell me about Wayne or Brad. There'd only been two men in Danni's life that she'd called boyfriends, neither of whom she claimed to have loved. The first, in high school, was named Tim. He'd been too timid for her liking, she'd told me one night, as we came down from a high while planted in my favourite stairwell. He was crazy about Ms. Pac-Man and the band A-ha, both of which I agreed were disturbing. They had to get drunk to have sex, and it'd come as a relief when after a year Tim had broken up with her for a girl in the chess club. She'd been cheating on him with a guy from the swim team. The other relationship, in university, had been with a long-haired and muscled physics major she'd met at a student hangout bar. They'd had an intense but mostly physical relationship that involved daily wall-slapping, sheet-clawing sex, almost always when they were high from pot. She'd ended the relationship when she left her graduate program, ignoring the daily texts and emails that he sent for weeks.

"I messed up," she said, still turning her pinky ring around and around. "I shouldn't've slept with that guy, with or without protection."

"We both messed up," I said. "That's why we're where we are." I pointed my thumb at the community centre and, reading her expression, changed the subject. "Hey, so, where are you staying, then?"

"In a dismal place on Sherbourne, about the size of this park bench. It's not as bad as some of the hellholes we've known, but pretty bad. Remember that time we crashed one night in that apartment on Jones near the Danforth? The one that Vicky and Tony rented before they got locked up?"

"Don't remind me. It might as well've had a revolving door!" The park filled with my explosive laugh, and hearing Danni's own laughter soothed me in a way that was almost as good as crack. It'd been such a long time since we'd laughed together. "Good God. You and I both need to get into supportive housing, am I right? I think I'm good for about two more months with Letty and Brian before their mom-and-dad routine makes me homicidal."

She pressed me for more, for details of what my life had been like since we'd parted ways. I sat on my hands, trying but failing to see the gratitude that the program wanted us to find in every small mercy. "It's hard. I don't know how long I can take living on so little. Freakin' minimum wage, man."

"Tell me about it. At least your job is full-time."

I told her about volunteering at Maggie's, how doing safety seminars with the girls was keeping me busy. I hadn't dropped my interest in the missing women issue, but that was more Olive's bailiwick, and I'd promised to take over her duties as safety mentor while she shifted focus. The seminars were connected anyway, and I liked the feeling of giving back. I clarified to Danni that I wasn't back turning tricks but didn't mention that I'd met two Maggie's members who were actively working the trade, if not the streets. Deedee and

Mariko did high-class outcalls for a much, much higher rate. They exchanged their tricks' contact info — got a trick's consent to do so as part of their conditions — as a kind of insurance against bad dates. They lived and worked out of a condo, a *condo* for Chrissake, on Wellington Street, and they freakin' owned it. I was slowly mining them for details as to how they made it work, how they lived their lives. They never touched drugs and were doing what I'd thought impossible: saving money. Building assets.

Instead, I told Danni about the compliment Deedee and Mariko had given me: that I was a good teacher.

"It's 'cause you feed on people idolizing you," she said, and I whacked her arm again. "No, good for you, Paulie. It doesn't surprise me. I've always been the chatty one, but you're the one people listen to."

I thanked her, let that sink in. Sometimes I didn't think Danni knew herself, but then comments like that told me there was a whole inner conversation I wasn't privy to, that she didn't always share. For the first time, I told her that I loved her stories. "I won't pretend some of them haven't irritated the shit out of me, but they never once bored me, I can tell you that."

Danni'd been thinking about volunteering herself, maybe at the People With AIDS Foundation in their Speakers' Bureau. Her ODSP worker had suggested it. She told me about her community centre job and asked me if I'd come by the street fair on Labour Day weekend, but I had shifts at the coffee shop all the way through the weekend and wouldn't be able to make it.

"I missed you," I said, when we were out of news.

She took my hands in hers. "You know, hearing you upstairs talking about Aaron, I couldn't help —"

"Hey, I needed to get that off my chest, up there in group. But you and me?" I waved my finger in the air between us. "We're good. We do not need to be dwelling on that."

"I wish I could make things right."

I must've looked at her the way you would a lunatic, a person delusional enough to believe there was any possible way to get over a lost child. I squeezed her hands. "Look at me. It wasn't your fault."

This time, Danni changed the subject, maybe resigned to that truth. At least giving us temporary relief from the miserable topic.

When, after a while, she told me she had to get some groceries, I pointed up at the building. "Will you come back?"

"Don't know. I'll have to think about it." We stood, hugged good-bye, and exchanged numbers. "I'll call soon," she said, and hurried away.

Eight Ball

DANNI MADE IT THROUGH THAT WEEKEND BY TAKING A LONG-distance walk each day, pushing herself until she felt a blister forming. That day, she set out along the pedestrian path up the Don River. Cyclists whizzed by, taking advantage of the late summer sun. She deviated from the path at one point to get closer to the water. Maybe Borka, Sara, Philip, and Wayne would be at their camp across the river.

Nobody was there. A streak of partridgeberries had turned red over the summer down near the shore, and on the other side, next to their camp, long grasses swayed at the river's edge. Sara's chair was blown over by the firepit. The tents were zipped, the fly on Wayne's hanging on a clothesline, flapping in the wind.

What would he do, she wondered, if she told him she was pregnant? Make a stupid show of chivalry that'd embarrass them both? No way she'd tell him. She walked back to the path, continued north until it forked, and followed it to the end of Taylor Creek Park. She was home again by late afternoon, to a modest meal of pasta with oil and grated cheese. She sliced a tomato that had almost gone mushy. The urge to do shots of mescal washed through her. Why mescal, she had no idea. Maybe, she thought, instead of pickles covered in chocolate, pregnant addicts got urges for strange-tasting booze. She resisted. It helped that she had no alcohol in the place, and that she was so exhausted.

Sunday morning dawned long after Danni did. At six o'clock, after tossing for an hour and a half, spinning the day out, reeling it in, and spinning it out again, she tired of listening to CBC radio, capitulated, and made coffee. She promised to haul off to another meeting if she could motivate herself to have a shower. She made toast and downed her HIV meds. She hoped it was true what the doctor'd said, that they were preventing the virus from replicating in her bloodstream, not killing it but knocking it out for the count, so that maybe, maybe she wasn't infectious. That maybe she hadn't given it to Wayne. It wasn't for sure that after one time you'd automatically get it, was it? Even if the meds weren't working? She grabbed the NA White Booklet from the drawer in her bedside table, and her eyes fell on a quote: *There may be times when a relapse lays the groundwork for complete freedom.* Why would they write such a stupid, tempting thing?

She spent the rest of the morning watching the Home Shopping Network and reruns of *Friends* and *Murder, She Wrote* and by noon was ready to be around other human beings. She decided against an NA meeting. She went on another hike, but this time took David Balfour Park until she reached St. Clair, then walked west to Spadina and up into Forest Hill. She drew her hoodie close in case someone recognized her. When she reached her mom's street, she quickened her pace. She hunched down as she approached the house. A *For Sale* sign was spiked into the lawn.

She glanced into the living room, but there was no movement, and the car wasn't in the drive. Was her mom going to send an email to let her know? Danni hadn't considered that one day, when she was ready to talk to her mom again, her mom might have moved on — literally. Her panic wasn't logical; there were always ways to find her.

She wanted to go inside, to snoop through the house for old time's sake. Was her old room being used for storage, or for an exercise bike? Unfortunately, she'd lost her key some time ago.

A car turned at the corner, and she pulled her hood farther forward.

She took Avenue Road downhill and made her way through the downtown, towards her apartment. On Gerrard, in front of Allen Gardens, she passed anti-abortion protesters outside of the Brock Clinic. At Parliament Street, more protesters stood opposite the women's centre. It was all she could do not to run over and bash them with their own signs. Satisfying as that might've been, she wanted to get home, and besides, Serena popped out of the Maggie's offices and nearly ran into her.

She was in ordinary street clothes, her long hair brushed back, and had slapped on some makeup. Stubble showed through the unenthusiastic effort. Had she gone off her hormones? Serena was crying. She fell onto Danni's shoulder, blubbering wetness all over her shirt. Her friend Babs had been arrested. There'd been a messy breakup between Babs and her sugar daddy, Bob, and a week later, the police had come by to charge Babs with aggravated sexual assault. Danni knew about that charge; it'd been used against a man in Peterborough who'd raped a woman on campus and who'd beaten her to a pulp while doing it. The woman had nearly died.

Apparently, Babs hadn't told Bob that she had HIV, at least not at the beginning. Later, he'd found out and hadn't made an issue of it, but now that they'd broken up, he'd decided Babs needed to be punished. "He doesn't even fucking have HIV!" Serena shouted, and buried her face again in Danni's shoulder.

There was nowhere to sit on the sidewalk. Danni propped Serena up against a lamppost while she stroked her arm and told her all would be okay, but Danni's breathing quickened. She hadn't known this could happen — that it could happen to her — simply because she'd withheld information. Wasn't it everyone's responsibility to protect themselves? When she'd slipped up and suffered the consequences, Danni hadn't stopped cars on the stroll to find someone to blame. Could Wayne — or those two other guys — come after her, if they ever found out? Serena said the meeting upstairs was people organizing to get legal help. Danni comforted her more before giving her her email address and cellphone number. She made Serena promise to call if there were any demos, and Serena in return slapped a string of condom packages into Danni's hand and said, "And you promise to use these." Danni stared at the condoms. "Hey, I don't know if you're HIV or not," Serena continued. "I'm giving them to everyone. I might even give them to those church ladies over there." She pointed to the protesters. "We've gotta protect ourselves." Serena was wild-eyed, on a mission.

Danni pocketed the condoms and walked home. Monday morning couldn't come soon enough. They had five days to get ready for the fair. She couldn't think of her mother, of Babs, of Brad, or of anything else. She had to work through the next weekend, and she was glad for the overtime. For having something to occupy her. She'd finished her first trimester — it was the third week in May that she'd slept with Wayne — so she needed to figure something out soon. But this job mattered, and another week wouldn't be too, too late. She resolved to put her pregnancy to the side and deal with it after the fair was over.

Carlotta got tenser and snippier as the weekend approached. If she'd progressed, over the course of Danni's contract, to speaking to her in full sentences, she reverted to one- or two-word yaps to release her stress. "Delivery!" she snapped when a FedEx man was standing at reception with a package and Danni didn't jump out of her chair fast enough. "Politicians!" she yelled, remembering they weren't confirmed. Danni told her the local city councillor and school trustee had assured them they'd be there, and though the mayor's office was still dithering, she was on it. "Sound checks?" Organized. "Food vendors, Christ!" Her colleague Marcella had taken care of it, and the kiosk set-up was all planned. "Hydro?" All permits received, and set-up crews were in place. "Entertainment update?" Danni reassured her the performers were lined up and double-confirmed: the four bands, the magician, the dub poet who'd been eluding them, and a whacky, aging French-Canadian bottle-blonde psychic with a cable show who'd nicknamed herself Coquelicot and whose nauseating English catchphrase was, "We are love, we are light, like a dove, take flight!"

During lunches, she'd check her phone for texts. Nothing. On Wednesday night, when her regular NA group met, she decided not to go. It wasn't a forever decision, but this week was nuts, and she didn't need the stress of running into Brad, nor did she want to cause him embarrassment. Instead, she pulled out her copy of the NA White Booklet and came to a line that read, *We may tire mentally in repeating our new ideas and tire physically in our new activities, yet we know that if we fail to repeat them we will surely take up our old practices.* This one was less puzzling than the last, she decided; it was a small comfort to know others recognized the tedium she felt trying to get her life back on track, tedium that was broken up by this busy week.

On Saturday morning, the fair exploded; from the opening moments, people poured in as though to a timed shopping spree. They were lucky to have good weather; there'd been a chance of rain earlier in the week. The grounds filled with hundreds of souls — families, couples holding hands, children with face paint holding cotton candy chased by parents holding bags of popcorn. The air smelled of hot butter, beernuts, curry, and grilled jerk chicken. At one end of the grounds, the small merry-go-round played tinny melodies from another time, almost drowned out by the bands playing at the opposite end. In the middle, Danni stood at an info booth, aided by two eager community volunteers, tiny old Guyanese lady friends named Shirley and Betty who'd known each other since their childhood in Georgetown. Carlotta crackled orders through the walkie-talkies, and occasionally she'd stride by, her event T-shirt rolled up at the sleeves, lanyard of keys dangling at her neck.

At eleven o'clock, Danni stood from fetching brochures from a box and there in front of her stood Yen Mah, wearing a summer dress with an orange polka-dot pattern and carrying a large teddy bear. Beside her, holding her hand, stood the same younger man who'd answered Yen Mah's apartment door, towel around his waist, nearly a year before when Danni'd gone to ask if she knew where I'd gone. He wore his hair in a quilt of short Congolese braids and had beautiful smooth skin.

"Danni! You're so official! I hardly recognize you."

She shrieked and ran out from behind the booth. "Yen Mah, how are you!" The teddy bear's fur tickled her when the scruff of its neck touched hers. Danni held their hug so long that when she released it, poor Yen Mah scuffed a shoe in the dirt.

Danni stuck her hand out to the boyfriend. "I'm Danni. We've met, but you probably don't remember."

"Ethan." He shook her hand. "Nice to see you again."

She told Yen Mah all about her recovery, about her job.

"So you and Paulette, both on track. So good. You need a place to stay?"

Her unfaltering, bewildering generosity. "I'm okay, Yen Mah. I can't believe, after everything, you'd still be willing to let me move in."

"You're nice person. The place is big for me."

This was completely untrue. "What about Ethan?"

"She's an independent woman," he said. "I keep trying to get her to shack up, but she won't have me."

Yen Mah elbowed him and smiled. "Ethan will grow tired of his older woman soon." He shook his head. They were crazy about each other, anyone could tell.

They spoke a while longer — Danni filled her in on me and where I was working. From a distance, Carlotta frowned at Danni, so she told Yen Mah she had to get back to work and she hoped they'd enjoy themselves. "Check out the woman selling the spicy beef patties. They're delicious." They hugged again, and Yen Mah and Ethan disappeared into the crowd.

The day zoomed by, with lots of minor problems to solve and a steady stream of people asking for directions. At seven, Danni took her break, grabbed two slices of pizza that Carlotta had ordered for staff, and went to sit on a plastic chair near the stage. She people-watched for fifteen minutes, listening to a reggae band with a female bass guitarist. When the crowd drunkenly shouted the chorus to "One Love," she spied Borka and Wayne swaying up near the front. The fair was only blocks from their daytime hangout; it made sense they'd take a break for some fun. Borka wore a sleeveless hausfrau dress that she'd accessorized with a clashing headscarf. Wayne sported a loose tank top, khaki shorts, and Jesus sandals; when he moved his hips, Danni's hand went unconsciously to her belly. Small backpacks lay at their feet.

She'd promised Borka a visit, and hadn't been by. They'd spy her for sure; her booth was in the centre of the grounds, and the grounds were small. After being approached by Yen Mah, she couldn't face another encounter where people she'd sponged off and later abandoned made the first move. She wove through the crowd and put her hand on Borka's shoulder. Borka flinched, but then, recognizing her, covered her mouth with both hands. "Danni! This is nice surprise!" She enveloped Danni in her meaty arms. A rank odour: she'd forgotten how challenged they'd all been in the area of hygiene.

"Hey, stranger." Wayne gave her a light tap on the arm. His scent was more pleasant; perhaps he'd bathed and done laundry. And he'd definitely splashed something on before coming to the fair — Old Spice and patchouli mixed with a heat that wasn't from the late summer air.

She moved back for a better vantage point, as far as she could, given that they were boxed in by others watching the band. "Did you get a haircut?" It was shorter than it'd been, neatly trimmed and parted at the side. He told her Sara did it, that she was quite talented but hated it, so he only imposed every two months.

"You never visit us," shouted Borka. Her bluntness came as no surprise.

She apologized, told her things'd been busy and that she had a job. When Wayne asked her to repeat herself, she shoved him. "Yes, I have a job! Don't be so surprised. I helped to organize this street fair."

Borka crossed her arms. "No excuse. You should still come visit."

"I know. I will. But ..." She was going to say she was in recovery, but she wasn't practised in this. What was the convention so that she wouldn't sound judgmental of Wayne and the others? "Maybe in a few weeks when we wrap things up." In a few weeks, if she did nothing about the pregnancy, she'd be showing. What would Wayne say, what would he do, if he knew? Hug her, excited to be a father? Blanch and run away?

"Come here, *dragi*, I cannot stay mad." Borka enveloped her again, pressed hard, and messed up her hair in the back with her hands. They danced together until the song ended, Danni doing the bump between them. She told them to come by before they left.

As the sun dropped below the red brick Regent Park homes, her shift dragged more and more. Hardly anyone came to the booth. Carlotta released Shirley and Betty, telling them they could return tomorrow. It was a steamy end-of-August night. People were getting louder and rowdier and cared less about where to go and what to do.

Burly volunteers dealt with boozy scuffles, including one between an idiot who swung the mallet used for the high striker strength test at his friend. Fortunately, he didn't have Danni's drunken aim. He was escorted off the grounds.

She was more on edge with the scent of warm spilled beer all around her. She recalled a family friend telling a story about aversion therapy she'd done to kick smoking, in which they filled a jar of water with cigarette butts, soaked it for days in the heat, and passed it under her nose to revolt her. Instead, the smell was delicious. That was how it was for Danni: the spilled draft was syrupy, hoppy, and while it wasn't her drink of choice, it wafted a warm familiarity. The scent of a kind of fun that would never again be hers.

There was still another day of this to get through, and when eleven o'clock neared, Danni was glad it'd soon be over — for now. At a quarter to the hour, Wayne returned. He was more than half in the bag. He sauntered behind the booth to stand with her, pretending to be there to help.

"Moron," she said and shook her head. "Where's Borka?"

He laughed and grabbed her by the waist, his hands moving down over her ass. "She left." Danni placed her hands against his hips, at first to push him away, but he pulled her tighter and she let herself enjoy the intimacy. For a moment.

"Wayne. You're drunk."

"It didn't stop you last time."

It should have, she thought, but she closed her eyes and breathed him in. When she opened them, off in the distance was Brad, standing with a hot dog, alone near a carnival game, staring. He turned and left. Shit. Yen Mah, Borka, Wayne, they'd all come by the fair because they lived or hung out in the neighbourhood, but not Brad. She pushed Wayne off her. "I have to finish my shift."

"Okay, I'll be over by the stage if you want to find me."

She had no intention of doing so. Her stomach tightened, and with it came a memory of her childhood gastric problems. Fifteen minutes later, the music died mid-song. Danni pictured Carlotta behind the stage, fed up, yanking the power cord from its socket. The crowd thinned, but fairgoers lingered as volunteers picked up garbage and stray plastic beer cups. She didn't need to be on cleanup duty; they'd organized another crew for that, so Carlotta released her. She grabbed her shoulder bag and was leaving when Wayne sidled up.

"Show me your apartment."

"You're happy tonight," she said, looking away.

"And you're beautiful."

"Corny," she chided.

"Horny," he shot back.

They fell silent. She let him walk next to her. She couldn't bring herself to invite him back to her place, but she also said nothing to get him to leave. She shoved her hands in the pockets of her shorts, in case he grabbed one. When they got to her building, she stood between him and the door, and he raised his eyebrows. "Ah, fuck it," she said, and unlocked it. It hadn't been what she'd hoped, last time, but it never was the first time. Didn't she deserve closeness, tenderness? Did life have to be a series of denials? Abstinence in all areas? He followed, hands on her waist, two people in a conga line.

In her apartment, he cast his eyes about and declared it nice, which she supposed it was, in comparison to where Wayne lived. He pulled off his shirt. Undressed Danni while she fixed her eyes on his toes. She grabbed one of the condoms that Serena had given her, made sure he used one this time, alarmed by what she'd learned about Babs. Maybe out of concern for Wayne, though she didn't want to admit it. Lying on her back, she readied herself for him.

But in that moment, she didn't want him there anymore. Embarrassed to be so hot and cold, she faked it and went to a special place —

a white sand beach in Bali. She'd seen a picture in a magazine. When she closed her eyes, a tan parasol covered a pair of chaises longues. Wayne moved in her, but she saw palms swaying, heard aquamarine waters lapping the shore. When it was over, in a matter of fifteen minutes, he rolled on his side, facing her, and drifted off.

Her arm was stuck under him. She counted her breaths. His back was to an open window through which a breeze ruffled the gauze curtains. His snoring — supposedly impossible if you lay on your side — was extra loud because it was in her face. Not to mention foul. Beer and sauerkraut. The snoring competed with the shrill meowing of a tomcat in the back alley. The after-scent of his Old Spice-slash-patchouli was annoying. She concentrated on loosening her lungs and ridding herself of an intense pressure pinning her to the mattress, strongest on her left arm, the one underneath him, but all down her body. Her arm was paralyzed, not part of her. If she could've cut it off, she wouldn't have missed it.

Dizziness. The floor next to the bed sloped away. Maybe all her breath counting had made her woozy. Her legs dimly ached. She felt pulsing from above, from the side, from underneath. Like when she'd done K once in a loud club and got stuck in a trance while time passed unnoticed. She'd been standing close to a speaker, the music too loud to recognize any kind of melody. The bass's seismic vibrations had rippled her flesh.

Another snore, and Wayne rolled onto his back. His snoring amped up, but Danni's muscles unclenched as her sense of being pinned eased — with the exception of her left arm, still trapped by her mind, despite the fact that he'd released it when he'd rolled away. The rest of her entered a state of sensory confusion. Either she was racked with pain, the hurt so widespread that she was experiencing it as white noise, or else nothing ached anymore. It angered her that she couldn't tell which it was.

Her lower abdomen cramped again. She lifted her head from the pillow and followed her body's landscape. Her stomach was flat, no sign yet. Perhaps the twinge was the beginning of a miscarriage and she wouldn't have to go through the trouble of an abortion, or the greater trouble of raising a child. A child who might be born with HIV, maybe doomed to a life of sickliness. And later, when it grew up, to celibacy, for fear of becoming a sex offender.

Danni felt foolish; it was ridiculous to entertain this pregnancy for a minute, let alone three months. If she'd ever believed it'd help her stay off drugs, well, what a laugh. If anything, it'd weakened her resolve. If she'd ever had a fantasy of the child knowing its father, the man snoring beside her had woken her from that daydream. Worst of all, this pregnancy had stolen her control of her body, control she'd fought for years to regain. No, that was another lie. She'd never been in control; at best, she'd coped. She'd been managing — everything, everyone — which, as any streetwalker knew, was a poor substitute for real control. Each step she'd taken to achieve control, each life decision she'd hoped would be a door to an up staircase, had ended with her tripping, tumbling down. When she'd black-mailed her stepfather, she was crafty and powerful, but one day, at twenty-three, she was hooked on painkillers, her relationship with her mom devastated.

The stripping away of these last self-delusions felt like a flaying. She was raw; her life's losses, and each of the past few months' gains, were seeping into the dense air of the apartment. She turned to Wayne, still snoring, wishing he was Brad. Danni lifted her arm to feel between her legs. It was wet, and not with blood. The touch released a flash, which she smothered by snapping her eyes open and blinking in the shadowy gloom. She wiped her hand on the sheet. Nausea shuddered through her.

When she first went to NA, an addict had likened the long road ahead of her to baking a cake, to combining measured ingredients into something rewarding. It was an unsanctioned analogy, so the woman had whispered it. Officially, the twelve steps were a process never finished, unlike a pie or a batch of brownies. The advice had seemed helpful until weeks later when Danni ruined an actual cake by mixing the dry and wet ingredients in one fell swoop, and by opening the oven to check on it every ten minutes. When she pulled out the dense, weapon-like object, she understood that baking was more complicated. Skill, patience, and the sequencing of those damned steps were crucial. If kicking drugs and alcohol was like baking a cake, she felt the oven door opening too soon.

She closed her eyes to quell a prickliness in her chest cavity. When she reached a count of two hundred, she pulled back the covers and sat up. The air was close. She shook Wayne. "You have to go. I can't sleep."

Without protesting, as if this'd happened to him often, he picked up his clothes and dressed. "I had fun," he offered, still groggy, and made his way to the door. "I wish we could've spent the night together." Did he think this might convince her to change her mind? Or maybe see him again?

"I want to, I do. But I can't sleep."

Shame and sadness pulsed in equal measures. The white lie that she wanted to spend the night with him had blown apart her pretence of toughness and reduced it to rubble. Was there no way for her to have sex anymore without its feeling like she was pleasing a trick — or worse?

"You had fun too, didn't you?" he asked.

"A bit full of yourself, aren't you?"

He laughed, but in a way that told her she'd hit her mark.

She waited until he left, lay still a minute and tried to fall asleep. She continued counting her breaths. It wasn't working. Her resolve was waning, a timer counting down with each heartbeat.

Collapse

DANNI PULLED ON HER BLOUSE, CARGO PANTS, SANDALS, AND HOODIE, and grabbed her purse. Shortly afterward, she stood on the street listening to a distant siren. The 505 streetcar stopped near her; its doors hissed, and a woman exited. It must've been the last one for the night, or close to it. There was a telltale twitchiness to the woman. The streetcar clattered on its way. The woman headed east at a fair clip; Danni watched her for maybe thirty paces as she hurried to her next fix.

From there on in, there was no thinking. Her muscles contracted, revived by a secret code. She walked head down in the direction the woman had gone. She clamped her eyes shut to stem the onset of tears. They'd be cooling on her cheek, but she wouldn't allow herself the pleasure. She counted the blocks until she reached Parliament Street, banishing all feeling except the growing anger that she had no money.

At the corner, she had to call someone. Her sponsor, maybe, though she'd never called her like this before. Maybe me. Maybe I'd talk her back to her apartment or invite her to mine. She reached into her purse and cursed. She'd forgotten her cellphone. She grabbled for cash in a pocket of her cargo pants, then another, and another.

If she were to find a quarter and a phone booth nearby, she'd take it as a sign she should swallow her pride and call me. She had fifteen cents, not enough. Staring at the coins, she accepted the uselessness of it, of believing she could ask for help, the stupidity of thinking to call in the first place. It felt like what remained of her free will had evaporated in the night heat.

She couldn't go to Mario until she had cash. A dilemma balanced in front of her —whether to use the rest of the little money in her bank account or earn quick cash. Savings or income, simple as that.

Back in the day, when we were in it together, when she and I didn't have a bank account, there wasn't this option of an ATM from which a fix could be funded. We knew only one way to get it fast. If she had to stand on a street corner again, well, there was no dwelling on it. It'd been five years since her first time, nearly four months since the last. A strategy to get back on track later by not draining her measly assets. *There may be times when a relapse lays the groundwork for complete freedom.* She got it now. Now it was comforting.

Ignoring the doughy thickening in her throat, she walked back west along Dundas, to Jarvis, and up the street. Her group had warned her that she couldn't expect to use once and go back to abstinence with a snap of the fingers. It depressed her that she'd have to fess up to everything. She'd deal with the silent criticism: you didn't judge people in NA, but it was frustrating knowing that all her time drug-free would ultimately get discounted, ignored. What about a cumulative count? From a harm reduction perspective, wasn't any time not using better than none? It wasn't fair that the clock had to be reset.

She searched her purse again and applied mascara and lipstick with long, shaky strokes, fixing the mistakes in her compact mirror. She rubbed a touch of the lipstick into the apples of her cheeks and fought a rising nausea. The rouge would compensate for the weak street lights and promote the fantasy that drew men away from wives, girlfriends, or the loneliness of rejection to a showier, more shameless sexuality, one that said, "My business is pleasure, my pleasure is you, and I'm a sure thing — for a price."

Not much had changed on Jarvis Street, except that some girls were new and some had moved on, or maybe were in jail, like Babs. There was a measure of pavement that wasn't being worked, and she hesitated before stepping towards the curb. Hooking wasn't unlike the theatre, and she'd applied her greasepaint. She took off her hoodie, tied it around her waist, tightened her shirt strategically, and stood on her mark.

An hour and a half later, she tried but failed to find Ülle, so she walked back to Parliament Street, to the building where she knew she'd find Mario, at the entrance to 200 Oak. He was still dealing.

He left the glow of the creepy, over-bright lobby and approached Danni in the gloom, scanning her head to toe.

"Look at you! We figured you were dead."

"Forty worth." Enough for a half of an eight ball, which would do her for a while. She hunched into the warmth of her hoodie.

He leaned in, waited for more. She'd been a talker, that Danni. I shifted easily to street talk when I needed to, but Danni'd been known for using big words and telling jokes, so when she shouted, "Now!" he was taken aback. "And I lost my pipe if you've got one. And if you've got screens, I'll take those too." She handed him money and held out her palm. A cooling wind had kicked up, but it carried the faint stench of garbage from a dumpster. She curled an arm around her waist.

"Okay, keep your panties on." Mario pulled baggies from his inside coat pocket, handed her one with small discs of metal screen, and a wooden push stick, and reached into his other pocket for a blade to divide the chunk of rock. Working on the edge of a planter, he had the focused concentration of a pharmacist. The fingertips of his gloves were severed, and his nail beds were blue and cracked.

She fidgeted. "I've always wanted to ask you: why do you work here, Mario? I mean in this spot. The cops can see you, the tenants harass you, and your poor clients are hideous in this light." She considered her pasty skin, the fresh acne that stippled the space between her brows.

"Meh." He shrugged. "It's good business." Mario had vampire-blue veins and dark circles under his bloodshot eyes. *The Lost Boys* was his favourite movie. He gave zero shits about standing under fluorescent light.

She fanned her nose, grimacing. "Goddamn, your breath smells like turds. You better not breathe on any of the girls while they're blowing you or they might puke all over your dick."

"I'm so huge, that sometimes happens anyway." His smile exposed his stained teeth. He pulled a stick of Juicy Fruit from his jeans pocket, popped it in his mouth. "I missed you. You always make me laugh. Where you been, Danni? You and Paulette up and disappeared. You didn't go and try to get yourselves clean, did ya?"

She opened her palm again and stomped her foot. The gum barely improved his breath.

He held the pipe and baggie of rock, taunting her. "Well?"

She snatched them. "I've been around!"

He raised his hands and backed away.

Ten minutes later, nerves supercharged, eyes blinking, thighs tight and keen as jackhammers, Danni walked to the stretch of Gerrard Street between Sherbourne and Jarvis. The Brock Clinic was housed in a three-storey red brick building that'd been a family home at one time. The street was barren. There might've been protesters if she'd come during the day. The clinic's front room had a picture window. A security cam surveyed the front yard and sidewalk, so she pulled up her sweatshirt's hood and tucked her hair down. Coming here might not help her make up her mind, but she needed to touch it, to imagine one outcome to her dilemma.

A car raced the light at Sherbourne and whizzed by. She ducked into the gap next to the clinic. Her nostrils crinkled from the smell of piss as she cradled her pipe and made sure the screen from her first hit was still in place. She nudged a piece of rock into the tip of the pipe, and lit up. The sweetness reached her before she wrapped her lips around the opening. Cotton candy mixed with burning plastic and a hint of cleanser. She drew the delicious, stinging smoke into her lungs. The euphoria set in, and she leaned against the house next door. Once again, her chest soared, her body eased.

Fifteen minutes later, slumped forward, ass in the dirt, she pressed her soles against the opposite wall. She sucked on a breath mint to get rid of the metallic tang left from the smoke. A car drove down the lane behind the building, its headlights flooding the gap, and Danni within it. An old Chevy, maybe an Impala. Its engine fell silent, a door clicked open. A dozen or so short hisses followed, like paint being sprayed — someone spraying graffiti? Footsteps approached the back of the clinic. In the distance an ambulance whined.

Danni clenched her ass, one cheek at a time, in order to shift her body side to side, a metronome working at a frenzied pace. From behind the clinic came the unmistakeable squeal of a drill hitting metal. She stilled herself, a near impossibility. The street was lined with houses. Why weren't neighbours complaining?

After the drilling came another sound she couldn't identify followed by the *glug-glug* of running liquid. Danni stuffed her pipe and the baggie with her last bit of rock into the front pocket of her sweatshirt. Her legs twitched and bounced until she pushed them back against the opposite wall and wriggled her way up to vertical. She crept to the back of the alley. Words were spray-painted on the fence behind the clinic's parking lot, but they were too dark to read. A post blocked her view of whoever was still making noise.

She stepped sideways. A floodlight fixed to the building's corner illuminated a shallow stoop at the top of stairs leading to the back door. The figure, just shy of six feet, stocky and broad-shouldered, was clearly male. A hood hid his face. His head was lowered, his feet rested on different steps.

The drill, horror-movie huge, hung at his hip. A can of spray paint stood on the top step beside a red plastic jug with a long-necked spout. The man fiddled with the end of a candle. He took a match, lit the candle's twisted wick, and shoved it through the hole he'd made in the door.

Dread and a surge of bile. The jug held gasoline. The candle was to set a fire. The man gathered his things and ran to the car.

Danni's limbs seized, but she pressed them into service. Hot again, she wanted to tear at her clothes, at her raw, tender skin.

Her instinct being to avoid him, she didn't flee down the lane but instead backtracked to the gap between the buildings. She ran towards Gerrard Street, down the narrowing, tilting space that was barely wide enough for her shoulders. Her drugs and pipe fell, and she stooped to find them in the dirt. Over the sound of her wheezing breath, Danni heard the car tires spinning and scraping.

Then the building blew.

Obliteration

I COULDN'T BLAME DANNI FOR ONE LAST STUPID, AWFUL, BEAUTIFUL night. Who could blame any of us for surrendering to such mercy?

When Danni awoke, her left leg was under a pile of rubble. The blast had hit her from behind, its force thrusting her diagonally into one of the gap's brick walls. Obliteration-wise, this was better than crack. More efficient. She chuckled, a low rumble broken by coughing. *Lying. Under. Rubble.* She spoke the words aloud. She yelled, *Crack hooer!*

Carlotta would be disappointed in her, she thought, when she didn't show up for work, when it turned out Danni was a hot mess who'd died in the wreckage of a building.

The night sky was so lovely. She winced from the throbbing in her temples, felt her forehead, sucked blood off her fingertips. They were cold. Her mom's face. But she wouldn't be standing there above her. The announcement of a grandchild might've been the reason Danni'd been searching for — a pretence to call after the estrangement. She could reach her in time before the move. No, she couldn't call, not after this. Even if she hadn't been blown into a pile of bricks, the idea would've been unwise. Her mom would recognize the pregnancy for the slip-up that it was and be further disappointed.

It was still dark. The spring air left a chalky coating on her face, cool and soothing. Maybe the universe was telling her something. Maybe she'd miscarry and there'd be no decision to make.

Looking up at the stars, Danni floated into nothingness.

The Rest of Your Life

RECOVERY IS LIKE BEING TOLD, SURPRISE! YOU'RE A BUILDING FOREMAN for a house that you're raising, and that house has to withstand the rest of your life. There are instructions, you're told, but — and with zero training — you still have to build it yourself. What do you think is going to happen on the first try? When I heard Danni was in the hospital, the circumstance surprised me, sure, but not the fact that she'd relapsed. I wasn't smug. I'd had my first relapse and was trying like hell to learn from my mistakes.

The police searched Danni's pockets for identification. An officer had gone to her apartment, powered up her phone, and my number was in it. The call came midway through my shift at Timothy's, and I ignored it because I was serving customers. At my break, I checked messages and said, "Holy shit, Gregor!" — I used his real name to show I was serious — "Please can I leave early? My good friend was injured in that Brock Clinic bombing." Minister was sympathetic; there were times when he needed to take his manager hat off and be a human being. He released me, and off I went to St. Mike's.

She was in rough shape: a sprained ankle, a head bandage, an IV pole and tubes attached to her arm, and a catheter. But she'd been lucky. No serious injuries. A minor concussion.

She didn't see it that way. When the nurse said, "Don't worry, you didn't lose the baby," Danni spat, "Fucking hell" and closed her eyes. The nurse eased herself out of the room.

"All those years of not getting pregnant, and a bomb couldn't dislodge this goddamned sprog," she said when we were alone. I asked what she'd been doing in that alley, pretty sure of the answer, and her story croaked and squawked from her gravelly throat, maybe driven by shame and frustration. She remembered her job and cursed more. The second day of the fair had already started, she was extremely late for work, and this was not just any workday.

I went to talk to Carlotta, to tell her what'd happened, or at least a prepared, semi-fictitious version of it. Carlotta was in the middle of the fair madness, wearing a sleeveless tank top and cargo shorts, a thousand keys jangling around her neck. She passed a hand through her short, dark hair and handled a logistics problem with a firm gentleness that sent a flush fanning upwards from my collarbone. I detected baby powder and a spicy cologne.

I introduced myself, shook her hand, and gave her the news that Danni was in the hospital, that she was the one they were talking about on TV. Carlotta put a hand in her pocket and the other over her mouth. The story I gave was that Danni was restless, couldn't sleep, went for a walk, thought she heard a dog whimpering in the alley, followed the sound, and was at the wrong place at the wrong time. I assured her Danni wasn't seriously hurt. If my instincts about Carlotta were correct, she smelled the whimpering dog story as the load of shit it was but didn't let on. I had a good sense about this woman. She had the carriage of someone who'd known hard times herself and had pulled out of it through hardscrabble stick-to-it-iveness.

"Danni's very upset not to be here today," I said, and made my pitch that she not be fired, that maybe they could have her job waiting for her when Danni was released from the hospital.

"Unfortunately, Danni's job was all about this fair, which is over today, and then we have a week of wrap-up and it's all done. I can't do anything about that, but Danni's a good worker. I was meaning to offer her another contract in the youth sports and rec program. You tell her to get better and swing by on those crutches."

"Thank you. What a great party you've got going here. So do you do this every —"

She put her finger up to cut me off because two people were waiting to speak with her, and one of them was asking a question over top of mine. She was busy, and at this point I was wasting her time.

I stepped back, pretended to tie my sneaker, knowing I should leave. A waft of cotton candy and beernuts overwhelmed me. By the time I stood, she was free. "Hey, do you need help with anything?" I jumped forward again. "My boss gave me the rest of the day off, and with Danni not here, you know, if you need a volunteer ..."

"Okay. Gimme a minute here." She smiled and turned to deal with another three fires that were burning in line. She had beautiful teeth, with sexy lines around the edges of her mouth. "Sorry." She came back to me. "I'm grateful for the offer. Normally we do a big orientation with volunteers, but I shouldn't look a gift horse in the mouth. You see those old ladies over there behind the booth?"

"The ones I could fit in my pocket?"

"Those ones. They could use a hand, and that's where Danni was stationed. The job's easy, just point people to their destination. It's all on a map behind the booth. Anything major, and Shirley and Betty have a walkie-talkie." Another problem announced itself over said walkie-talkie. She smiled again, handed me a lanyard from her pocket that read *Volunteer*, and ran off.

I flipped open my cell and called Danni to tell her that despite the fact that she'd neglected to tell me how smoking hot her boss was, I'd overlooked this and helped secure Danni's next job. And that on top of that, I was doing her current one for her. I might've over-stated things, but Danni was happy. She said, "You are not allowed to date my boss. Besides, I don't even know what her situation is."

"You are in no position to call the shots." I felt bold. "Besides, you owe me big-time. I put in a good word for you. Now maybe you can do the same?"

"I hate you."

"You love me, because I'm adorable and I'm your best friend." I ended the call and walked over to the booth.

They released Danni three days later, and in between she endured police questioning. Grainy stills from a security cam showed that the bomber was a much taller person than Danni, probably a man, and that only one person had emerged from the car that had delivered him to the back laneway. Even so, they needed to determine if her suspicious presence meant any connection. What helped Danni was discussing her pregnancy and her political views, and disclosing her intentions: she'd made an appointment at the Mendelssohn Clinic on Harbord, where the Brock procedures would be performed until they could rebuild in a new location.

It took Danni two weeks before she was ready to go back to work, but before she did, I picked her up for her appointment. We took a taxi, a breeze ruffling her hair through its window. It was mid-September, but there was still not much relief from the heat, except at night.

She hung her head outside the taxi window like a spaniel. "Maybe it'll break once this is done."

"Yes, the universe does revolve around events in your life." I laughed.

"Can you let me have this fantasy?"

I put my hand on her leg. "You okay? You ready for this?"

"Oh, sure. Hey, can you put on the air conditioning?" The driver did so and rolled up the window. Then to me, "These cramps from the hoo-ha they put in my cervix yesterday, holy moly. Who would've guessed that a tiny stick of dried seaweed could be so fucking painful?" We passed two more lights. "I should've had it done on Labour Day, you know, for the irony. But I was busy that day getting treated for a concussion."

What she didn't say was that she should've done this long before that, or not at all, but maybe those were my feelings. She was having an abortion in the second trimester, and each additional week meant a more invasive, more complicated procedure. Another week where I imagined a baby like my Aaron or my Chantelle. I took a deep breath. "It's okay to be nervous. It's gonna be fine."

The taxi stopped down a side street. With her gripping my arm, Danni and I made our way to the front of the clinic. Protesters paced across the street. "Buffer zone," mumbled Danni. She didn't look. "They can't come any closer." One of them, a man, held a sign with a gruesome bloody picture that read, *Abortion: the ultimate child abuse.* Danni's eyes fixed themselves on the clinic door, and I followed suit.

Once inside, we sat in plush chairs and she distracted herself with magazines. Four other women waited beside us. Two appeared to be in their early forties and wore smart business attire. A young woman in jeans and a T-shirt sat with her mother, who was wearing a hijab. A counsellor named Sheri came to the waiting area and asked how Danni was. She leaned forward in her chair and winced.

"That's the laminaria doing its work. It's normal. It'll be over soon." She showed Danni to the changing area, where she put on a gown before the nurse took her into the procedure room, and I went back to my chair to wait for her.

It took about an hour.

When she emerged from the recovery room, the relief showed on her face, in her shoulders, and in the way she relaxed into the chair beside me. They gave her antibiotics, pads for any bleeding, medicine to help her uterus contract to its regular size, and Tylenol for the cramping that she'd feel with the contractions. The receptionist handed me a package of information about how she was supposed to take care of herself afterwards and a number to call if needed.

Back at her apartment, I settled Danni into her bed and asked how she was.

"I know I should feel guilty." She pulled a pillow to her stomach. "But I don't."

"Guilt's overrated."

"You know, those protesters. The fuckers." Her voice rose. "They say that women like me are selfish, choosing my own life over the life of another. But for me, and I don't mean any offence by this, Paulie, 'cause we're all different, but having a baby in my circumstances would've been more selfish."

"Why is that?"

"Because I kept hoping it'd help me stay in recovery."

I nodded. "I deluded myself with that one, too."

She closed her eyes, and her head settled into the pillow. She reached out to squeeze my hand. I told her there was lots of time for her to be a mother.

"When it's right," she said. "I mean, we couldn't have loved Aaron more, but ..."

Her voice trailed off. Thinking it might be better for both of us if I finished her sentence, I added, "... it wasn't enough."

On Monday, Danni went into the community centre and spoke to Carlotta about the sports and rec job. Carlotta hired her on the spot and gave Danni her paycheque, which included pay for the missed time. Danni threw her arms around Carlotta, who raised her arms in the air and endured the hug.

Danni must've put in a good word for me, too, that day, because later I got a call from Carlotta asking if I wanted to go for coffee. I'd always had to be the one taking the lead, and this was new and awesome and terrifying. What would this woman make of my history? Of my future? I hadn't told Danni this yet, but nine to five for minimum wage and no benefits was not gonna be my life. What would happen the next time I suffered another spell of depression?

Deedee and Mariko were willing to bring me into their arrangement, though I'd have to find a nice apartment of my own, one that said high-class call girl, not two-bit ho. These girls were teaching me how to carve myself a new niche market, using ads and word of mouth. How to recreate my image to attract a different kind of clientele. How to vet tricks properly. They were smart as hell. With cellphones and the internet changing the business, it was becoming common for girls to post ads and do outcalls from their apartments. Deedee and Mariko didn't hang around the streets. And they swore they'd cut me loose if they caught one whiff of my using drugs. I was never one to bend to threats, but that one I liked.

Danni and I were different birds, she'd get that. Once I explained it, she'd see this wasn't backsliding. For one thing, she was the one who'd had trouble with the sex, not me. It was the other shit that got me down: the risk of assault; the sketchiness of a life chasing drug money; the grinding poverty; the streets. The winters. There'd still be danger, but if I was clever, stayed with the program, and enrolled in the City Adult Learning Centre, I'd get ahead. Make myself a life. Put aside a healthy contingency fund for those times depression buried me alive. For when I got too old for the business in another fifteen years. That was my window, and I'd make sure I had some other skill before it closed.

That night in my room, I shut my eyes in a chair beside my bed, appreciating the quiet. After a while, I called Danni to check in. Her voice was tired, but calm and centred. In not so many words, she announced that she'd decided not to be an idiot who squandered her blessings because of one pervert who was long gone. She was going to get her ass into therapy. And she'd contact her mom, rebuild connections. The advantages Danni'd grown up with were a set of misplaced keys, and when she found them, doors would fly open again. It'd already started.

I asked how she was feeling about the procedure. Completely fine, she said. What was clear was that it was done and, unlike so many decisions she'd made — from a place of greed, arrogance, spite, or plain old fear — she'd have no regrets, not this time. She reassured me it had been no worse than a bad period. Nothing she couldn't handle.

"That," I said, "I never doubted."

Notes and Acknowledgements

Early inspiration for this story was the too-short life of Kim Johnson, a woman whom I had the pleasure of working with and calling a friend. When I met Kim in 2003, we were colleagues at the Toronto People with AIDS Foundation, where she was coordinating their Speakers' Bureau. She spoke publicly and engagingly about her then former crack cocaine use, her previous sex work, the joys and struggles of motherhood, and being a woman — and a lesbian — living with HIV. The dignity and power of her storytelling inspired many, in part because she refused to be seen as a victim.

In the two years after we worked together, Kim was generous enough to grant me several long interviews in aid of this project. The first consisted of her reflections on a life she thought she'd left behind, but the last, most painful interviews occurred in December 2007, after she began using drugs again and wanted to stop but couldn't. At that point, worried she couldn't properly parent her son, she sent him to live with her ex-partner. In the end, Kim's and my conversations were far more intimate than I could have predicted. She described her in-the-moment life without censorship or self-pity. She spoke with breathtaking self-awareness and a heartbreaking mixture of self-deprecating humour and sadness. Kim Johnson died in July 2009 from an overdose.

Kim's is only one story of drug use. In sharp contrast, some drug users handily and happily manage their drug use for years, even decades. I've had the pleasure of meeting, working with, and supporting some of these people in my local and international global health work as they fight for better rights and services. For these activists, lumping all frequent drug users into the category of "addict" is a problem. And, given that many are parents of healthy and successful adult children, they are understandably concerned that the oft-repeated narrative of the neglectful drug-using parent will only bring further misunderstanding and stigma upon them.

They worry not only that this narrative leads people to believe it is true of all drug-using parents but that, even in real cases of child neglect, it places the blame squarely on the parent, on the drug, or on both. It tends to absolve our society of the responsibility to find better ways to keep children safe and keep families together. As for the large, hidden, overlooked population of capable and attentive drug-using parents, Imogen Byrne, daughter of my friend Jude Byrne, has written an enlightening thesis on her mother and others like her, who lovingly raised their children in safe and stable homes.

These contrasting stories — Kim Johnson's on the one hand and Jude and Imogen Byrne's on the other — are parallel truths. Some people manage drug use well, and others cannot. The common thread of these parallel truths, at least for parents, is how stigma and criminalization conspire against them. They are the double whammy that isolates families from services and support and that facilitates the endangerment of drug-using parents and their children. The same can be said of sex work. Colleagues who are current or former sex workers have taught me much about dignity and courage in the face of scorn, about what it means to make a living in a social and legal environment stacked against you. And about a social service system without appropriate child care that then blames sex worker mothers who must choose between two terrible options: do I feed my child, but risk leaving her in a situation that may or may not be safe, or do I stay with my child and let her go hungry because I can't take her to work?

Finding solutions to these social and legal failures is our collective responsibility.

One of this novel's challenges was how to use narrative voice to achieve my storytelling goals without misappropriating other people's stories. This book is a tribute to dear and courageous friends and colleagues, living and dead. My friend Kim Johnson started her life with white, middle-class privilege, as I did, but other friends have faced far greater social or systemic barriers. When one is a male writer, writing from a female perspective is already an exercise in imaginative empathy, but choosing Paulette as narrator instead of Danni was an intentional exercise to help me see Danni from a social location very different from my own. Writing in the first person is an intimate process for a novelist. Seeing Danni through Paulette's eyes allowed me to viscerally explore and critique the unconscious biases of people who wish to be allies — as I do — but who may not yet fully recognize how our privilege shapes our world view. In that way, it was a literary and a socio-political project, the success of which won't be mine to judge.

An exercise of imaginative empathy requires research and a generous community of people willing to lend you their stories. These are the many people in that community that I must thank for their trust:

- On the subject of managed drug use, harm reduction, and activism related to people who use drugs: Jude Byrne, who read with an eye to drug use authenticity, and Julia Barnett, Imogen Byrne, Jay Levy, and Maria Phelan;

- On living with or recovering from unmanaged drug use, or on the subject of detox, treatment, and twelve-step culture: Bryan Grant, Tammy Mackenzie, Tatiana Russell, Vanessa Russell, Darryl Wright, and, of course, the late Kim Johnson;

- For general mentorship in my understanding of the issues facing sex workers: my colleagues across the globe fighting for sex worker rights and services, and in particular Duduzile Dlamini, Ruth Morgan Thomas, Daisy Nakato, and Erastus Ndunda — and also the Maggie's Toronto Sex Workers Action Project for their excellent online resources;

- Of all the challenges in writing this story, perhaps most daunting was writing a believable Black female narrator. I'm therefore extremely grateful to Beth Jordan and Kimahli Powell for their gentle critiques and for their specific and helpful notes and edits;

- On the lives and struggles of transgender women living in poverty: colleagues Leigh Davids and JoAnne Keatley;

- For insight and information into HIV treatments between 2003 and 2008, and their particular effects on women: Maggie Atkinson and Tim McCaskell;

- On issues related to incarceration and criminal trials: my uncle, Bob Kellermann;

- On the subject of Canada's history of overly broad criminalization of people living with HIV in sexual relationships: Edwin Bernard and Richard Elliot;

- On the difficulties that HIV-positive women face, because of stigma, in finding sexual and romantic relationships, I looked for inspiration to Laurette Lévy's brilliant and achingly personal

2007 novel *Debout en clair-obscur*, and to conversations with Laurette and other friends at the time of her novel's release;

- On abortion procedures, and on the historical threats faced by the Toronto clinics: Sharon Broughton, Maria Corsillo, Carolyn Egan, Sheri Krieger, and my mother, Ruth Miller;

- Regarding the investigation into the unsolved 1992 bombing of the Morgentaler Clinic: Staff Sergeant John Boyce of Toronto Police Services;

- On child protection services and proceedings in Ontario, and on eviction procedures under the Ontario Landlord and Tenant Act: Patricia Swerhone and A.J. Pittis, respectively;

- For her careful copy-editing, thanks to Andrea Waters.

Finally, for their encouragement, comments, and reading of early drafts, thanks go to Sally Cooper, Emily Donaldson, Elizabeth Ruth, and my agent, Beverley Slopen, but most of all to my editor, Marc Côté. In 2013, Marc read a very different manuscript. He saw its potential, he saw mine, and, while we hadn't previously worked together, he encouraged me along a difficult rewrite. For his having pushed me to another level, this novel is deeper, rawer, and — though nothing like my mostly charmed life — the most personal piece of fiction that I've ever written.

We acknowledge the sacred land on which Cormorant Books operates. It has been a site of human activity for 15,000 years. This land is the territory of the Huron-Wendat and Petun First Nations, the Seneca, and most recently, the Mississaugas of the Credit River. The territory was the subject of the Dish With One Spoon Wampum Belt Covenant, an agreement between the Iroquois Confederacy and Confederacy of the Ojibway and allied nations to peaceably share and steward the resources around the Great Lakes. Today, the meeting place of Toronto is still home to many Indigenous people from across Turtle Island. We are grateful to have the opportunity to work in the community, on this territory.

We are also mindful of broken covenants and the need to strive to make right with all our relations.